Llyfrgelloedd Caerdydd
www.caerdydd.gov.uk/llyfrgelloedd
Cardiff Libraries
www.cardiff.gov.uk/libraries

KU-050-853

ACC. No: 02352372

SPECIAL MESSAGE TO READERS

This book is published under the auspices of

THE ULVERSCROFT FOUNDATION

(registered charity No. 264873 UK)

Established in 1972 to provide funds for research, diagnosis and treatment of eye diseases. Examples of contributions made are: —

A Children's Assessment Unit at Moorfield's Hospital, London.

•

Twin operating theatres at the Western Ophthalmic Hospital, London.

•

A Chair of Ophthalmology at the Royal Australian College of Ophthalmologists.

•

The Ulverscroft Children's Eye Unit at the Great Ormond Street Hospital For Sick Children, London.

You can help further the work of the Foundation by making a donation or leaving a legacy. Every contribution, no matter how small, is received with gratitude. Please write for details to:

**THE ULVERSCROFT FOUNDATION,
The Green, Bradgate Road, Anstey,
Leicester LE7 7FU, England.
Telephone: (0116) 236 4325**

**In Australia write to:
THE ULVERSCROFT FOUNDATION,
c/o The Royal Australian and New Zealand
College of Ophthalmologists,
94-98 Chalmers Street, Surry Hills,
N.S.W. 2010, Australia**

WILHELMINA

'That was a remarkable performance, Miss Wilhelmina. I shall look forward to working with you.' The speaker was Frederick Chopin addressing the budding young concert pianist before him. But it was not to be. There were plans for this German family to migrate to Australia — to the Upper Hunter in New South Wales. Yet dashed dreams and family tragedy would not dampen Wilhelmina's spirit. Her faith and courage would be tested by the trials of pioneering in nineteenth-century Australia — not to mention a wayward husband — but these qualities would contribute to an amazing outcome . . .

Books by Daphne Saxby Taylor
Published by The House of Ulverscroft:

CAROLINE

DAPHNE SAXBY TAYLOR

◆

WILHELMINA

Complete and Unabridged

ULVERSCROFT
Leicester

First published in Great Britain in 1995

First Large Print Edition
published 2006

The moral right of the author has been asserted

Copyright © 1995 by Daphne Taylor
All rights reserved

British Library CIP Data

Taylor, Daphne Saxby
Wilhelmina.—Large print ed.—
Ulverscroft large print series: family saga
1. Frontier and pioneer life—Australia—Fiction
2. Woman pianists—Fiction 3. Domestic fiction
4. Large type books
I. Title
823.9′14 [F]

ISBN 1–84617–559–3

Published by
F. A. Thorpe (Publishing)
Anstey, Leicestershire
Set by Words & Graphics Ltd.
Anstey, Leicestershire
Printed and bound in Great Britain by
T. J. International Ltd., Padstow, Cornwall

This book is printed on acid-free paper

To Mathilde Wilhelmina Maria Helena,
whose life inspired this story

Contents

Acknowledgements

My thanks to all who have assisted me in the gaining of knowledge and local colour of the Allyn and Williams Rivers and the people who settled there in the 1830s and 40s; to those whose memories of old times and old tales have been stirred and the results shared with me; to Ida and Jess and Laura and Edna, now all octogenarians; to Ann for her untiring help in securing research material; and the Queensland State Library for information, particularly that relating to the political and social situation in the German states at this period in history; and to my faithful encourager, researcher, proofreader and critic, my husband Harry: my heartfelt thanks to you all.

1

The grand duchess' offer

The Grand Duchess stood still, her head tilted to one side, listening. 'Who is that, Maria? Who is that playing the piano?' She paused, listening intently. 'Not since Mr Chopin visited us have I heard such music. The notes are like drops of water falling into a still pool — so clear they are crystal-like.'

'I believe, Your Grace, it is the younger daughter of Colonel Johann Gerhardt, Wilhelmina,' her companion replied.

'A young girl?' She was silent again. 'Her music is so touching — so much feeling!' They walked out into the courtyard. The afternoon was balmy and the notes wafted across from the music room.

'I fancy she is playing some of Mr Chopin's compositions, Your Grace. I know she greatly admires his music.'

The two women sat down beside the fountain. The grand duchess did not often venture into this wing of the castle. It was occupied mostly by the army officers and their families. As the court was now in session with the grand duke and duchess in residence, there were many occupying this section. It was a close court, the grand duke knowing his officers by name. There was almost a family feeling.

The music came to a climax and the notes drifted away into silence.

'Maria, go. Fetch the girl to me. I wish to speak to her.' Maria rose and hastened away, entering the building by the door near the ceremonial arch.

The sun was warm. The courtyard, now such a delight with the exquisite gardens ablaze with colour and perfume, would soon be clothed in autumn foliage preparing for winter's sleep and blankets of snow. The fountain sparkled in the sunlight and the drops of water tinkled into the pool.

The grand duchess sat musing: a young girl to play like that! What maturity! What understanding! The feeling expressed in her music drew out a response in the listener. Her own heart had swelled with emotion: pain, yet delight. She must encourage such talent — extend it — bring out the gift this girl possessed.

She would offer her patronage, give her the opportunity to fulfil her potential. She would make her a protégé. How exciting it was to discover such a one! She could even build a concert hall here in Heidelberg. It would be to honour this gifted artist if she excelled under her patronage. It could become famous throughout Europe; the world.

Already the university was rapidly gaining a reputation as a world famous institute of learning. This was thanks to the grand dukes of Baden who, after a period of decline of the university during the period of the Thirty Years' War, had granted their patronage and involvement in its affairs.

Now, if she could be a true patron of the Arts, building a superb concert hall and taking under her patronage this girl, Heidelberg could gain a reputation as a centre of musical excellence. And it would be her own project. She smiled. 'The Grand Duchess of Baden Music Hall. The Heidelberg Grand Duchess Music Hall.' She would have to think about the name. It would carry on for many years, long after she was gone from this earth.

She must talk to the grand duke, then the architects at the university. What a project! It would keep her happily occupied for some years.

★ ★ ★

Maria waited outside the music room. Wilhelmina had begun to play again. As the

3

last notes died away she entered, moving swiftly across to the piano where the girl sat absorbed in the pages of music she was studying.

She jumped when Maria spoke. 'Good afternoon, Wilhelmina. Come with me, please. The grand duchess wishes to see you.'

The girl looked up in alarm. 'The grand duchess? Is anything amiss? Should I perhaps not have been using this room today? Have I disturbed her?'

'You will see,' Maria replied. 'Come at once. We must not keep the grand duchess waiting.' She turned and went quickly towards the door.

Wilhelmina rose and followed hastily. Why ever would the grand duchess send for her? Her mind raced. Where had she been this morning? What had she done? Was there any point of courtesy or protocol she had transgressed?

She ran a few steps to catch up to Maria. They turned down the long corridor, their footsteps echoing from the walls and lofty ceiling.

As they emerged into the courtyard, the sun was bright after the dim corridors. The grand duchess was still seated by the fountain. She turned when she heard the approaching footsteps.

So this was the girl. What a striking face! Her broad forehead was surmounted by thick dark hair which was caught high on the crown of her head with a wide ribbon bow and fell in a cascade down her back. The eyes were wide, observant, yet had a dreamy depth — a deeply intuitive and sensitive girl, thought the grand duchess. Yes, she could believe she was capable of such emotion in her music.

She held out her hand. Wilhelmina moved forward and curtsied. Her Grace did not look annoyed. Perhaps she had not displeased her, after all. What then?

'Come here, my child,' the grand duchess said, smiling. 'I have been listening to your music.'

'I trust I did not disturb Your Grace with my playing. It was such a beautiful afternoon and the light was so clear in the music room. I sat down to play. I did not stop to think I may be disturbing the quiet.' She lifted apologetic eyes.

The older woman was looking at her with interest. 'You like to play, Wilhelmina?'

'Oh yes, Your Grace. That is the trouble. I begin to play and I forget everything else. I do not mean to be rude or annoy. It is just that everything else goes out of my head. There is just the piano and me and the sounds that we make together.'

'You speak as though the piano has an entity of its own,' the grand duchess said. 'It only produces the sounds you determine with your hands.'

'Yes, Your Grace. But it is like a child or an animal. It is the way you approach it, the way you handle it that makes the difference. If you treat it with love and caress it, if you speak to it with your fingers, then it responds. The beautiful sounds come back to you. There is an empathy.' She paused, hoping she had not spoken too much. 'You make it together, the piano and the pianist.'

What depth this child had. What age would she be? Perhaps fifteen: almost a woman — and mature; mature for her age, yet still with the innocence of the child in her eyes.

'I see you love the piano, Wilhelmina. Do you have a piano of your own at home?'

'Yes, Your Grace.'

'And you practice diligently?'

'It is not a task, Your Grace. I do not think about playing as practice. I just like to strive till I get the sounds I feel the composition calls for. It is not always achieved quickly — I am afraid I sometimes become so involved I lose count of time and I may be annoying those within hearing.'

The grand duchess gave a little laugh. She held out her hand again and patted the seat near her. 'Sit down here, Wilhelmina. I have not been annoyed. I was delighted by your music.'

The girl's heart gave a leap of joy. She had delighted the grand duchess with her music. Wait till she told Mama and Papa. How pleased they would be.

The grand duchess was speaking again. 'Was that one of Mr Chopin's compositions you were playing just now?'

'Yes, Your Grace.'

'You admire Mr Chopin and his music?'

'Oh yes, Your Grace. There are so many wonderful composers, but Mr Chopin loves the piano, too, and his music speaks from the heart of the piano.'

'You are a discerning, perceptive little soul, aren't you? I do believe you are right, even though I would not have expressed it so poetically. I believe Mr Chopin is a genius. Even Mr Schumann states such. Mr Chopin is an unchallenged master in his field. No-one speaks through the piano with so rich and varied a language!'

There was silence for a few minutes, broken only by the birds in the trees and the bees buzzing in the gardens. 'Would you wish to devote yourself fully to your music, Wilhelmina?'

The dark eyes swept up in surprise. 'I do

devote a great deal of my time to my music, Your Grace — as much as ever I am able.'

'I mean, Wilhelmina, would you wish to make a career of your music — become a concert pianist — give your life to the piano?' She hastened on. 'This kind of life, if you are successful, brings great fame, great prestige. You may have Baden, Germany, Europe, the world at your feet, begging to hear you play, crying for more and more and more. You could be feted, given accolades, be at the pinnacle of the world.

'But it would be you and your piano. There would be no room, no time for anyone or anything else. You would belong body and soul to your public. Would you wish to do this? To devote yourself wholly to the piano?'

A puzzled expression had creased the girl's brow. What was the grand duchess saying? What was the meaning of all this? 'It would be very wonderful to do this, Your Grace, to give my whole time and attention to my music. When Mr Chopin was here, my tutor, Mr Rhyngold, secured a short time with the master for me. He seemed pleased with what I achieved in the time spent with him.'

'You played for Mr Chopin? You say your tutor arranged this?' the grand duchess exclaimed in astonishment. The girl's tutor must believe she had great potential. If only she had discovered her while Mr Chopin was here! Never mind. She would invite him again.

But first she must ensure the girl's dedication to the demands entailed. She was young yet, but not too young.

'Yes, your Grace. I was working on some of Mr Chopin's compositions. Mr Rhyngold believed time spent with the composer was of great value. Mr Chopin is a great teacher as well as a great composer and pianist. I was very lucky to have such an opportunity.'

This girl obviously had no idea of her potential — or what I believe is her potential, thought the grand duchess. Neither did she have any idea of what the grand duchess was leading up to.

'Wilhelmina, if you had the opportunity to study under the great masters, to devote yourself wholly to your music, to become, as I said, a concert pianist of the highest order, would you take that opportunity? Or would you think the demands too great?'

Thoughts, possibilities raced through Wilhelmina's mind. What was the grand duchess suggesting, asking these things? Oh, how wonderful it would be to do as she suggested. But what of Mama and Papa? What would they say?

Her heart thudded against her ribs and she

9

felt her pulse searing through her veins. What a dream! To study under someone like Mr Chopin! But how silly she was to get excited like this. It was just that the words awakened untold dreams.

But dreams they were. The grand duchess was speaking hypothetically. She had enjoyed her music and flattered her by sending for her to discuss her music. How gracious of her.

'Well Wilhelmina, what would you do?'

'Oh, Your Grace. If I had such an opportunity as you describe — I don't know how that could ever be, it is just a dream — but if I did, I would find it no burden to lose myself in my music. It speaks to the very soul. I would not think the demands too great.'

'Then, my dear young lady, I intend to invite Mr Chopin to visit us again presently. I want him to spend time with you. I shall ask him if he is willing to accept you as a pupil with the view of grooming you for a career as a concert pianist. You could become famous.'

She watched as amazement and incredulity suffused the girl's face.

'In other words, Wilhelmina, I am offering you my patronage. What do you say?'

2

Troubled times

The two officers strolled slowly down the great hall. They were deep in conversation. Though the hall was unoccupied except for themselves, their voices were hushed and their footsteps were barely audible on the tiled floor. The sun slanted in obliquely from the high window.

'I tell you, Heinrich, I am concerned. These are turbulent times. What is going to happen?'

The taller of the two men glanced briefly at his companion. The sun caught the glint of the gold epaulettes and heavy fringe on their uniforms.

'That I cannot tell you, Johann. It would be a wiser man than I who could answer you precisely. I think one would need to be a clairvoyant. One can look at events, situations, the movement of society around us, but there is no saying for sure how things will go.' He was the shorter of the two, though both men were well-built, upright figures.

'But we must use foresight. We must look to the future, prepare for what may come.'

They walked a few metres in silence.

'That was a nasty clash a while back — remember?' continued Heinrich. 'I refer to the weavers' revolt. Factory workers in the towns are feeling the power of their numbers and are not going to accept things continuing as they have been in the past.'

His companion agreed. 'That was badly and harshly handled, too. They were put down this time, but I believe it will only be temporarily. Times are changing, towns are growing. These people will not accept the standard of life they now have. They have little to lose or to risk in an uprising.'

'We must not forget the horror and the bloodshed in France. It is not so long ago.'

'We were not old enough to understand at the time, but my parents were.' Johann paused. 'Many of their friends and some relatives perished in that bloody time. It was a bloodbath we do not want to see here in Baden, my friend.'

'Indeed, no.' Heinrich looked up at the vast ceiling, the soaring columns, the great chandeliers. 'It is understandable,' he said, 'this questioning of all this beauty and magnificence compared with their squalor.'

'There are some, too, who laud their mastery over the lower classes. It does not help the situation. If all men are equal in the sight of God, then some change must come. God will see to that if man does not.'

Heinrich nodded. 'That is another issue, of course: the turmoil in the church. A man cannot be told how he must worship. We are told in the scriptures a man must worship from his heart. The way he does that is his affair. There is great division not only between the Catholics and Protestants, but between Protestants themselves.' He shook his head. 'These are man's deepest feelings, his motivations and aspirations.'

Johann hastened to add, 'Many of the Lutherans are suffering. This united church of Lutheran and Reformed will not work. There are men who are suffering imprisonment for their stand, a stand made in conscience. They will not become part of a church which does not comply wholeheartedly with their beliefs and teachings. Some are resisting and suffering the consequences; others are leaving the country. In any case, however admirable the intention at the beginning, the union is today largely a political and administrative ploy.'

They had walked through the great doors into the courtyard and gazed out over the town.

'There is tension between our countries, too. The states are in disarray. Agreements cannot be reached.'

Another officer of the army approached the two by the wall. 'You are taking the air for the good of your health?' he called. 'You both look decidedly gloomy. What ails you?'

Heinrich replied, 'We have been discussing the state of the kingdom — or rather, the whole country. There is much that troubles one.'

The new arrival waved his arm in a motion of dismissal. 'Do not worry. All these lower class uprisings will soon be squashed. The army just has to flex its muscles and they'll come to heel again.' He slapped his gloves on his thigh. 'To happier tidings. We are required to dine in the great hall tonight. The grand duke has some special entertainment for us.' He turned to go. 'I must move on to carry the good news to others.'

Johann and Heinrich watched his departure. They watched as he bounded up the flight of stairs and disappeared into the palace. 'We must be careful, my friend,' Heinrich said. 'We would not be looked on favourably if it were generally known our feelings in some of these matters.' He paused a moment. 'The very walls have ears.'

'You are right, Heinrich. There is much intrigue. Concern for all men could be interpreted as disloyalty at best and treason at worst. We must not speak openly of this.'

The two friends parted, each deeply troubled.

Johann left the palace grounds and descended to the town. He would go for a long walk to clear his head. A foreboding of things to come and the urgency for action made his step heavy as he wended his way down.

If the factory workers were to rise up again, as they well might, if they were joined by others of the lower classes, there would no doubt be violence. Once violence begins, the mob mentality takes over. Reason, logic, compassion all fly out the window. The mentality of the mob, the hysteria of mob rule takes over. This was what had happened in France. There had been other lesser revolutions since, but that was the one that had rocked Europe, the world.

Johann strode along the narrow, winding streets. He was aware of the looks of suspicion cast in his direction. As he passed one man leaning in his doorway, the man spat on the ground in contempt. Johann ignored the action. Such actions were rare as yet. It was possible the man had not meant it for him. More likely he had though, he thought. He was in uniform. He was associated with the palace and, in the mind of the lower people, 'one of them'.

That would be the case, should it all come to the point of full violent revolution. Not only he, but his family as well would be classed with the ruling family and would no doubt receive the same treatment.

The situation here in Heidelberg was not so volatile as in some states. The grand duke had done much for Baden. The university was evidence of this. But the revolt would come, if it came, from people who had no connection with places like the university. There were many things that needed review, attention. For instance, both his girls had bright minds. They had both had a good education. Both spoke several languages. Wilhelmina particularly had a bright, enquiring mind. Yet they were denied access to the university. Was it not unfair that women were excluded from enrolment in the university?

He would be classed as a radical if he spoke these thoughts abroad. Then he could be in danger from the palace. He was caught between the two, he thought. He could see the good and the bad, both in the government and administration of the state and the reactionary movement. The danger beyond all other for him and his family, though, would be in the event of mob rule.

He turned and made his way back through

16

the town. The late afternoon sun was losing its warmth. The castle, set high above the town, dominated the surrounding country-side — almost symbolic of its place and the place of its occupants in society.

He climbed the hill, twisting and turning up the steep path. The red sandstone building loomed above him.

What should he do? How could he protect his family from the turmoil and danger he felt so surely were coming? He had lost his first wife, Sophia. She had died so soon after their daughter was born. Then he had been so lucky to find his second, Sophia. They had another daughter, Wilhelmina. She was now fifteen years old and doing so well with her studies and with her piano.

What a funny little person she was with her great love of her music. She forgot everything when she sat down at the piano — even her mother's bidding and tasks assigned to her. He smiled, remembering. Nothing must happen to them. He must protect them.

He had reached the grounds of the castle. He must hurry in and change for the dinner and entertainment. Sophia would know if the ladies were to be included or if it was only for the officers.

He had been remiss going so far and being so late back. He hurried down through the courtyard towards his rooms.

As he entered the corridor, he almost collided with a woman, one of the servants he realised. He helped her pick up the things she had dropped. 'We were both in too much hurry, Frederica,' he said, smiling. 'Where are you going in such a hurry?'

The girl looked both ways, wary. Seeing they were alone, she spoke softly. 'I am going to my room to collect my things, Colonel. I am leaving Baden. My family are all going.'

'Leaving? Why are you leaving?' he asked.

The girl spoke almost in a whisper. 'We are going to the colony of New South Wales to find freedom, Colonel — freedom to worship God in peace — and freedom to build a future. My father is a vinedresser and winemaker. We have very little money now we have prepared for our new life, but we believe we can progress and prosper with hard work when we get there.'

Going to Australia! They were going to a faraway colony, an outpost for sending convicts to relieve the state of prisons in England, this girl and her family! They — ordinary people — must also be seeing the restrictions and dangers. What courage they had! 'It must call for a great deal of courage to set off to a colony like Australia,' he said.

The girl returned his direct honest gaze.

18

'Yes, sir. It is . . . it is frightening.' She paused, then added, 'But God will take care of us. He will prosper us. We have prayed and believe we should go. After all, Abraham went out into the unknown country, didn't he? God called him and he obeyed God's prompting — and he reached his promised land and he prospered. We believe we will prosper.'

She bobbed a little curtsy. 'God be with you, Colonel, and with your family. I hear your daughter play the piano in the music room every day. It is beautiful to hear. Goodbye, sir.' With that, she was gone.

Johann stood watching her in amazement. What presence the girl had for one of the uneducated. What dignity and purpose. Australia! A penal colony! He recollected the time and hurried up the corridor to his rooms. He must not be late for the dinner.

3

Mr Chopin

Wilhelmina's mind was whirling as she left the grand duchess. It was unbelievable! The grand duchess was offering her patronage. The great lady would arrange and provide for her every need, leaving her to concentrate solely on her music. She would steer her career; promote her.

Mr Chopin had been pleased with her when she played for him before. The thought did not cross her mind that he may refuse to take her as a pupil. There had been a mental and spiritual harmony between them, the young inexperienced girl and the master musician. Their feelings towards their music were in tune.

What was it he had quoted to her? 'My dear Miss Wilhelmina,' he had said, 'music hath charms to soothe the savage breast.'

She had reached the other end of the courtyard. She looked back and saw the grand duchess and Maria moving away down the garden amidst the trees and statues. They were deep in conversation. The grand duchess was moving her hands excitedly as she talked.

I must pinch myself to see I am really awake, Wilhelmina thought. This must all be a dream. Did she really have the ability to become a concert pianist, as the grand duchess had said, 'of the highest order'?

Visions of great halls filled with ladies and gentlemen in evening dress, jewels sparkling in the light from the great chandeliers, flashed through her mind — and of herself seated at the grand piano on the stage, playing, playing, rapt with the sounds that emanated from the instrument.

She saw through a haze the faces uplifted to her, all attention riveted on her. She saw the audience rise to its feet in acclamation; the deafening thunder of applause. And she saw herself bowing low in gracious acknowledgement.

Oh, it was too much! Could this really happen? The grand duchess said it could. She would have to work hard, of course. But what work! It was something she loved doing, more than anything else.

She had come to the door of her home, but decided to walk a little further to try to sort out her thoughts and control her racing emotions.

The grand duchess would send word to Mr Chopin inviting him to her court. He had enjoyed his previous visit and would no doubt be pleased and flattered to receive an invitation for a return visit.

When would he come? She must speak to Mr Rhyngold. But no, the grand duchess had said she would send for him and inform him of her intentions. He would be pleased. He was most encouraging always.

She turned at the end of the pathway and walked back the way she had come. What of Mama and Papa? What would they say? They would be proud, but would they be keen for her — a girl — to undertake a public career? They would see all the demands, all the pitfalls.

She tried to visualise their reaction. Perhaps they would feel they had lost her if she undertook this great thing. She would be dependent on the grand duchess and have her life, her decisions, ordered by her. She would no longer be under her father's care and guidance.

He may not like that. He was very conscious of his responsibility to his family. He took it very seriously. He may not consent to her accepting the offer.

She walked along, musing, trying to realise all the implications. Perhaps she would wait till she had played for Mr Chopin and see what he said before mentioning it to Mama and Papa. Was she being secretive, even deceitful in doing that? Should she be open and tell them now all the grand duchess had said? That was what she had intended to do. But now . . .

Papa had seemed somewhat worried of late. It may cause him concern if she told them. And there was no certainty, really. Yet. It all depended on Mr Chopin's acceptance of the proposal. It wasn't definite. Yet.

Perhaps it would be wiser to wait, to say nothing for the present, to wait till the offer was formal before saying anything. There would be plenty of time when the master had been and accepted her to tell them the exciting prospects awaiting her.

No, she would say nothing. But oh, it would be hard to appear normal with the exciting visions racing through her mind. Mama would know there was something. She would have to keep busy so her mind was occupied. She would dream when she got to bed.

She turned in the door now when she reached it. The afternoon was drawing away. Mama would be looking for her. It was some time now since she had been playing the piano and the grand duchess had interrupted her. Her steps hastened along the corridor.

★   ★   ★

It was two weeks before Mr Chopin was located, the grand duchess' communication sent and an answer received. In just three weeks he would visit Heidelberg and entertain the court with his music.

He was, he said, most conscious of the honour bestowed on him by the grand duchess in inviting him again so soon after his last most enjoyable visit. He was most gratified to be made aware of her appreciation of his compositions and rendering of them.

He would be delighted to hear again the young lady, Wilhelmina, play and would be most willing to assess her suitability as a serious pupil with a view to grooming her as a concert pianist.

The grand duchess sent for Wilhelmina and told her the news. 'Mr Chopin remembers you and your rendition of his music,' she said as she folded the letter and placed it in her secretaire. 'Are you practising well, Wilhelmina?'

'I play every day, Your Grace. I wonder what Mr Chopin would like me to play?'

'Something of his compositions, I should say,' smiled the grand duchess.

'Mr Rhyngold is pleased with me,' added Wilhelmina. 'He is quite excited the master is possibly going to take me as a pupil.'

'I am quite excited myself, my dear.' She

stood up. 'However, we must just wait for his verdict.'

Realising she was being dismissed, Wilhelmina bobbed a curtsy and left the room. As she went down the lofty corridor, she thought of the time — three weeks! Then she would know the course of her future — depending, of course, on how Mama and Papa received the news.

What would they say? Perhaps she should have told them before. But no. Papa seemed quite preoccupied and worried. What was wrong with him? Was there some trouble? His concern had increased these last few weeks.

No, she had done the right thing in not telling them yet. Soon she would know if there was really anything to tell.

Please God there would be.

★ ★ ★

The master had arrived. Wilhelmina had seen the carriage draw up at the palace entrance when she was returning from a visit to the dressmaker. She saw the frail little man descend from the carriage and enter the palace. What a nasty cough he had, poor man.

Her heart thudded as she made her way back to their apartment. When would he want to hear her play, to talk with her? The grand duchess would send for her when she was required. Perhaps it would not be until the next day. Mr Chopin looked very tired when he arrived. He would need to rest.

It was two days before the awaited summons came. Wilhelmina heard the knock on the door and the servant's answer, then her mother's voice. 'The grand duchess wishes to see Wilhelmina? Why?' Her mother's face was creased with concern.

'I am sure I have not done anything amiss, Mama.' She thought quickly. Perhaps she could introduce a note of the interest the grand duchess had shown in her. 'She sent for me a few weeks ago when she heard me playing in the music room. She was very kind and said she enjoyed my music. Perhaps she would like to hear me play today.'

She rose from her desk and straightened her skirt. 'She complimented you on your music and you mentioned nothing to us? Oh, you are a strange girl, Wilhelmina. Your father would be so pleased to hear that. How good of her to bother to send for you to tell you.'

She ushered her daughter out into the main salon. 'Hurry along, now. Don't keep her waiting.'

When she arrived, Wilhelmina was immediately shown into the grand duchess' music salon. It was a beautiful room with a southern aspect. The sun streamed in the windows, making the room light and bright.

A frail figure was standing by the window with the grand duchess. They turned when Wilhelmina entered the room. 'Ah, Wilhelmina. There you are. I have been talking to Mr Chopin about my ideas for you.'

Wilhelmina curtsied to the grand duchess and inclined her head to the master. He held out his hand. 'It is a great pleasure to meet you again, Miss Wilhelmina. I await with joyful anticipation your rendition of some of my music. Your tutor has told me you are acquainted with many of my compositions.' He indicated the open grand piano. 'Please delight us with my 'Fantasy Impromptu'.'

Wilhelmina stepped confidently to the piano and seated herself calmly. Her mind was racing ahead through the music. It was one of her favourites. She could express her feelings in this.

She settled herself.

The compelling introduction shattered the silence of the room as she began to play. Then softly, caressingly, the sparkling cadences followed. There was movement, brilliance in the sound. The Largo section wooed the listeners, the piano singing the melody under her fingers. And so it flowed.

At last, the crescendo mounted into a

frenzy of sound as note after note, full *fortissimo*, filled the room. Then, with gathering lightness, it tiptoed and faded, faded until the last notes were barely audible and finally died away. Her fingers lingered on the beloved keyboard. Then her hands dropped to her lap.

4

The menace of the unknown

As he made his way to the great hall, the colonel's thoughts returned to the servant girl Frederica. So the people on the estates were aware of the dangers, too, and taking action. People like her father, good men of conscience, Christian men with their strongly held beliefs were not going to accept a dogma forced upon them. They may not take violent action as was more probable from the factory workers in their situation, but they would deal with it in their own way.

He had reached the hall and turned in at the great ornate doors. The hall was ablaze with the lights of a multitude of candles, the great crystal chandeliers sparkling and glinting, the long tables laden with the banquet food. The ladies had not been included tonight.

He glanced around the room. Everywhere, the uniforms of officers displayed the glamour of the court, the gold aglow against the dark material, the young officers like young cock birds as they strutted in their tight breeches.

As he walked among the throng, he was struck by the number of visiting officers from neighbouring states. There must be a good deal of discussion going on between the grand duke and his advisers and the emissaries of other countries. Again his mind went to the critical social and political situation around him.

He had been greeting acquaintances as he wended his way down the hall. Suddenly, to his surprise, he noticed an unexpected familiar face. This man was an Englishman. What was Sir Percy Rutherford doing here in Heidelberg? The man looked up. Catching sight of Johann, he excused himself from his companions and made his way towards him. 'Colonel Gerhardt!' he called. 'How very good to meet you again. I trust all is well with you?'

The two men greeted each other enthusiastically and stood talking till the grand duke entered and they all seated themselves at the table.

The chefs had excelled and course after course was served. The wine flowed and the clamour of voices rose as the evening wore on. As they applied themselves to the fish course, Johann turned to his companion. 'How goes it in your country, Sir Percy?' he asked.

The Englishman looked searchingly at him. 'Better than in yours at present, I believe, my friend,' he said softly. 'Our young queen has brought a stability to the throne that was sadly lacking after the tragedy of her immediate predecessor and the scandals of the previous two.

'She is presenting a model of unimpeachable private life: a deep-rooted sense of responsibility, warmth and kindliness; and a great capacity for hard, conscientious work. It is felt throughout the nation and she is admired and copied widely.'

Johann shook his head. He glanced along the table. The group to his right were involved in a heated discussion and those on his left equally taken up. 'I fear we are not in such a happy position,' he said. 'I tremble at what might happen. There is unrest among the lower classes, in the church and in political circles. We could see tragic times, I fear. Unless change is achieved very quickly, I fear it will be too late to avert bloodshed.'

There was a silence between them for a few minutes. Then the Englishman raised his glass and peered at the wine, twirling the glass in his fingers. He said softly, 'Some of these things you have mentioned are indirectly the reason I am here.'

Johann glanced at him quickly.

'We are aware in England that some of your people are not, shall we say, content in their homeland today, that they see no future. We are in the process of facilitating certain passages and positions, covering a wide range of employment. We are looking for a breadth of expertise, of skills, of profession, from shepherds and vinedressers to veterinary surgeons and doctors.'

'You are short of all these people in England?' asked Johann, mystified.

'No, Colonel. We need these people to go to the colony of New South Wales. It began as a penal colony peopled with convicts and soldiers. But it is growing. Many are finding it a land of opportunity — and making a great future there.'

Johann's attention was riveted on his companion. 'And you are here in connection with this?'

Sir Percy smiled. 'That is one of my assignments on this visit. There are several.'

'And are you getting a response? People are accepting such a challenge?'

'Those with big hearts; those with fortitude; those with dreams. Yes, they are going. They will make good settlers. They are prepared for hard work. They have determination. They will make good Australians.'

He paused, then added, 'And they will be

free — and safe from the turmoil here.'

'That is what I fear: the turmoil. I remember all too clearly the consequences of the French eruption. I want to protect my family. They are innocent of any aggression. But we will all be lumped together in the minds of those with heavy grievances. And if it comes to mob rule . . .'

His companion leant towards him. The parties on either side were imbibing freely, but one must be careful. 'Consider what I have been saying, Colonel.' He smiled. 'You may decide to emigrate. We need people of your calibre.'

Of a sudden, Johann realised that this thought had been hovering in the back of his mind ever since his interchange with Frederica, though he had not consciously acknowledged it. But to leave his homeland, to cut the old ties completely, to start a new and strange life in a strange country, a country undeveloped, a wilderness without any of the attributes of civilisation as he knew it was such a big step!

To go to India, or China — anywhere in the East, even — would be one thing. But to go to a British colony devoid of the trappings of civilisation was another!

Sir Percy watched him, a faint smile playing around his lips. 'Your roots are deep in this country?' he said softly.

'Deep indeed,' replied Johann. 'My family has worked the estate at Wiesbaden for centuries. My brother now administers it. Our vineyards have been producing for generations and our wine is famous. It has been in our very blood.' He lifted his glass to his lips, sipped his wine and replaced the glass. 'To leave the fatherland!'

'Think about it,' Sir Percy said again. 'If you believe it may be an answer, here is where I shall be in the next few weeks.' He wrote on a card he had extracted from his pocket. 'I can be contacted at these places. There are places waiting to be filled now. It is a challenge. It could be exciting. And it is an alternative, albeit drastic, to staying here and risking,' he paused, 'perhaps your life and that of your family.'

The grand duke had risen. The assembly rose. The banquet was at an end. The opportunity for the *tête-a-tête* had vanished.

★ ★ ★

Johann walked the corridors thoughtfully as he made his way back to the apartment.

What would Sophia think of this idea — and the girls? He did not know what to think of it himself. He let himself into the apartment and went quietly to the bedroom. The girls' rooms were in darkness. They were already asleep. He undressed and slid into bed beside Sophia. She stirred and turned towards him. 'Did you enjoy the banquet, Johann?' she asked sleepily.

'It was a very good meal,' he answered.

'What is it? Did something happen? You have something more to tell me.' She was awake now.

'I am worried, my love.'

She lifted her head and looked at him. 'Worried? What about?

'I am worried about our country — the situation with the factory workers and many of the lower classes. I fear there is going to be trouble, Sophia; really big trouble. The shadow of the French Revolution is not far removed from us.'

'Is this what has been ailing you these last weeks? Do you think it is so serious?'

'I do, indeed. I become more and more filled with an urgency to take action to protect you and the girls.'

'But why are you thinking particularly of this tonight, at this time of night — after a banquet, when I would think your mood would have mellowed?'

Johann's mind whirled. Would he confide his thoughts to his Sophia? It affected her as much as himself. He made a sudden decision. 'I met tonight an old acquaintance, an admirable man, Sir Percy Rutherford from Britain. He is an emissary for the Queen and the British government.'

He stalled a minute, hardly daring to voice Sir Percy's suggestion. 'He tells me the young Queen Victoria has brought stability to her country. He spoke most highly of her.'

'Yes, but what has that to do with your being worried at this time of night?' she asked, cutting through his diversionary tactics.

'He told me one of his assignments in this visit to our country is to recruit emigrants for his government.'

'Emigrants?' exclaimed Sophia. 'Emigrants to where?'

'To the colony of New South Wales. Australia.' The words were out.

'To the colony of New South Wales? I don't see . . . '

'We talked of the troubles of our country, the turmoil. I don't know if you realise the severity of the turmoil we are facing. The lower classes are demanding change. We could face a bloody revolution. You know what happened not so long ago in France.'

He heard Sophia catch her breath. 'You think this could happen here, Johann?'

36

'I believe there is every possibility it could happen. Pray God it does not. But if it does, we will be classed with the nobility, the royalty we serve. Not only me, but you and the girls also.'

'Oh Johann, I had no idea it was quite so serious,' she exclaimed. 'Whatever can we do? Are you sure you are not taking a too pessimistic view?'

Johann told her of his chance meeting with Frederica and their conversation. 'So you see, it is not only my thoughts. These people are making their decisions; they are taking control of what can be done about their future — and they are leaving. I believe there are also people going to Russia. But I do not see any lasting improvement there. All of Europe is like a volcano seething underneath ready to erupt. There will be trouble in many quarters.'

The enormity of the state of affairs that was so troubling Johann filled Sophia's mind. So this was why he had been so preoccupied — so unlike himself. Ensconsed in the castle and life of the court with all its plenty, she had been unaware. They talked for some time in undertones. Johann explained to her the violence of the uprising of the factory workers, of the persecution in the church and the imprisonment of clergy and people who held out for their beliefs, of the strained relations between the states. She was trying to take it all in and the implications for themselves.

After a moment of silence while she digested all this, Johann said, 'Sir Percy said he has positions from shepherds to doctors to fill. He suggested we might consider emigrating.'

Sophia sat bolt upright. 'We emigrate?' she expostulated. 'We emigrate to the colony of New South Wales?' She could not believe her ears. She had not come this far in all this revelation. She had not seen what Johann was leading up to. 'But that is a penal colony. There is no court! No society! Whatever could we do? Oh, it is unthinkable.'

'There, there. Do not distress yourself, my dear. I have not said we would go. He has suggested we might consider the possibility — look into it, see what is really involved, get facts as to what we may be going to, should we make that decision.'

Sophia fell back on her pillows. Oh, it was unthinkable, positively unthinkable, to leave the life she knew, the prestige she enjoyed as a member of the court, her place in society. For what? The unknown loomed menacingly.

They talked far into the early hours of the dangers; the little they knew or surmised

38

about the colony; what they would be leaving; the effects on the girls; their future.

At last Johann said, 'The thing is, my love, if we remain and do nothing, we may none of us have any future.'

There was silence as Sophia grappled with the devastation of her secure world.

'We must pray for God's guidance and protection. As Frederica said, Abraham went out into the unknown at God's calling and God prospered him. Let us pray now, my darling. Then go to sleep, secure in his care, that he will guide us and direct us in what to do. We must be alert, looking for that direction. It will come.'

5

A dream beyond all expectations

There was silence in the room as Wilhelmina became aware of her surroundings. The clock on the mantel chimed the hour.

What had Mr Chopin thought of her rendition of his music? The master left the window and walked slowly across the room to where she was seated. She looked up, trying to gauge his reaction.

He stood looking at her silently for what seemed to the girl to be minutes. Then he sighed softly. 'That was a most remarkable performance for one so young, Miss Wilhelmina. You have great perception, great sensitivity. You have gone straight to the soul of the music.' He smiled. 'I shall look forward with delight to working with you.'

A rush of pure joy flooded Wilhelmina. The master was going to accept her as a pupil! All this wonderful dream could come true! Oh, thankyou, Lord. Thankyou. Her face flushed as she remained seated, feeling weak with emotion.

The grand duchess, who had followed Mr

Chopin across the room, gave a little cry of pleasure. 'So, you are pleased with Wilhelmina's ability?' she asked.

'More than pleased, Your Grace. To groom such a one will be a delight.'

The grand duchess looked at Wilhelmina. 'Well, my dear young lady, what have you to say?'

'Oh, Your Grace, I do not know what to say. I am overwhelmed.'

'And well you may be,' said the grand duchess. 'Mr Chopin has paid you a great compliment.' She turned to the master. 'Wilhelmina has assured me it is no burden to her to practise for hours per day, Mr Chopin.'

'I am sure that is true, Your Grace. No-one plays as she does if it is a burden.' He smiled at Wilhelmina.

'You may go and tell your parents now of Mr Chopin's decision. We must look to the business side of our arrangement — how long you will need to be under his tutelage before you can give a concert, where you should make your debut. Oh, there are a thousand things to be decided.'

Wilhelmina was looking bewildered by the grand duchess' enthusiasm and plans. However could she fulfil all the plans for her? The thought of all these arrangements frightened her.

The grand duchess saw her confusion. She hastened to reassure her. 'But you do not have to worry about any of this. You just have to put yourself in our hands and, between Mr Chopin and myself, we will arrange everything. You just have to think of your piano and work hard to absorb and achieve all Mr Chopin instructs you in.'

'Oh, I will, Your Grace, I will. I just can't take it all in yet.'

'We will speak to your father later. You have told your father and mother of my hopes for you, of my interest in you?' The grand duchess raised her eyebrows in question.

Wilhelmina flushed with embarrassment. 'No, Your Grace. I did not mention it. I thought it best not to mention it until Mr Chopin had said he was willing to accept me as a pupil.'

'Then you will need to tell them all now,' she replied. 'I will send for you and your father later when I have the details decided upon.'

Wilhelmina left the room in a daze. Her thoughts were a maelstrom. They alternated between visions conjured up by the prospects of her future and the need now to procure her parents' consent. She hugged herself in disbelief. Oh, how could this be happening to her? It was only a few weeks since the grand duchess had called her to her and talked of her ability.

What would Mama and Papa say? They would be pleased, very pleased that Mr. Chopin thought so highly of her ability as a musician, as a pianist.

But would Papa be happy to place her future in the hands of someone else — even the grand duchess? He admired the grand duke and duchess and their involvement in many things in the kingdom, particularly the university. The grand duchess (as well as the grand duke) involved herself in various projects. These plans she had for her were typical of her vision and energy. She would see it all through. She would organise and encourage — and she would also demand what she expected from all involved. Her commands must be obeyed.

Wilhelmina's step slackened as she approached the apartment. How would Papa view it all? She opened the door and let herself into the apartment.

Her mother and father were seated by the window. Henrietta was standing near her father, one hand on his chair. Her posture indicated some agitation. She turned as her sister entered the room. 'Wilhelmina, come and listen to what Papa is saying.'

'Hush, my dear. Close the door, Wilhelmina.' Her mother had risen.

'What is the matter?' Wilhelmina secured the door and crossed the room. 'Whatever is wrong?'

'I wish to talk to you both, my dears.' Her father rose and paced a few steps. 'I feel you must be aware of the dangers we could be facing. Everywhere there is unrest.'

He stopped in front of the girls. 'We could be confronted with violence before very long if change does not come quickly. I fear it is already too late.' He calmed himself. 'But sit down, my dears, sit down. I do not wish to alarm you, but you are both young ladies now. You are no longer children. I must confide in you my fears, my predictions — and tell you of my plans for your protection and that of your mother.'

He seated himself again and wiped his handkerchief over his face. Papa is upset — he is really concerned, Wilhelmina thought. This must be the reason he had been so preoccupied these last weeks.

What of her own news? She must let him speak first before divulging her great prospects.

Johann began again. 'I do not want you to divulge or discuss anything I say to you with anyone outside this family,' he said firmly. 'I must impress upon you the importance of this. There are some who would not hesitate to harm us if it would progress their own benefit. Have I your word to that account?'

The girls nodded solemnly.

'Your mother and I have talked much about this, trying to arrive at the right decision.'

'But what is the danger you are so worried about, Papa?' It was Henrietta the elder sister who spoke. She was already 'out' and receiving the attentions of many of the younger officers.

'You know and have studied the French Revolution. I fear — pray God it does not — but I fear a similar situation could arise here.'

He watched the effect on his daughters. The astounded girls reeled before the shock. 'You cannot be serious, Papa,' exclaimed Henrietta. 'Why, we have had no threats. We can go freely abroad. This is a wonderful place!'

'Your world is wonderful, my dear, but the world of many is very different. You may not be aware of that, but it is so. They are asking why. There is a seething under the surface of our society.' He went on to tell them of the factory workers, of the violence already evidenced in the weavers' revolt. He spoke of the turmoil in the church, of the persecution of those who would not forsake their teachings and join in the union church being thrust upon them. He told them of the political unrest and of the man who had spat on the ground as he passed.

'You see, my darlings, you must understand that in the eyes of these people, we are classed with all those of privilege or authority. We live part of the year here in the palace. We are guests of the grand duke and duchess. My very uniform flaunts before them that I am close to them and serve them.' He paused. 'You know what happened to those in such positions in France.'

Their eyes were wide with shock. Horror. Incredulity. 'Then what are we to do, Papa? You say we must prepare for our own protection. How can we protect ourselves from all these terrible things?' cried Henrietta.

'I have been trying to discern that these last weeks. I wanted to settle on a course of action before mentioning all this to you. It is very difficult. The unrest is not only in one quarter.'

He sighed. 'Then I met Frederica the servant girl in the corridor one day.' He looked up. 'You know her?'

They nodded.

'She and her family, like many others, are also seeing the writing on the wall. They have made their decision and are pursuing it.'

'What are they doing, Papa?' asked Wilhelmina.

'They are emigrating.' He watched to see if the girls perceived what he was about to suggest.

'Emigrating? Where to, Papa?'

'They are emigrating to the British colony of New South Wales. Australia.'

'The penal colony of New South Wales? Whatever for? How can that be a solution? What can they do there? How can they live there?' Henrietta's brow was furrowed in bewilderment.

'They have positions to go to, many of them. It is not only a penal settlement now. In fact, the transport of convicts has ceased except in two places. There are free settlers going there. The British government is assisting people willing to risk their fortunes. Frederica's father is a vinedresser and winemaker. Such people are now required in the colony.'

'New South Wales. To go so far! Why, it is not even a civilised country! It would be like going to somewhere . . . ' Henrietta floundered, searching for a word, 'somewhere off this earth!' she exclaimed.

47

Obviously they had not caught the drift of his conversation, Johann thought. How could he tell them gently? He had thought they may see the connection and come to the conclusion themselves.

'Well, that is Frederica's family's decision. They will certainly be out of this place of possible danger.'

'But Papa, what do you suggest we should do?' Wilhelmina looked trustingly at her father.

How could he tell them? How could he say he had come to the decision to do likewise? They had not guessed what he was leading up to. He had not yet contacted Sir Percy to see if a suitable post could be found, but in his heart he could see no other alternative.

Perhaps he would leave it at that for the moment — let them ponder on the things he had said, become aware of the world outside their own circle and the security and comfort of life at the castle and at home at Wiesbaden.

Yes, he would say no more at present. But he would send word to Sir Percy enquiring what positions may be available should he decide on that course of action.

He passed his hand over his eyes and forehead and looked at them, giving his head a little shake. 'For the moment we must pray,' he said. 'Pray with all your heart. We must pray together for guidance, for God's guidance. We are not alone. He is with us.'

He reached out his hand to them. 'You trust him. We know he will care for us and protect us. My concern only is to be aware of his guidance, that I may have eyes to recognise it. You must pray for me, too, that my decision may be in accordance with his will. It is my responsibility to make that decision.'

There was silence for a moment. A log on the fire crackled and broke, sending a little shower of sparks onto the hearth.

Johann rose and attended to it. 'And did you play for the grand duchess, Wilhelmina? Did she want to hear you play again?' Sophia had realised Johann was going to say no more at present and changed the subject accordingly.

Wilhelmina caught her breath. Even her wonderful news had vanished from her mind for the last little while in the wake of her father's communication. How would she tell them now? What was to become of all the grand schemes, the duchess' patronage, her acceptance as a pupil by Mr Chopin, her debut, the concerts, her career?

Sophia looked at her questioningly. 'Well? Did you do well? Or not? Is that why she sent for you?'

Wilhelmina tried desperately to gather her thoughts.

'There was no trouble?' Sophia's alarmed voice cut into her thoughts.

She realised her father and sister were now looking at her also, waiting for her answer. 'Oh no, Mama. There was no trouble, no trouble at all.'

Should she tell them now? It was not at all as she had planned it. 'You see,' she hesitated again, taking a quivering breath. 'You see, when the grand duchess sent for me that day when she heard me playing, she asked me all sorts of questions about my music. Then she asked me . . . ' She looked at them, their attention riveted on her. 'She asked me if I would like to be a concert pianist and perform at great concerts. I thought she was just being kind — telling me she liked my music.'

She swallowed nervously. Her mother's eyes were wide in surprise and expectation. 'Then she talked about all the bad side of that sort of life — as a concert pianist, I mean — in the public eye.'

She glanced away and back to her mother, her heart beating furiously. It was hard to get enough breath to continue. 'Then she said if I was prepared for all that, for the hard work of perfecting my music to become 'a concert pianist of the highest order' — and if Mr Chopin, after he had heard me play, would accept me as a pupil — she would offer me her patronage.'

There: it was out!

'Offer you her patronage? She believes you have this potential?' Sophia's hands covered her mouth, her eyes wide, looking incredulously at her daughter. 'Oh Johann!' She reached out her hand to him. 'Whatever is to be done?'

'Be calm, my darling. Be calm.' He turned to Wilhelmina. 'I had no idea your gift was so great and your development so far, my dear. I enjoy your music, but I am no judge of quality such as this. Is the grand duchess such a judge, to offer you patronage? I hope she is not playing with you. Are you sure she is serious?'

Wilhelmina let out her breath. She must disclose the rest of it. 'Yes, Papa. She is serious.'

'But you said nothing to us of all this, Wilhelmina. Why did you not tell us before?' her mother interrupted.

'I wanted to be sure Mr Chopin thought I had the potential and would take me as a pupil to groom me for this career. The grand duchess said she would invite Mr Chopin back again to entertain the court and she would arrange for him to assess my ability.'

'You must realise Mr Chopin is a very great musician, composer, performer, pianist and may not think you quite able enough to accept you,' Johann ventured, worried that his daughter could be badly let down and enormously disappointed.

Wilhelmina smiled a little shaky smile. 'I know, Papa. But you see, I saw Mr Chopin arrive two days ago. And today Her Grace sent for me. Mr Chopin was there in her salon. I played on her grand piano.' She hesitated.

'And,' cut in Henrietta excitedly, 'what did he say?'

Wilhelmina took a deep breath. 'He said he would 'look forward with delight to grooming me as a concert pianist'.'

The emotion of the afternoon was too much. Wilhelmina burst into tears.

'And the grand duchess?' cried her mother, jumping up to throw her arms around her daughter.

Wilhelmina lifted her face from her mother's shoulder. 'She has offered me her patronage and will send for Papa and me shortly to discuss it all and make the formal offer!'

6

Remember France

The card Johann extracted from his inner pocket had writing on both sides. His eye ran down the figures till it rested on the current date. It would take two days for a rider to reach the address listed there. Where would he be by then?

He scanned the card again. Another seventy-kilometre ride. Better allow another day. If he sent word tomorrow, his note could reach Sir Percy in four days from now.

Then he must wait to receive a reply detailing what was offering. He would need to talk to Sir Percy again to learn all the details — conditions on arrival, prospects for the future, conditions on the journey, what it would mean to the girls.

His mind reeled with the questions he wanted answered. Now, this great opportunity for Wilhelmina was further complicating the whole situation — in better times, what a wonderful prospect for her.

And yet, a nagging reluctance to become excited by it lingered. The grand duchess was a most worthy lady and the compliment she had paid Wilhelmina was very great. Yet she would call the tune and Wilhelmina would have to dance to it. Didn't it mean giving the responsibility of his daughter into another's hands . . . ? And besides, as Her Grace had apparently pointed out, the life of a famous artist was not one to be envied. She would have no privacy, no peace. It would be a lonely life.

Yet if God had given her this talent, was it for him to deny that gift its fulfilment?

But it was not the best of times. It was far from good times. There were other forces to be considered. If things went as he feared, there would be no place for concert pianists.

He pulled open the drawer of his desk and took out a sheet of paper and an envelope. Placing it on the desk blotter, he dipped the quill into the ink and began to write. He requested to speak further regarding matters discussed at the grand duke's dinner. If Sir Percy could graciously accede to his request, he would be at his home in Wiesbaden one week before Christmas and would be honoured to receive a visit from him then. His wife and two daughters joined with him in urging him to pay them a visit.

He remained his obedient servant, Johann H. Gerhardt.

He blotted the note, folded it, placed it in the envelope and addressed it. He must now arrange for his messenger. If the note should fall into the wrong hands, it was sufficiently ambiguous not to arouse suspicion, he thought. Sir Percy would know what the matter to discuss was and would have the necessary information.

As Johann pushed back his chair from the desk and rose, he felt better than he had for some weeks. There was no doubt that indecision was the worst state to be in. It was certainly not decided yet that they should emigrate, but the first step to a life of greater stability, no matter what lay in between, had been taken.

A voice spoke from the door. 'What have you been doing at your desk at this time of day, Johann?'

He came towards her and said softly, 'I have been writing to Sir Percy.'

Sophia looked up at him quickly. 'So you are decided?'

'I have asked only to speak with him again. I have invited him to Wiesbaden while we are home the week before Christmas.'

'You were circumspect in your wording?'

He nodded. 'If we are to do this thing, it must all be finalised before anything is known.'

She shook her head. 'We will not be popular here. We will have to speak and go quickly.'

'If all goes well, I see this as God's opening for us. I did not seek this. Sir Percy suggested it. I have been seeking and asking God's guidance and this is what has come up.' He paused. 'I must talk more with the girls and prepare them.'

As he passed the globe on its stand by the window, Johann stopped. He turned the globe, tracing his finger across the channel to England, across the Atlantic. Then he followed down the coast to Rio and east across the Atlantic to South Africa, then across the vast Southern Ocean to Van Dieman's Land and up the coast to New South Wales. His heart lurched.

Of course, there was also the settlement in Victoria and now South Australia. Sir Percy had not mentioned these. It seemed to be New South Wales that he was specifically involved with. In any case, it was a long, long way from the fatherland. He dropped his hand and left the room.

Sophia went back to her sewing. Johann was deeply disturbed, she thought, though his step seemed brisker as he had left the apartment. Perhaps some of his tension was relieved in at least taking this step.

The door was thrust open and the girls burst in. 'Oh Mama, it is starting to snow. I do so love to see the first snow falling!'

Wilhelmina unbuttoned her cloak and, flinging off her hat, hung them on the stand. She hastened to the fire and held out her hands to the warmth, then turned and, with a mischievous glance at her sister, giggled, her eyes sparkling with fun. 'Oh Mama, you should have seen that new young officer we met yesterday. We met him on the way home and he escorted us the rest of the way.' She giggled again. 'He is absolutely smitten with Etty!'

'Really, Wilhelmina, you imagine things,' her sister cried, flushing crimson. 'I'm sure he was most polite.'

'Oh, he was polite,' chortled Wilhelmina. 'He was so polite he was almost tongue-tied. He almost fell over his own boots, because he couldn't take his eyes off her.' She went into peals of laughter again.

'Willy, don't tease your poor sister,' remonstrated Sophia, laughing in spite of herself. 'Any young man would find it hard not to be captivated by Henrietta. She grows so pretty and, with such apples in her cheeks from this exhilarating air . . . I am not surprised.'

Henrietta flushed again at this praise from

her stepmother. 'Mama' she called her, and 'Mama' she was in all but the physical fact. She was lucky.

Wilhelmina was bubbling on. 'We met Papa as we came in. I was glad to see him looking happier. He even joked with us when he noticed our escort — ' she said, glancing at her sister and giggling again, ' — or Henrietta's escort,' she corrected herself, 'leaving the entrance hall.'

'Oh Will, do stop it,' protested Henrietta.

'Yes, I think perhaps he is feeling better,' rejoined Sophia quickly. Perhaps she could at least prepare the ground for Johann. 'I think perhaps he has been coming to some conclusions and getting closer to making decisions about our future.'

The girls now were all interest. 'Do you know what they are, Mama?'

'I know he is writing requesting a British emissary to visit us when we are at home the week before Christmas,' she said, choosing her words carefully. 'Whatever your father decides, be certain his decision has not been arrived at lightly or without a great deal of deliberation.'

She paused then continued. 'Rest assured that whatever the decision, if it is going to take us out of this situation he fears will come, our lives will be thrust into very different paths. There is nothing quite like court life. We will not be in another court. There is unrest throughout this country.'

Wilhelmina looked at her searchingly. 'Mama, do you know what Papa has in mind? Is it something you think we will not like?'

'I will say no more now, my dears. Your father will speak to you when he is ready. I just want you to realise that whatever his decision is it will mean change — big change — possibly catastrophic change. But I know you both have great courage. It has perhaps not as yet been really tested. But I am confident it is there — and I am confident you will accept a challenge and even perhaps be sparked by a spirit of adventure. There,' she said as she jabbed her needle into the pin cushion, 'I will say no more.'

Ten days passed before the waited-for answer came. A commonplace acceptance letter, it simply stated Sir Percy Rutherford would be pleased to accept the kind invitation of Colonel Johann and Mrs Gerhardt to visit them at their home in Wiesbaden the week before Christmas. He would bring with him some interesting items he had collected for their diversion.

'The girls must now be told without delay,' Johann said to Sophia when he read the letter. 'It seems to me Sir Percy may have everything ready for us. He must be confident he has a suitable position for me.'

Sophia's inner calm was shattered. So Johann had made up his mind to accept should a suitable position be offered. Her heart thudded. What would it all entail? 'Oh Johann, I am afraid,' she said softly, putting her hand on his arm.

'Not as afraid as you may be if we stay and do nothing, my love.' Johann put his arm around her. 'God will lead us and protect us. We will go to freedom and opportunity and peace. We will make a new life.'

He was seated by the fire when the girls came in. He heard them coming along the hall. He would tell them now. 'My dears,' he called as they came to the door, 'come in. It is cosy here by the fire.'

They came in, rubbing their hands to warm them. Henrietta kissed his cheek and seated herself on the arm of his chair. Wilhelmina sat on the stool at his feet, holding her hands out to the fire.

'Have you had a pleasant afternoon?' he asked.

'Oh yes, Papa, thankyou. And Papa, it is so nice to see you looking happier.' Wilhelmina looked up at her father. 'Have you come to a decision about what we are to do?'

Her directness took him by surprise and

undermined his carefully prepared introduction to the subject. 'I have moved along that path, yes. Remember I mentioned Frederica to you and the decision of her family to emigrate to New South Wales?'

They nodded.

'Well, it so happened that same night I met an old acquaintance at the grand duke's banquet. He is a very influential Englishman, an emissary for the British government and the Queen of England. He is a man I hold in the greatest respect.

'We sat together at dinner. On both sides of us were parties imbibing rather too freely, but it gave us the chance for a confidential discussion. He is aware and holds the same view as I do regarding the state of our country. He is carrying out various assignments for his government while visiting our country.'

'What sort of assignments, Papa? Are they concerned with your decision?' Henrietta asked solemnly.

'Yes, my dear. The assignment he is entrusted with, which may be of concern to us, is to enlist people from all walks of life, all manner of occupations, to take their courage and their expertise and help to build a new world in a British colony.'

'Not . . . not New South Wales, Papa?'

Henrietta's eyes were wide in her stunned face. 'You do not think of going to New South Wales?'

'It is not decided yet, my dear. Sir Percy Rutherford is the Englishman I mentioned. He has accepted my invitation to visit us in Wiesbaden the week before Christmas. I conclude from his reply that he has something he believes will be of interest to us.'

'But Papa! The grand duchess! Her offer of patronage! What is to become of that? She has not discussed it further with us yet, having gone to Paris. But she will call us as soon as she gets back. Oh Papa, what of my music?'

Wilhelmina was blinking back the tears. Surely Papa was not going to take her away to some uncivilised place, from her career, her concerts, her music. Oh, it would be too bad, too bad — away from all her prospects and the grand duchess' patronage.

Johann's heart ached for her. He drew her to him. 'My darling, if we stay and the volcano of bitterness and hatred erupts, there will be no place for concert pianists.' He stroked her hair.

'But what about the grand duchess? Her promise?'

'My darling, in the ferment of what I

predict, there will be no place for the grand duchess either.'

Wilhelmina caught her breath. 'You can't mean . . . ?'

He nodded. 'Pray God it does not come to that. But I keep saying, 'remember France'. It happened there. It could happen again.'

7

The English visitor

The snow continued to fall intermittently right up to the week before Christmas when the family were to go home to prepare for the festival. They would then return to Heidelberg for Christmas at the castle.

The journey from Heidelberg had not held the usual joyous expectation. The thought uppermost in all their minds was, what would Sir Percy put before them? Would this be their last Christmas in their homeland? It was a subdued homecoming.

Wilhelmina sat now by her bedroom window, looking out at the cold scene. It would most likely be a very white Christmas.

She had been playing the piano all afternoon. The time had gone so quickly — as always, she thought, when the black and white keys made her fingers captive at the first touch.

If they did go to New South Wales or some such place, what would happen to her piano? She would die, just die without her piano. She thought again of Mr Chopin's words: 'Music hath charms to soothe the savage breast.' It sounded, the way he said it, as though it was a quote from a play or some such.

But how true. She herself felt better after her afternoon of music. It lifted her soul, held out a promise that all would be well. It offered hope.

The sound of a carriage and horses carried up to her from the street. She looked out to see a tall man in a heavy cloak alighting. He spoke to the driver and turned towards the door. The bell sounded throughout the house.

Johann, too, had heard the carriage. He stirred the fire. The servant came and announced that Sir Percy Rutherford had arrived and his carriage was waiting at the door.

Johann hastened to greet his guest. 'Sir Percy. I am so glad you could come,' he said, extending his hand. He spoke to the servant, directing him to attend Sir Percy's men and the horses and carriage. He ushered his guest into the study and motioned to the chairs beside the fire. 'You had a good journey, I trust?'

'A very cold journey, I'm afraid. The snow has been quite heavy. It impedes our progress somewhat. However, we were able to get through,' replied Sir Percy, seating himself and holding out his hands to the blaze.

He looked at Johann. 'I have some proposals for you to consider, Colonel,' he said directly. 'I will not prevaricate, but speak to you directly. I know you are deeply concerned about your future.'

He took the drink Johann was extending to him and sipped it appreciatively. 'I have perused the information I have been supplied by my government. There is one that seems to me to suit you eminently.'

Johann's heart leapt. Was this to be the answer he was seeking?

Sir Percy continued. 'It is a position offered by Mr James Montgomery. He has a large property on the Allyn River in the upper Hunter valley in New South Wales. He has a large establishment with 120 convicts assigned to him.

'He has been establishing his property for some years and is now seeking a competent and reliable man to be the veterinary surgeon and also to be overseer of his vineyards and winemaking. I thought this dual position would suit you admirably.' He looked at Johann enquiringly.

Johann's pulse was beating fast. 'Indeed, it seems a position designed for me.' He smiled, his eyes wide, hardly daring to hope the conditions would be as favourable. 'I have, of course, had many years experience in the army with our horses and the oversight of their care by the men. As you know, I have grown up with the vineyards and winery of my family. I know this industry like the back of my hand.'

He paused. 'Of course, I should have much to learn about the climate and soil, but I am sure I could do that.'

'Good. You are interested, then?'

'Very interested so far, Sir Percy.'

The Englishman sipped his drink and continued. 'There is a comfortable cottage for the person who fills this position. Also, such commodities as are produced on the property will be supplied. I refer to things such as meat and milk.' He smiled at Johann. 'And wine, of course, when you get it into production.'

He held up his glass. 'This is excellent wine,' he said. 'From your family vineyards?'

Johann nodded.

'There will also be a financial recompense commensurate with the position's responsibility and authority.'

'It sounds attractive,' Johann ventured.

'My government would conduct all arrangements with Mr Montgomery and also arrange and assist with the passage to the colony. It is, of course, possible to supply yourself with items to make your cabin and your passage more comfortable for the long journey.'

Sir Percy glanced at his host, noting the effect his words had produced. There was a light in his eyes that had not been there when he entered the room. A spark of interest, of adventure, of hope now glowed there.

'You must, of course, realise this is in a very remote area by European standards. The colony is still very young and, though great progress has been made since its ignoble beginnings, it is not Europe. Roads when you get out of the immediate town area, where there are roads, are tracks. Communication is slow in the extreme. Provisions are not always available.

'If the stock supplies run out, you must wait until the next ship arrives from England. For your family there are no stores such as they would be used to here. There are no theatres such as you know. There are, however, balls conducted in some of the grand homesteads and some concert halls in certain towns.'

He sipped his drink thoughtfully. 'One makes one's own entertainment in the colony. Settlers make long journeys for house parties, dances in woolsheds and such divertissements — staying overnight or longer, then making the long trek home. One is thrown back on one's own resources.'

Johann had watched his visitor eagerly as he was speaking, trying to absorb all that was being said.

He was stirred, there was no doubt about that. Something in him had awakened. The challenge beckoned. What had he to lose? His life in the army, his commission, his prestige? Where would they all be if revolution came?

Sir Percy was speaking again. 'There is opportunity in the new lands and freedom to shape your future. There is much to be said for that. For those who have courage and initiative and perseverance, there can be great prospects, far beyond those offering here. The climate, too, is very advantageous. Many who have had physical problems in our cold countries find their problems disappear in Australia.'

Johann's mind whirled, trying to visualise the country and the conditions Sir Percy had described.

'It is a great change, to leave Europe and emigrate to Australia. Nothing I can say can really prepare you for the change. I can give you facts. The rest has to be experienced.' Sir Percy rose. 'I will leave you now to consider all I have said.'

He handed Johann a card. 'I can be reached at this address if you wish to consult me further. I shall be in Wiesbaden until

Christmas Eve. I would appreciate your reply as early as possible. A ship, the *S.S. Parland*, is scheduled to leave London in early March for New South Wales. I would hope to have someone to fill this position on that ship. It is not very long. Then again, you consider your situation pressing, so perhaps it is advantageous.'

He smiled as they moved towards the door. 'You will have much to discuss with your family before making your decision.'

Johann helped him on with his cloak and handed him his hat. 'I wish you happy and profitable deliberations,' Sir Percy said.

Johann closed the door after him. He was gone. He retraced his steps to the study. Pouring himself another glass of wine, he sat down and stared into the fire.

He had such scanty details to make such a gigantic decision! Sir Percy had been most gracious, though, in giving him this time and in supplying, as far as he was able, a glimpse of the life he would be going to as well as the details of the position he was being offered.

He must call Sophia and the girls and tell them the news. In all probability they had heard the bell and were aware of the identity of his visitor. But he must sit for a few minutes and review it all. It would be an irreversible decision once made. He would not be able to retrace his steps. The fire burned down. He put another log on and scraped the coals together. He sat holding the poker in the coals, idly moving it, lost in thought.

The clock on the mantel struck. How long had he sat there? He must tell them. He pulled the bell cord. When the servant answered the call, he stood up. 'Please ask Mrs Gerhardt and my daughters to join me here in the study,' he said.

In a surprisingly short time, the door burst open again and Wilhelmina ran into the room. Henrietta followed her closely and shortly came Sophia, her face creased with concern as she caught her husband's eye.

'I perceive you may all have guessed who my visitor was,' Johann said with a wry smile as he closed the door firmly. 'You are right. It was Sir Percy Rutherford. He has offered me a position and has been very gracious in trying to give me a picture of conditions in New South Wales.'

He moved back to the fire. 'Sit down, my dears. Sit down. We must discuss all your feelings about this. We must be wise. We may not like the outcome. But it must be what is best for us all. I must make the final decision, but I want to know your feelings.'

He looked at Sophia, her anxiety clear on her face.

'Wilhelmina, pour your mother a glass of wine, then I will tell you all I know.' He paused. 'We must make our decision quickly. Sir Percy leaves Wiesbaden on Christmas Eve. I must give him my answer before then.'

He paused again. 'A ship leaves London the first week in March, bound for the colony. We must decide if we are going to be aboard that ship.'

8

An irreversible decision

The next hour was filled with questions, anxieties, doubts. Johann recounted again and again the scanty details he knew. They tried to build up a picture of what it would be like.

Always it came back to the same points. Here was a position offered to him, a position he could fill with confidence. A comfortable home would be provided. Their passage would be arranged and assisted in a comfortable cabin. There would be people to welcome them and help them to settle. And above all, it would be a solution to their dilemma of the threatening uprising and danger.

'And Sir Percy assures me that there are opportunities for those willing to seek and strive for them far beyond what is offering in Europe at this time,' Johann added. 'We may in time find ourselves very well situated indeed if we approach this in the right spirit.'

'But Papa, what about my piano?' wailed Wilhelmina. 'I will die, just die without my piano!'

Johann put his hand on her shoulder and looked into her eyes, smiling. 'There is no need to die, my darling, no need at all. We will, of course, take your piano with us. We will take some of our treasured pieces with us so we will not feel our surroundings are too alien.'

Wilhelmina lifted her face to her father in surprise. 'Take our piano? I had no idea we could do such a thing.'

'Oh, yes. If we decide to accept the offer, we will take a great deal with us. All that is feasible,' he assured them.

He saw Sophia visibly relax. How important her home was to her — all the precious pieces she had collected over the years.

He wondered just what the comfortable cottage would be like. Would their treasures be grossly out of place? Or would it really be as he hoped? All things were relative and what was considered a comfortable cottage in Europe may not be quite the same in this struggling colony.

He turned again to Wilhelmina. 'I am very conscious of the change you must consider after your excitement of the great prospects offered you by Her Grace the grand duchess, my dear. It pains me to have to speak to you like this. But as I have said, in the world that I fear will be upon us here in Baden very soon, there will be no place for years for a concert pianist, or even a grand duchess.'

Wilhelmina nodded. A tear slipped down her nose and fell on her hand. She lifted her hand and wiped her eyes, swallowing the lump in her throat with difficulty.

Johann turned to Henrietta. 'And what of you, my dear? You have been very quiet.'

'I have no great career prospect such as Will's to renounce, Papa. I am enjoying my social life here at the palace and at home since I came out.' She paused, solemn, then said wistfully, 'I dare say there will be some social life in New South Wales — or we shall make it, as Sir Percy says.' She paused again. 'I am sure there must be some young people we can make friends with.' She added rather desperately, 'There must be young people besides convicts, surely — people of our own social standing, I mean.'

'I am sure there must be, my dear.' Johann looked at her keenly. 'You have not formed any serious particular relationship with a young man here, have you?'

Henrietta looked directly at her father. 'No, Papa, no-one of special account. I have enjoyed the company of many of the younger officers, but no-one in particular.'

'They are all besotted with her, Papa,' chimed in Wilhelmina, wiping her eyes. 'You should see them. Really, they are almost sickening sometimes. They fall over each other to win her favour.'

'That is as it should be,' smiled Johann. 'She will take the colony by storm. There will be other young suitors in plenty.'

Sophia had been quiet for some time. Her fears were somewhat mollified by Johann's assurances. If she could make a home even something like she had been used to — the standard and comfort — she would manage. If they could maintain their social standing so she could keep her head high, she could adapt.

She lifted her eyes and met Johann's gaze upon her. 'So you have decided to accept?' she asked quietly.

He nodded. 'I think it is what we must do,' he said. 'We have prayed for direction. This is what has come. There has been nothing else. I could not find a position more suited to my capabilities. We should do well. It is a position of responsibility and authority and Sir Percy assured me the financial remuneration would be commensurate with the position.' He was silent a moment, gazing into the fire. 'It is just the break with the life we know, with our past, with the heritage from our ancestors.'

In silence they nodded agreement. Johann slapped his knee. 'But we must face the future, if we are to have a future. Then we must be brave and trust in God.'

He rose and paced the length of the room. 'We do not have much time for preparation. We must decide what we will take with us to the new world. Then we must pack.'

He looked at Wilhelmina. 'And, my little one, when I have handed my resignation to the grand duke, we must brave an interview with the grand duchess. We will say nothing of our fears of the future here in Baden, only that I have been offered an important position in the colony and have decided to emigrate.'

He pulled a face at his daughter. 'She will not be pleased. She will consider us most ungrateful, but we must accept that. Who knows?' he cried, waving his hand. 'You may become the first concert pianist in Australia.'

* * *

It was not easy, not easy at all to write his resignation. All his adult life he had been in the army. He had reached the rank of colonel. He was a good officer, respected by his men. The life was in his blood. He had welcomed the extra privileges and prestige as a member of the court. He admired and respected the grand duke.

No, it was not easy. The words would not come. But he must do it. He had Sophia and the girls to consider.

If he were alone, he would stay and face what he had to. But he was not alone. They were dependent upon him. At last it was done. He folded the page and sealed the envelope.

He rose and, putting the envelope in his inner pocket, left the room and made his way towards the grand duke's apartments to beg an audience with His Grace.

The grand duchess glared at Johann in disbelief. 'You are what, Colonel?' she rasped. 'Emigrating to the British colony of New South Wales? Are you mad?'

Johann bowed his head, then returned her gaze. 'It grieves me beyond words to displease Your Grace. I am most conscious of the favour you have bestowed upon Wilhelmina in offering her your patronage. She also is greatly in your debt and is anxious that you understand our position. We are most grateful for your beneficence.'

'Grateful! Grateful! Then why in heaven's name are you depriving her of an illustrious career, sir, and taking her to the wilds of an uncivilised country?' She glared at him, her face suffused with her anger.

This man was taking her protege, the artist

she had discovered, to the other side of the world! Her plans for Wilhelmina were to come to naught. What a fool she would appear to Mr Chopin! What of her plans to build a concert hall honouring the artist under her patronage? It was beyond belief! To refuse her patronage!

'The position I have been offered, Your Grace, is one of importance. I have given over thirty years of my life in His Grace's service in the army. I would not have too many more years in active service. I must think of the future.' Johann spoke quietly but definitely.

'Then if you must go off on this wild goose chase, leave Wilhelmina behind to fulfil the destiny of which I believe she is capable.' Perhaps she could yet save the situation. It may be possible yet to still bring to consummation her dreams and plans. 'When Wilhelmina is under my patronage, she will be well cared for. She will want for nothing.' Surely he must see how gracious she was being. He could not possibly refuse.

★   ★   ★

Johann looked at his daughter. He smiled slightly without mirth. He lifted his head and returned the grand duchess' gaze. 'Believe me, Your Grace, I deeply appreciate your

79

interest and favour towards my daughter. But I also feel deeply my responsibility as her father. God has given her into my care and I must discharge that sacred trust until she is of age and beyond need of my protection. With the greatest regret we must decline your most magnanimous offer.'

She could not believe her ears. She should have finalised all this before going off to Paris. Perhaps the delay between speaking to the girl after she played for Mr Chopin and this audience had caused him to be disinclined towards her proposition. After all, she had spoken only to the girl, not to her father.

'Then you are refusing my patronage?' she asked coldly.

'Regretfully and with the greatest consciousness and appreciation, yes, Your Grace.'

She looked at Wilhelmina standing quietly beside her father. 'And you, Wilhelmina. What have you to say?' She looked coldly at the object of her proffered favour.

Wilhelmina returned the grand duchess' gaze, her eyes great pools of unfathomable emotion.

'I am deeply grateful for your offer, Your Grace. I shall always remember your graciousness. But I must go with my family. My father has made his decision, believing it is for all our welfare and I must abide by it.'

The grand duchess threw down the book she had in her agitation picked up from the table. 'Your father, Wilhelmina, is a fool!' she cried witheringly. She turned on her heel and flung herself from the room.

9

The long journey begins

It was done. There was no turning back now. Sir Percy had been notified. Johann had sent a note by hand, stating that he would accept the position with Mr Montgomery at 'Llanflylhn' and that they would be on the ship *S.S. Parland* when it sailed in March.

The grand duke had been surprised and sorry to receive Johann's resignation but, though he could not understand anyone having a desire to emigrate to such a wild, uncivilised part of the world, he wished him well and congratulated him on his many years of faithful service to himself and the state of Baden.

There were no such pleasantries from the grand duchess. She was offended and affronted in the extreme. Wilhelmina sent a short composition for piano, which she had composed, dedicated to the grand duchess as a mark of appreciation. It was returned unopened.

Now the preparations were in full swing. Sophia stood in the middle of the gracious dining room. What to take? If only she could transport her house as it stood. But that was not possible. She must make choices.

The piano would go. That was the first priority. Wilhelmina must never feel she had been forced to forego her music. The chiffonier, the two tapestry set chairs, the credenza and her bed must all go. She would see what else it may be possible to take after the trunks were packed.

Their clothes would all have to be packed. What would they need in their new life? Never mind, they must all go. There may not be occasion to wear their court clothes, but if it so transpired, they could be modified to suit. The household items, the porcelain, glass, the crystal and the linen: oh, there would be so many boxes and trunks!

At last it was finished. The servants had been paid and dismissed. They were sad to go. It was not easy to find such a congenial position today. The Colonel and Mrs Gerhardt, though their standards were high, were fair and considerate employers. The girls, too, were pleasant and accepted their responsibilities in the smooth running of the house. They were interested and energetic young ladies, even though Wilhelmina was so outspoken.

Jost Gerhardt, Johann's brother, had been

greatly perturbed when acquainted with their decision to emigrate. What of the family tradition? Certainly Johann was not on the estate, but he was still a Gerhardt of Wiesbaden. Johann had a hard time explaining, telling of his fears for the future, of forthcoming trouble as he saw it, of the special danger to his family because of his position in the army and as a member of the court.

At length Jost understood. 'And you say you are going to be in charge of the vineyards and winemaking?' he said. 'You should do well at that. We have been steeped in it since babyhood.'

'I am confident,' replied Johann. 'Though, of course, the climate will be very different — and I know nothing of the soil.'

'If the soil is any good at all, it should go well. It will certainly not be worn out and impoverished. And it will be virgin soil as far as crops and especially grapes are concerned. I wonder what varieties grow there? Is the vineyard and winery established?' Jost looked at his brother.

'That I do not know,' Johann replied. 'The information I have is very sketchy.' He took a deep breath. 'I shall just have to find out all these things when I get there.' He passed his hand over his eyes and forehead. 'It is a very big step,' he added.

Jost looked at him with concern. Johann did not appear really well. He hoped when he got away he would relax. The long journey may provide a respite from the tensions of the last months.

'May God go with you, my brother,' he said, putting an affectionate arm around Johann's shoulders. 'Keep me informed of your progress — and how the girls fare. I care deeply for them. You are a Gerhardt of the Gerhardt vineyards. The Gerhardt coffers are not empty. Do not hesitate to notify me if you should find reverse. We are brothers.'

Johann's eyes misted. He clasped his brother's hand. He was a good man, a man of the soil. A Gerhardt.

The last trunk was closed. The last box secured. The furniture had gone ahead. The door was closed for the last time. They would stay with Uncle Jost tonight and tomorrow sail down the Rhine.

Sophia gave a little smothered sob as she turned away. The girls were surreptitiously wiping their eyes. Johann had an ache in his chest. I must calm myself, he thought. I am getting too emotional. It will be well.

The clouds had cleared when morning came. The sun sparkled on the snow-clad trees and buildings. The surrounding country was clothed in its most charming winter finery.

They boarded the vessel amidst clamour and scurry on the wharf. Only the cabin trunk for the time until they boarded the *S.S. Parland* would be placed in their cabin. The rest would be reallocated when they got to London.

Their farewells were said. Aunt Helena wept copiously as she kissed her nieces goodbye.

The ship's bell clanged, the ropes were cast off, the wind caught the sails and they were moving. The beautiful Rhine never looked more beautiful. The water sparkled and glistened as they moved. Johann stood at the rail. Sophia and the girls had gone below to organise the cabin.

The panorama of the Rhine valley unfolded before his eyes: the steeply sloping hills, covered with the famous vineyards, renowned throughout the known world; the buildings with their steeply pitched roofs; here and there castles, hundreds of years old, some built on lofty vantage points; and the monasteries: all the evidence of civilisation, of development over centuries — ordered, cultured, sophisticated.

He sighed deeply. Pray God he was doing the right thing. He put his hand over his eyes and rubbed his forehead. His head was throbbing again. He would feel better when they got to London and the homeland was left behind. He had not been aware of just how deeply he was steeped in his homeland.

They disembarked when they berthed at London and wended their way through the melee of the wharf. A cab was soon found and they were whisked away to the lodgings prepared for them by Sir Percy. He would, he said, call on them at their lodgings the evening of their arrival to acquaint them with further details for their journey.

The rooms were comfortably furnished, a warm fire burning in the sitting room. A buxom serving-maid brought their meal and placed it on the table in their rooms. She chatted cheerfully as she set the table and removed the covers on the food. The appetising aroma wafted through the room.

'If there's anything you might be wanting, if you'd just be pulling the rope,' she said, indicating the bell cord, 'I'll be here in a twinkling,' she said breezily.

They took their places at the table. Johann gave thanks and they partook of their first meal on foreign soil. The wine was good, but not their Gerhardt vintage.

The *S.S. Parland* was scheduled to sail on 8 March. They would have a short time to spend in London. Sir Percy, when he arrived, explained the arrangements and responsibilities, both of his government and the emigrants in this agreement.

'I am sure you will find little to complain of in this scheme,' he said. 'We are most anxious to have happy free settlers, anxious to prosper in the new land and thereby help to hasten its development and prosperity, both economically and socially. People of your calibre, Colonel, are what we are looking for.' He smiled. 'Custom dies hard. I should now say *Mr* Gerhardt, I suppose.'

The days dragged. They had few acquaintances in England with whom they were on visiting terms. The girls explored the shops but, under the circumstances, bought little. Johann checked again the money he had brought — all their money.

It would be better once they got settled and into the new position. Though it was a sizable amount, the uncertainty of when the next income would be received caused him a wave of unaccustomed insecurity.

During the first days of March, they took on board the *Parland* those things they had prepared for their comfort — the chest of drawers for clothes, shelves and books, the little harp and the flute (they must have some music) — and the wine — some of their own homeland wine. There was Sophia's medicine chest and the feather eiderdown.

The eighth dawned clear. Spring would soon be coming. The worst of the weather should be over.

They boarded the vessel. It looked frighteningly small to travel all that distance across the open seas. Those southern seas were almost unknown.

Only Sir Percy was there to see them off. He came, of course, to farewell all those brave souls of all social strata who were emigrating. They didn't know how many.

The crew were busy. Some looked very rough fellows indeed. Perhaps, though, they were good seamen. At last the bell sounded. The ropes cast off and they were moving down the Thames.

They moved slowly. There were other craft on the river. Wilhelmina and Henrietta stood beside their father, watching the passing vista as they moved. It was a vast city.

By mid-afternoon they had reached Gravesend. Here another delay awaited them. The wind had dropped and so the anchor was lowered. They lay at rest. Day followed day. Still the wind was not propitious.

As the 13th of March dawned, the longed-for favourable wind arose and they sailed out into the open sea.

They were on their way to Australia.

10

The doldrums

The meal had been good, the wine excellent. Since it had been from Johann's own supply brought from the ancestral vineyards, that was assured. The compliments had been enthusiastic and freely forthcoming.

The company had been congenial. Johann looked around the table. The officers were mostly younger men, ranging from the late twenties to early forties.

The ship's doctor was a man of possibly early fifties. A seasoned medico and sailor, he had spent several years on convict transports and had lurid tales to tell when encouraged of conditions below deck where these wretched dregs of humanity had been herded and of the poor wretches themselves.

The captain was the oldest of the assembled company. Johann guessed he would be well in his fifties. He was fit, though, and observed the world around him from steely blue eyes. His officers obviously respected him and he ruled the ship with an iron fist.

Three other passengers were enjoying the captain's hospitality at this dinner. They were an English couple by the name of Henshaw and a young Scot, Angus McKenzie.

The ladies, dressed to complement the captain and his dinner table, added elegance and a touch of unreality in the isolated world of the dining room of the small ship afloat in the vastness of the Atlantic Ocean. Johann's gaze moved to his wife and daughters. He had noticed the gaze of others in the company frequently returning to the two girls. How pretty and well groomed they were. Wilhelmina was not really grown up yet, but the promise was there. Henrietta was a real beauty.

'It is a pity there is not room enough to dance on board ship, Miss Gerhardt. We could have a right royal time with such beautiful ladies to partner.' It was the young second officer speaking.

'And what would you use for music, Mr Jones?' asked the ship's doctor, joining in the frivolity. 'Perhaps we could call up some mermaids from the deep to charm your feet.'

'Or King Neptune's court,' interjected the captain. 'We will soon be in the tropics.' He lifted his eyebrows and grimaced. 'That is when we shall need all the diversions we can muster. The heat and the uncertainty of winds can make it hard to bear the doldrums.'

'If there were an abundance of ladies, Wilhelmina could be spared to play the flute for us,' ventured Henrietta.

'Or I could unpack my bagpipes from my luggage in the hold,' suggested Angus McKenzie with a twinkle. There was a general laughter at the prospect of the bagpipes in the confines of the dining or ward rooms.

'In any case, Miss Gerhardt, there will no doubt be any amount of social life in New South Wales for you to enjoy.'

Mr Jones smiled openly, admiring Henrietta. 'Oh, for the good fortune of being the man who escorts you to such divertissements.'

There was a knock at the door. A duty officer entered and spoke briefly to the doctor. He rose and addressed the captain. 'You will excuse me, sir? I am needed below.'

The captain lifted his hand in dismissal. He turned back to his guests. 'This place you are going to, Mr Gerhardt: is it an established property?' he asked.

'It is established to some extent, Captain. There are 120 convicts assigned to Mr Montgomery for work on 'Llanfylhn'. I know it has been in operation for at least ten years.

'As far as the vineyards and winemaking

are concerned, which is to be my responsibility along with the veterinary work, I have only the scantiest details. I do not know even if there are any vines planted.' He took a deep breath. 'I shall just have to find all this out when I get there.'

'And you are going halfway round the world, knowing no more than that?' The first officer had not spoken before. His tone was deriding, his expression supercilious.

Wilhelmina glanced hastily at her father. Johann had flushed. His tone when he spoke was calm, controlled. 'There are many things to be taken into account when one considers a move such as we have taken,' he said, looking directly at the young man. 'The extent of the development of wine production does not seem to me a deciding factor.'

'It could be a deciding factor if the climate and soil are not suitable, or there is lack of water and they just don't grow.' He leaned forward and poured himself another glass of wine. 'You could find yourself without a position and little offering in the colony and a wife and daughters to support.'

'My father is not a fool, sir,' burst out Wilhelmina. Who did this upstart think he was to speak to her father in this way? 'Our comfort is being attended to in every way. We have a home waiting for us.'

There was a momentary silence of shock following her outburst and a few quickly concealed smiles from the older men. The officer in turn flushed angrily. To be chastened by this slip of a girl!

Johann cut in hastily. 'We shall do very well,' he smiled. 'We are indeed lucky to be going to such a position with a comfortable home prepared.'

The captain rose, the indication that the meal was at an end. 'It grows hot in here.' He turned to Fitzroy, his first officer. 'A turn around the deck may provide some relief, Mr Fitzroy. You will accompany me?' They trooped out. Sophia led the way to the cabin.

As they passed the companion ladder leading down to the crew's quarters, they heard moaning and Dr Cartwright's voice. 'Clean this up and swab the deck. If we're not careful we'll have fever spreading through the ship.' A door closed and footsteps sounded, fading away into the bowels of the ship. They exchanged alarmed glances.

⋆ ⋆ ⋆

The blue of sky and sea merged into haze at the far horizon. It was difficult to tell where one finished and the other began. The heat was intense.

Johann wiped his forehead with his handkerchief. If only a wind would spring up! The sails hung limply, uselessly as far as the ship was concerned. The vessel swayed slightly with only the movements of the ocean currents.

The doldrums were living up to the captain's description. Day after day they had hung motionless. Not a breath of wind rose to expedite their progress.

'You are feeling the heat, sir.'

Johann swung round. Dr Cartwright was behind him.

'Indeed, yes.' He sighed. 'How long must we endure this?'

The doctor shrugged and smiled ruefully. 'Who can say?' He looked out across the expanse of ocean. 'Oh, that we had some way of moving across the oceans without being dependent upon the winds!' he looked at Johann. 'However, it will come when it is ready. It always has.'

They moved away from the rail and continued walking along the deck.

'Our next port of call is Rio, is it not? Then Cape Town?'

The doctor nodded. 'That is so. You will all be glad of a time on dry land at both places. At the Cape, we take on stock for your Australian settlement. There is always demand for more cattle and sheep these days. The rural sector must be growing.' He smiled at Johann. 'No doubt you will be an authority on that before long.'

'It is surprising you can handle stock on a ship such as this,' Johann observed.

'Oh, we usually have pigs and poultry, too, in our cargo. The faraway colony has no other means of obtaining these farm essentials than our ships from England.' He corrected himself hastily. 'Although, I must add there is a small contingent of enterprising fellows from New South Wales who have purchased old ships and are making their fortunes buying up goods in Asia and bringing them back to their stores in Sydney. Some of these also sail to England. I feel sure some also carry stock back from the Cape.'

Dr Cartwright stopped to listen. 'There is music!' he exclaimed.

'That would be my daughters,' Johann smiled.

The sweet, haunting notes of the flute and the gentle sounds of the plucked strings of the harp wafted up to them. 'It is beautiful.' The lines of the doctor's face relaxed as he listened. Then a girl's sweet voice lifted in an old folk song.

The doctor stood as motionless as the sails above him. At last, as the sound died away, he turned to Johann. 'Our existence, those of us who spend the greatest part of our life at sea, is not renowned for an abundance of beauty.' He gestured to the hatch leading down to the crew's quarters. 'There is little of beauty down there at any time and less at present.'

'Is there any further spread of the fever?'

The doctor looked sharply at Johann. 'Fever?' he rapped. 'Who mentioned fever?'

Johann put out a conciliatory hand. 'We overheard a scrap of conversation the night you were called from the captain's dinner,' he said. 'Do not fear. We have not spoken of it except with each other.'

The doctor relaxed. 'It is worrying. They are rough fellows, not used to washing. Their work is hard. I am doing what I can. I do not want panic among the ship's company. We cannot get away from it.'

He grasped the rail. 'And the longer we wait here in this airless hell, the more chance there is of the spread of disease . . . and discontent.' He straightened. 'I must go down again and check the sick and conditions down there.'

He walked quickly away. Johann watched as he descended the ladder.

★　★　★

97

Their own cabin was as comfortable as could be expected in the small space possible on ship. They had brought their chest of drawers. It now contained their clothes, fitting neatly across one end of the cabin. Sophia had laid out her toiletries: the silver brush and hand mirror, her comb and perfume bottle, the pin tray and the little box with her jewellery. The silver-framed mirror was on the wall.

Shelves had been placed on the wall opposite the bunk and were now filled with books to while away the long hours. The porthole, through which they had a view of the smooth sea, provided fresh air and light. It was as comfortable as one could expect.

As Johann entered, Sophia was lying on the bunk wrapped in a loose, cool robe. The two girls were seated, one at the foot of the bed, the other on a small stool.

'You have been charming Dr Cartwright with your music,' he said, smiling at them. 'He thought it quite beautiful.' He sobered. 'I inadvertently asked about the fever when he alluded to the crew's quarters. He was immediately very guarded. I assured him we had spoken of it only to each other.' He paused. 'We must be very careful. It would be well to keep as far away as possible from the crew's quarters.'

11

Tempers frayed

The sound of shouting woke them as the first light filtered into the cabin. There was the clash of metal and thuds of something heavy on deck.

The heat was excessive. It settled over them all like an overweight blanket, oppressive, inescapable. Nerves and tempers were stretched to the limit. Wilhelmina lay looking up at the ceiling of the cabin. How much longer would they stay motionless in this never-ending expanse of salt water? She wiped the perspiration from her face. This was as bad as the heat, this perpetual wetness.

Oh, how she longed for the crispness of the air at home, the fresh tingling as snowflakes fell on her upturned face. Would she ever see snow again, ever run down the hill, gather up snow to a ball to throw at Henrietta as, laughing, they made their way home? What would become of home? Would Papa's fears be realised? She shuddered at the picture such an eventuality conjured up.

A scuffle sounded in the passageway and

something bumped the door. She sat up, startled, her eyes wide with fright. She glanced quickly to the door to ensure it was securely locked. 'Did you hear that, Etty?' she whispered.

Henrietta had jumped out of her bunk and was pulling on her robe. She put her finger to her pursed lips. Footsteps were receding and muttered oaths could be heard. Henrietta opened the door and looked along the passageway. An officer was disappearing, dragging one of the crew, his arm bent behind him.

'What was that about?' Wilhelmina whispered.

'I don't know. But there seems to be some trouble.' Henrietta closed the door and bolted it again. 'It must be dreadful down in their quarters,' she ventured. 'The heat is bad enough here, but it must be so much worse down there.' She proceeded to dress herself. 'As soon as Papa is up I want to go up on deck, before the sun gets too hot. I can't stand it in here all closed up.'

It was after breakfast when they were seated in their parents' cabin that a knock came on the door. Johann opened the door to find Dr Cartwright standing there. 'Good morning, sir. May I come in and have a word with you?' The doctor's expression was grave.

Johann moved aside to allow him to enter. 'Is all well, Doctor?' he asked.

'Unfortunately, no.' The doctor moved to the chair Johann indicated. 'There is trouble among the crew,' he said quietly. 'These doldrums try the control of us all, but these fellows live and work in a hard, cutthroat world. It is rather like the law of the jungle. Their work is usually hard and taxing on strength and energies and this idleness leaves them with pent-up emotions and excess of unused energy.'

He took a deep breath and looked from one to the other. 'Add to this the fear of this fever and we have a volatile keg of gunpowder. They have been fighting among themselves. One man will be lucky to survive after being stabbed and this morning one of the officers was attacked.'

He looked directly at the girls. 'I suggest you young ladies do not leave your cabin unless in the company of your father or some other escort.' He smiled grimly. 'They have been a long while away from home and the comforts of feminine company.'

The girls glanced quickly at Sophia and back to Dr Cartwright. Henrietta spoke for them both. 'Thankyou for warning us, Dr Cartwright. We will certainly take your advice.' She hesitated then continued, 'Has there been any spread of the fever?' All eyes confronted the doctor.

'A man died last night.' There was a shock of indrawn breath. 'He went overboard this morning.' His hands rested on his knees. 'This has done nothing to smooth the troubled waters.'

'If only we could get the wind we need to proceed on our journey.' Sophia picked up her fan. 'How much longer, Doctor?'

He shook his head, shrugging his shoulders. 'Things will certainly improve when the wind comes,' he replied, 'including the situation of the spread of fever.'

'Can anything be done?' Johann's concern was evident.

'Extra care with hygiene and fresh air,' the doctor replied. 'I see you have a small spirit stove. Boil all the water that passes your lips. Drink nothing that has not been boiled.' He smiled briefly. 'Except your wine, of course. That is safe.' He rose to go. 'I must go about my business. I wanted to warn you. I have already spoken to the other passengers. Once we get the winds, we will soon be in Rio and spirits will improve out of sight. Then the Cape — and we will be taking on quite a consignment of stock.' He smiled as he opened the door. 'We'll be a veritable Noah's Ark then.'

He turned back as he left the room. Smiling diffidently at the two girls, he said, 'Perhaps the young ladies could favour us with their music. It could do much to diffuse that keg of gunpowder I spoke of. It would lift the morale of everyone.' He closed the door and they heard his footsteps departing.

'Oh Johann, this is terrible!' wailed Sophia. 'Here we have left our homeland to escape danger and turmoil, only to find ourselves in this position.' Her distress was mounting.

'Now calm yourself, my dear. We have been warned. There are things we can do to protect ourselves.' Johann spoke in a decisive manner. 'Come now. Dry your eyes. We will take Dr Cartwright's advice to heart. Henrietta, set the spirit stove up. And Wilhelmina, perhaps you can find a jug to keep the boiled water in. I will fill the kettle.'

The decisive attitude and action helped them all. Sophia drew out a bottle of wine and set it on the tray with glasses. When the stove was lit and the kettle boiling, the feeling of panic had passed.

They played all afternoon — the haunting, sweet love songs of their homeland, the reels and folk songs they had all danced to. Their feet tapped in time with the music and, as Wilhelmina's nimble fingers found the tune on the flute, the others sang. They had left the door of the cabin open to help the sound of the music find its way throughout the ship.

Angus McKenzie and Peggy and Albert Henshaw soon joined the little party and added their voices to the melody, though many of the songs were unknown to them.

'Now what about a good old Scottish song?' pleaded Angus McKenzie. But the girls were unable to oblige. 'Then I shall just have to unpack my bagpipes and go up on deck. You've awakened my musical soul now and I won't be content till I've expressed all these pent-up feelings in the music of the highlands.'

And so the afternoon flew. As they finished one song, someone was heard whistling with them from some far corner of the ship.

As the sun dropped into the ocean, they all left the cabin and mounted the companion-way. Was there a fresh breath of air? They strolled along, the girls following behind Johann and Sophia. Jones the young second officer joined them, exchanging pleasantries with Johann and Sophia, then offering his arm to Henrietta.

Wilhelmina slackened her pace, pretending interest in something else far out on the water — and moved over to stand by the rail. Really, it was laughable how every young man fawned on Henrietta. They made such ninnies of themselves mooning around her. She turned to follow, realising suddenly with alarm how far they had gone.

A rough fellow, a crew hand, was standing behind her, leaning towards her. She could smell the stench of his unwashed body. He leered at her, smiling, his eyes glistening. He moved his hand stealthily towards her, making lewd gestures.

'Don't touch me, you filthy reptile.' In her alarm, her voice was high. 'And keep your eyes to yourself.' She swung past him and almost ran along the deck.

Jones and her father, having heard her raised voice, were hurrying towards her. 'That imbecile there tried to accost me,' she gasped loudly. 'The impertinence of him!'

'Hush, my dear, hush. You are making a commotion.' Johann took her arm. 'Did he touch you?'

'No. But he would have. Ughh! The smell of him! No wonder there is fever aboard!'

'For goodness sake, Wilhelmina, be quiet. You are drawing attention to yourself. We don't want more trouble.' The sound of her mother's voice scolding quietened her.

They all went below and closed the door of the cabin. Jones had gone about his duties. 'Now what actually happened?' Johann asked.

'He made suggestive gestures to me!'

Wilhelmina exploded. 'The impertinence! The cheek!'

'But he didn't actually touch you? Or threaten you?'

'No-o,' she agreed. 'But if I hadn't told him off, he might have.'

'You shouldn't have noticed him, Will,' added Henrietta.

'But I did notice him,' she answered indignantly.

Henrietta lifted her eyebrows and smiled. 'Yes. I know. But a lady wouldn't have noticed.'

Wilhelmina's eyes widened. A lady? Wasn't she a lady?

Sophia intervened. 'He was very remiss to approach you like that. But Henrietta is right. A lady would have ignored him and walked away. You were turning heads to look at you, making a fuss.' She put her arm around her daughter's shoulders. 'You must learn to keep your dignity — to be a lady, my dear. It will be your protection.'

There were no more walks on deck without the girls in front. Johann was disturbed. This was just the sort of thing Dr Cartwright had warned them of. If Wilhelmina had been alone, it may have been a much more serious occurrence. His heart failed him as he thought of the

106

possibility of such harm to her. They must be more careful.

★ ★ ★

The ship rose and fell as one shaking, stretching after sleep, as the skirl of McKenzie's bagpipes was borne out over the Atlantic Ocean. There was something incongruous in the sound, so far from the hills and crags of its native Scotland. And yet, Johann thought, it clutched at your heart.

The stillness, the isolation was becoming more and more unbearable and the longing for land insufferable. But this journey wasn't half over yet. They would have to muster their reserves.

12

The Cape

Rio was left behind. The winds had come and carried them on their course to the busy bustling seaport. The noise and crowds of people had been a shock after so many weeks encooped in the confines of the *S.S. Parland*. Rio was an exotic place. The people, their dress, their city were so different from anything they had ever experienced. Yet the many churches, the bells ringing the angelus (evidence of the Portuguese origins), the mountains behind the city all stirred memories of home.

The weather, though far more bearable than they had experienced in the doldrums, was still hot and humid. It had been a relief to go ashore, to feel solid land under their feet and to exercise their legs.

It had all been very interesting, but they were glad when the ship's business was completed and they were again on their way.

'When we need to stir up wind again, we shall know what to do.' Henrietta glanced at Angus McKenzie. He raised his eyes in question. 'We shall simply request you to play your bagpipes again,' she laughed. 'When we were becalmed back in the doldrums, the breeze rose as you started to play and it's been a good, useful wind ever since.'

They had been standing by the rail watching the receding city disappear from view. Once again, their horizons were nothing but water. They were joined by Dr Cartwright. 'Well, back to sea again,' he commented. 'That stretch ashore and the fresh food we were able to take aboard have done wonders, though.'

'Do you think the danger of the spread of fever has been averted then?' Johann said softly.

'I hope so,' Cartwright replied. 'We have been able to open up the quarters below to the fresh air and thoroughly fumigate.'

He looked directly at Johann with a slight smile. 'The fear of contagion amongst the crew has greatly diminished. That in itself is a big step in the right direction. A positive outlook makes a big contribution to health and immunity to disease.'

★   ★   ★

It was surprising, Wilhelmina mused, how quickly they recrossed the Atlantic. Today they would berth in Table Bay, Cape Town.

Wherever would they stow the livestock it was said they would be taking on board? What of the noise — and the smell? She wrinkled her nose in distaste. How she hated bad smells! Thinking of it reminded her of the sailor who had accosted her. She could still recall his stench. He had been working on deck when she went up yesterday, but had averted his eyes as she approached.

But cattle, pigs, sheep, roosters and hens! How would they cope with it all? Oh, how good it would be to reach this New South Wales they were bound for.

'A penny for your thoughts.' Mr Jones had come up behind her.

'Oh, I was thinking of the livestock we are to take aboard.' Wilhelmina smiled. 'However are you able to cope with them on ship? The smell alone must be dreadful.'

He laughed. 'We do our best,' he said. 'It may not be as bad as you think.' He looked at her, his eyes twinkling. 'You are not a keen farmer, I think. Do you ride?'

'Oh yes. I love riding. Papa has taught me since I was very small. He is very particular. But then, you see, even though I had to groom my horse, I did it in a clean stable with fresh straw on the floor. It just smelt of horse and fresh straw. I didn't mind that very much.'

'And what of Miss Gerhardt? Does she ride as well?'

She knew this would happen. Sooner or later he would turn the conversation to Henrietta. Here she had been having a sensible conversation with him and what does he do? He must ask about Henrietta. The man was besotted with her. 'Oh yes. She rides very well,' she replied.

'I'm sure she would do anything she attempts very well.' He paused, a thoughtful expression on his face. 'She must have many beaux.'

Well, really!

'She had many admirers among the young officers of Papa's company,' she said airily. 'But no-one special, as far as I know.'

There. That was what he really wanted to know. Now perhaps he would be satisfied.

A shout came from the crow's nest. 'Land.'

They turned eagerly to the east, straining their eyes to see what the lookout had seen from his high vantage point. Gradually the hazy vision of the African continent appeared over the horizon — one more step on this interminable journey. Wilhelmina felt an unaccountable sense of foreboding. 'Is the next stage of our journey, after Cape Town, very dangerous, Mr Jones?' she asked softly.

He looked at her quickly. 'It is not the safest, smoothest, most uneventful part,' he replied. 'Why do you ask?'

Wilhelmina avoided his gaze. 'You may think me fanciful, or childish. But I,' she paused, 'I cannot explain. But I have a presentiment, a feeling of imminent danger, trouble.'

Mr Jones thought for a minute. 'The southern sea is a forbidding area,' he said. 'Between the Cape and the South Pole stretches the ocean — nothing else. There is no land.' He paused. 'Sailors are on the whole a superstitious lot. There is a dread of going down into the southern seas. It is possibly because it is the unknown.'

'It is a very long way from the Cape to Van Diemen's Land, isn't it?'

'Yes. The longest stretch of the voyage. The crew are rather edgy, in anticipation.'

A bell sounded. Jones drew himself up. 'I must go to my duties, Miss Wilhelmina.' He smiled. 'Don't be too worried. Most likely it will be an uneventful crossing. In any case, we will do our best to get you to Sydney town safely and in good time.'

Wilhelmina watched him as he strode away. He is really quite a nice young man. If he didn't make such an ass of himself about

Henrietta, he would really be quite interesting.

It was sunset by the time the anchor had been lowered and the ropes secured. There was great activity with the sails. There was movement and purpose on the part of the crew.

Wilhelmina watched with interest. She admired the skill and agility of the sailors as they clambered among the rigging — like a tree full of monkeys, she thought — as relaxed and confident, moving from point to point.

Someone was coming up the companionway. Henrietta emerged. Wilhelmina waved and patted the plank beside her. 'Come and watch,' she cried as her sister drew closer. 'They are very clever.'

They watched the activity in silence for a while. Then Wilhemina spoke. 'I had quite a talk with your Mr Jones earlier.'

'Oh Will! He isn't *my* Mr Jones. I wish you wouldn't say things like that.'

Wilhelmina laughed. 'Well, he'd like to be your Mr Jones,' she giggled. 'I told him you didn't have any special beau.'

Henrietta sprang up. 'Wilhelmina, you didn't! Whatever did you say? Oh, he will think I am a real hussy.'

Wilhelmina went into peals of laughter.

'Calm down. I'm only teasing. Actually, he is a very nice man. I had a pleasant, sensible conversation with him. Yes. I think he's very nice.'

Henrietta looked up and smiled, relieved. 'Yes. I think so, too,' she said with a quiet twinkle.

★   ★   ★

Mists hung around Table Mountain as they looked out across the water to the town. It was so much cooler, the temperature being quite pleasant.

Already there was great activity, with long boats bringing cargo to be loaded and transported to the new colonies in Australia. This being the last possibility of purchasing fresh foods before reaching Sydney town, its strategic importance was very great.

Most of those not actively engaged in the business of cargo were gathered on deck watching or preparing to go ashore to explore, trade or do business of one kind or another.

Most of the officers not on duty had already gone ashore. Most had trading ventures of their own to attend to, bargaining and selling exotic items bought on their last trip to the East, or buying goods from the

Cape to trade in Sydney town. It could be quite a lucrative sideline.

At last, a boat was ready to take the passengers ashore — and to enable them to feel the solid earth under their feet.

Johann and his family explored the town. It was pleasant to sit in the cool, green parks after walking the streets. They bought little, but enjoyed the change, returning to the ship before nightfall.

They lay at anchor for eighteen days. It was in the last few days that the livestock was being loaded. The loading of cattle was a slow, laborious and precarious business. Each beast was lifted individually, winched up with a wide belt like a girth behind its forelegs, the rope over the davits being rhythmically hauled by several crewmen.

Unexpected struggles of a beast while still in the longboat could reduce the exercise to chaos. It was a triumph when a beast was safely lowered through the hatchway to the prepared hold. Cattle, sheep, pigs and poultry were all in the cargo. The bleating of sheep and squeals of pigs as these were held down forcibly added to the general melee. The poultry confined in wire cages were usually no problem, apart from the startled shrieks when the cages were moved.

On the last morning of loading, however,

an incident occurred which afforded the watching passengers comical entertainment. Tensions among the crew were mounting again. They had now to face that longest stretch of the journey, the dreaded, unknown southern seas and the change of weather as they moved nearer the Antarctic Circle.

This had communicated itself to the passengers. Vague fears of the unknown stirred in them. Wilhelmina was not the only one who was wishing that this part of the journey was over.

A longboat approached the *S.S. Parland* and drew alongside. It was laden with poultry. Cages of hens, roosters, ducks and geese made up the load.

All was going smoothly despite the din, when two cages, one of geese, the other of hens and two roosters, was lifted. The side of the cage forming the door flew open and, amid an overwhelming escalation of the noise, the birds made their terrified escape. Shouts, oaths, commands, shrieks of hens and honks of geese rent the air.

Crewmen swiped the air in efforts to catch the escaping birds. The longboat jerked from side to side as they tried to catch those still in the boat. Two men had fallen into the water and were thrashing about, grasping at the wings or legs of those overboard.

Two or three hens had made safe landings on longboats from other shipping in the bay engaged in trade with the *S.S. Parland* and were now caught by crew of those boats and being handed over.

The man in charge of the cargo was red-faced and furious amidst the mirth and jibes around him. After the first moment of shock, the watching passengers rocked with laughter. Was anything as silly as a wet hen?

Sophia wiped her eyes. 'Oh, that has done us the world of good,' she gasped when she could make herself heard.

'What chaos!' exclaimed Johann. 'I'm sure that poor fellow in charge is very relieved the valuable cargo has all been retrieved.' He chuckled again. 'Oh, he is embarrassed — and the others make the most of his embarrassment. I feel sure someone, if the culprit is found, will get a hefty punishment for not seeing those doors were securely fastened.'

It was good to laugh and to chuckle every time they thought of it later.

The loading continued by lantern light until it was all complete and the hatches closed.

The wind stayed with them and, as the tide changed, they sailed away from the town, out of the bay. They steered now for the Southern Ocean.

13

The endless Southern Ocean

Wilhelmina shivered — partly from cold and partly from the fact that, as they used to say at home, 'someone walked over her grave'. She could not rid herself of this sense of foreboding that had dogged her since the day she had talked with Mr Jones as they approached Cape Town.

There was a tension among the crew, too. They were sullen. Quarrels were breaking out frequently over the most trivial things.

The cold winds whipped up mountainous waves and the deck was constantly awash. The time spent in the open air was becoming less and less. 'We must get a trunk of our warmer clothes up from the hold.' Sophia had noticed Wilhelmina's shiver. 'We must keep warm. We must not get ill. It would be unthinkable in these conditions.'

Henrietta leaned back on her chair. 'Oh, but this pitching and rolling makes me feel so ill right now, Mama. I don't know how I can endure it. It was quite all right until we came into these rough seas.' She managed a little smile. 'I could even endure a day of the doldrums again.'

There was a knock on the door. Wilhelmina rose to open it and was surprised to see Mr Jones in the passageway, holding a tray of drinks. 'I thought you may be feeling the bad effects of this patch of weather we are going through,' he said. 'A drink to warm you may be useful.' He put the tray down on the chest of drawers.

'Oh, Mr Jones, how kind of you.' Sophia approved of the manners and thoughtfulness of this young man. What a pity he was a sailor. He was showing real interest and attention towards Henrietta and she might do well to encourage the attentions of such an agreeable, pleasant young man. But marry a sailor? What sort of life would she have? True, there were times now when a captain's wife may accompany him on some of his travels, but that would be impossible when children came. Their father would be a stranger to them. It would be a lonely life for a sailor's wife.

And what were his family, his prospects?

Henrietta was looking brighter since the advent of the second officer into the room. He handed round the drinks and raised his glass. 'To the most beautiful ladies in the southern seas,' he said, his eyes on Henrietta.

They all drank to his toast. Really, he was such a nice man, so suitable in every way — except for his profession.

Sophia brought up the subject of getting the trunk of woollens from the hold.

'Certainly, Mrs Gerhardt. It will be no trouble at all. Perhaps you would be good enough to come along with me and fill in the necessary paperwork. Then I can get it for you.' He gathered up the glasses and Sophia followed him along the passageway.

Wilhelmina cast an enquiring glance at Henrietta when the door closed. 'What,' she said, 'are you going to do about him?'

Henrietta smiled, looking down at her hands in her lap.

'He seems to me to be getting really serious about you. Who would have thought? A shipboard romance.' Wilhelmina looked searchingly at her sister. 'What do you think about him? You obviously like him. Do you think any more of him than that?'

There was silence as Henrietta tried to phrase her answer.

'Well, come on. Do you think he is courting you really? Do you want him to?' Wilhelmina cut in.

'I like him very much. He's such a gentleman — a true gentleman, I mean. He's so thoughtful in every way. But we may be reading more into his attentions than he intends?

'Oh Etty, for goodness sake! Where are your eyes? He's been head over heels about you ever since he set eyes on you.' A thought suddenly occurred to her. 'He hasn't asked Papa's permission to court you openly, has he?'

'Oh, no — at least, not that I know of.'

'Well, I shall be very surprised if he doesn't do so very soon. He'll probably want to announce a betrothal when we get to Sydney.'

'Oh Wilhelmina, you are impossible,' expostulated Henrietta. 'You'll have me married before we get to 'Llanfylhn' if we're not careful.'

The trunk brought up from the hold provided some diversion for the afternoon. They had not seen these clothes since they left home and the change was welcome.

Johann joined them late in the afternoon and watched the girls as they pulled out skirts and dresses, jackets and shawls, trying them on and exclaiming about garments they had forgotten.

His head was aching and he felt slightly giddy — possibly being inside too much. It was impossible to be out on deck in this squally weather with the waves breaking over it. One would be drenched in a few minutes.

'Did you have a pleasant afternoon with the officers, Papa?' Henrietta looked enquiringly at her father.

Johann hesitated. 'It was quite pleasant,' he said. 'But I am afraid some of them are imbibing rather too freely for my liking. They are certainly exceeding their rum ration.' He paused a moment then added, 'As always when rum and card games are combined too well, there are disagreements and arguments.'

'Is that why you look so weary?' Wilhelmina ventured, coming to her father's side and putting her arm around his shoulders.

She looked up with a beguilingly innocent expression at Henrietta. 'We had a visit from Mr Jones. He obviously wasn't in your party, Papa. He must have found more attractions here than at the card game.'

Henrietta watched Wilhelmina apprehensively. Whatever was she about to say? Oh, don't let her say anything embarrassing in front of Papa.

'Oh, Jones is a different kettle of fish from some of those fellows,' Johann said airily. 'I must say Fitzroy doesn't impress me any more favourably on further acquaintance.'

He passed his hand across his forehead and covered his eyes. 'I wonder what will be on the menu tonight? The salt pork is being served rather frequently, isn't it? We must be running low on fresh provisions.'

That night, as they lay in their bunks after they had prayed together, Sophia looked into the darkness and listened to her husband's breathing. No, he was not asleep yet. 'Johann, are you awake?' she asked softly.

'Yes, I'm awake,' he replied. 'What do you want?'

'I am thinking of Henrietta,' she said. 'You must have noticed Mr Jones' attention to her.'

'One could hardly fail to notice.' He smiled into the darkness. What young man could fail to be attracted to her?

'Has he spoken to you regarding her?'

He was surprised at the question.

'I mean, has he asked your permission to court her openly? It is almost that now.'

'No. He has not been so definite, my dear. He has openly admired Henrietta, but that is all.'

'He is a most agreeable, thoughtful young man. His manners and personality are without fault.' Sophia pondered. 'But to marry a sailor! It would be a lonely life. And what about his family? And his prospects? I suppose he has the prospect of rising to master of a vessel. But his family prospects? If he speaks to you, Johann, you must be sure to ask him these things.'

'Oh, be sure I shall, my dear.' Johann

smiled to himself. 'I shall be sure to ask him all the things I think you would want to know. But then, it may just be a shipboard attraction when they are thrown together so much with so little other young company. In any case, if we believe it could be serious, we must seek God's guidance in the matter. It is a most important matter if anything develops.'

Sophia gave a sigh of relief. It would be all right then. Johann could be depended upon to handle the matter.

The next morning, the seas were somewhat abated. The waves were not pounding the deck and a weak sun was trying to pierce the clouds.

Johann took advantage of the respite to venture on deck. He had not long emerged from the companionway when the hatch to the hold housing the livestock was raised and a sling was lowered. He watched, concerned as the crew, with much grumbling and disagreement, hauled up a dead beast and proceeded to throw it overboard.

'Died o' the rats' disease.' Johann realised he was being addressed by one of the crew who had noticed his concern. 'Won't be much of 'im left for long now 'e's gone down there.'

He looked down into the surging sea. 'Feed's gettin' low and rats is in it.' He considered for a moment. 'Bad things, rats. Devil's things they be.' His eyes wandered to the southern horizon. 'Devil takes 'is own in these 'ere seas.' There was fear in his eyes — fear of the unknown.

'When them waves come up and there's great beasts out in the sea . . . ' He shook his head knowingly, moving closer to Johann. ''Tis the devil reachin' out to grab thee.' He rolled his eyes. ''E was after that poor beast — and 'e got 'im.'

Johann could smell the stench from the man, a stench of unwashed body, of rum, of cattle, of rotting stock feed and dung. The man leant closer till he was almost touching Johann. 'An' 'e'll maybe get one of us next.' He slunk away, his bare feet making little sound on the deck.

The encounter had startled Johann. The man was uneducated, superstitious. It all meant nothing more than that. But yet he, too, felt the danger, the power of the elements; the isolation.

The tightness in his chest was back again.

He stayed a while, watching the crew as they went about their duties. There seemed to be a bad mood running through the company. There were no jokes, no whistling as when they had all enjoyed the afternoon of music. It must be this fear, permeating and corrupting the entire body.

He must suggest the girls bring out their instruments again.

But Henrietta was suffering from sea sickness. Henrietta. What of this young fellow Jones? He seemed a fine sort of fellow — certainly was showing a great deal of attraction to Henrietta. And Sophia wanted some more information about him — about his family, his prospects.

He smiled to himself. Dear Sophia. She would feel the loss of court life severely. What this young man's family connections were would be extremely important to her.

And what of Henrietta herself? He must have a private conversation with her and try to ascertain her feelings. It was hard to think of her being old enough to be contemplating courtship, marriage.

What if the young fellow did want to marry her? When they disembarked at Sydney he would go on his way with the *S.S. Parland*, and how long would it be before he came back again? And how long would that be for?

He swayed slightly. The tightness was coming back again and the world was starting to spin around him. He stood up and took an unsteady few steps. He tried to call out. Then his legs buckled beneath him and he slumped onto the deck.

14

Family crisis

Johann lay on his bunk, unconscious. He had been carried down to the cabin and Dr Cartwright called. He had examined Johann carefully and now turned to a stricken Sophia and her daughters. His face was grave. 'I'm afraid it is very serious, Mrs Gerhardt. Your husband has suffered a major stroke. It is most unfortunate to have occurred in such a position as we are in. There is no possibility of getting him off ship and into more peaceful surroundings until we get to Sydney.' He shook his head. 'It is a long way to go yet.'

Sophia's face was ashen. 'He will recover though, Dr Cartwright?'

'That is impossible to tell yet, madam. He will need the utmost constant care, particularly in these next few days.' He looked back at the still figure. 'If he shows any signs of recovering consciousness, please call me at once.' He closed the door behind him.

Sophia moved to Johann's side. 'Oh, my poor Johann.' She turned to the girls. 'This has come about because of the strain of these last months. He was not well before we left home.'

'But he seemed better once he had made the decision to emigrate, Mama,' Henrietta said gently. 'Poor Papa.' She stroked his forehead gently. The boat lurched and she clasped the upright. 'Oh, if only this bumping would stop!'

Wilhelmina was watching her father. A stroke, Dr Cartwright had said. Did that mean that Papa may even, if he recovered, not be an able man? People who had strokes were often left paralysed, or unable to speak. Sometimes their brain was affected. Oh, Papa — dear, loving, caring, able Papa. Please God, don't let that happen to him. Better he died now than that. The lump in her throat grew bigger. She held back the tears that were threatening to overflow.

Mama seemed calmer than she had expected. Had she perhaps not yet faced the possibility of these things? What would they do in such an eventuality? What *could* they do?

Mama would be useless. She always handed decisions and responsibilities over to Papa. He always looked after everything, did everything for their welfare and comfort. And Henrietta? She was a darling sister and she loved her dearly, but she was not the sort of person to take charge in a state of emergency.

That only leaves me, she thought. Her agile brain raced ahead, facing the possibility of her father's incapacitation, conjuring up this scheme and that for the solution to the dilemma.

For days, Johann lay as in a coma. They nursed him ceaselessly, taking it in turns to watch and rest. The strain was telling on Sophia.

At last one day, as she sat looking sadly at him, his eyelids fluttered and opened. 'Oh, my darling. You are awake. Oh, thank God. Do you feel better?'

Johann blinked his eyes.

Sophia put her hand on his head. 'Tell me, my darling. Are you better?' She turned and picked up the glass of liquid and the spoon. 'Open your mouth, dearest. Take a little drop of this.'

The girls were beside her.

Johann looked at her, but otherwise didn't respond. 'What is the matter, my darling? Come, open your mouth.'

Papa is paralysed! Paralysed! He cannot open his mouth. Wilhelmina looked with horror at her father. 'I will go and get Dr Cartwright immediately, Mama,' she gasped, turning and running down the passageway.

The doctor hurried in and, after examining

Johann and speaking softly to him, turned back to the women. 'I am afraid, my dear ladies, that Mr Gerhardt is at present paralysed down one side. He is unable to speak. I say 'at present', because that could change in time. It is unlikely that he will be restored to full health and vigour. I must tell you this so you are prepared. He may recover his speech. He seems a man of strong will and that is a big factor in his favour.'

Sophia's expression revealed her shock and horror. Mama hadn't even considered this could happen, Wilhelmina marvelled. Oh, I know she will just go to pieces. O God, help me deal with this. I'll have to be Papa and look after her.

Henrietta was silent, but her eyes showed her shock and feeling of helplessness.

'A stroke is caused by a haemorrhage, or a clot in the brain,' the doctor explained. 'If it is possible for the brain to heal, or find a way around that part of itself that has been affected, then he will recover to some extent. Continue with your nursing,' he said kindly. 'You are doing all the right things. If he shows any change at all, let me know immediately.' He left them to their commiserations.

As soon as the doctor had left the room, Sophia collapsed into the chair. She threw her hands up and rocked herself back and forth.

'Oh dear, oh dear, oh dear!' she wailed. 'What shall we do? Oh, whatever shall we do? Here in a strange country and not even there yet! Oh, what shall we do?'

'There, there, Mama. Please don't upset yourself. I'm sure we'll think of something.' Henrietta looked anything but sure of anything. 'Please don't cry.' She was blinking back her own tears.

'But who will take care of getting accommodation in Sydney till we go to 'Llanfylhn'? Who will see to the luggage, to all our furniture being taken off the boat? Oh, what shall we do?'

Surely Mama had now looked further ahead than Sydney. Did she not realise yet that there was a great probability that Papa would not be able to work, that they may not even go to 'Llanfylhn' — ever?

Dr Cartwright had said that it would be a long time before Papa was able to move and speak — if he ever improved to that degree. There were greater things to consider than temporary accommodation and the unloading of their possessions.

'Mama, please stop that wailing. I know you are upset. We all are. But we should think what we are going to do. We must think and make our plans for the future.'

The shock of Wilhelmina's tone calmed her

mother. She looked at her with startled eyes, tears still coursing down her cheeks.

'We are at least fortunate that this has happened here and not as we were leaving the ship,' Wilhelmina stated firmly. 'We have sufficient time to look at our situation calmly. Our first thought must be to make provision for Papa's care. If he is to make any degree of recovery, he must be cared for.'

'Yes. Yes. You are right, my little one. Oh, you are like your Papa — so clear-headed.' Sophia wiped her eyes.

'I have been thinking about this ever since Papa became ill,' Wilhelmina said.

'You have been thinking about it?' cut in Sophia in amazement. 'You guessed he may still be ill when we land?'

'Mama.' Wilhelmina spoke gently to her mother, coming and sitting on the stool by her chair. She placed her hand on her mother's knee. 'Mama, Papa will most likely be ill for a very long time.' She watched the effect her words were having on her mother. 'He may not, in all probability, be able to take up the position offered to him.'

Sophia's mouth flew open. 'Not take up the position!' She started to wail again. 'Oh, whatever shall we do if that should happen? How will we survive?'

'Mama, do stop that noise and listen to

me.' Wilhelmina spoke sharply. Really, Mama was being impossible. 'If Papa is unable to work, we can hardly expect Mr Montgomery to supply us with a house. That went with the position.'

This pronouncement sent Sophia into a further fit of hysteria. Wilhelmina brought her hand down on the arm of her mother's chair. 'Mama, stop it! You are becoming hysterical. We must face these things and prepare ourselves.'

Henrietta, with her arm round her mother's shoulder, was gazing at Wilhelmina in amazement. Where had this outspoken little sister gained all this foresight and capability?

'When we reach Sydney, you must stay on board and look after Papa, while Etty and I go and look for accommodation for us, where we can care for Papa. We must find a doctor who will have the oversight and prescribe for him.' She turned to Henrietta. 'I am sure Mr Jones will accompany us if he is able. If not, we shall find our own way around. We must contact Mr Montgomery immediately and wait for his reply. Then we shall know how to go on.'

Her mother was becoming calmer. Someone was making decisions. 'But if your Papa cannot work and we have no home and no income, no relatives in this strange country . . . ' She threatened to go off into hysterics again.

Wilhelmina cut in. 'If we are not able to go to 'Llanfylhn', then we must find a house and settle in Sydney,' she stated emphatically.

'But we will have no income,' wailed Sophia. 'We brought all our money with us, but it will not last long in this country after we have set ourselves up in a home.'

'We must arrange for an income,' stated Wilhelmina flatly. 'Etty and I are both ablebodied and will earn an income.'

'Earn an income? Oh, that my daughters should come to this! Whatever are we coming to? We shall be destitute.'

'Rubbish, Mama. We are not destitute at all; far from it. We have several options.'

Henrietta spoke. 'What options do you suggest, Will?' she said softly, now looking less helpless.

'Well first, we could, if the positions are offering, find work as governesses. I believe there may be a demand for governesses in Sydney town.'

Henrietta had brightened considerably.

'Or,' continued Wilhelmina, 'we may find positions as companions to some lady in high position. I think there may not be too many educated ladies available to fill the post of companion. Then again, we could advertise and take pupils in music and language.' She smiled a little ruefully. 'Perish the thought that I should have to endure pupils murdering the music of the masters, but it is something we can do. I could teach piano and the flute and Etty could teach the harp — and she could do the theory part,' she added.

'Well, that certainly would be a perfectly respectable and ladylike solution,' Sophia conceded.

'And yet again,' pressed Wilhelmina, 'if we could find a large house with sufficient room, we could open a school for young ladies. Then we could include music in our curriculum. And we both speak five languages, Mama. It is quite a possibility.'

Henrietta threw her arms around Wilhelmina. 'Oh, my little sister. You are wonderful,' she gasped. 'And you have been working all this out ever since Papa first became ill.'

'Of course,' Wilhelmina replied. 'You've got to look ahead and face up to things. I'm just thankful we have time to make our decisions calmly.'

'I'm sure Mr Jones will give us any assistance he can,' said Henrietta.

Wilhelmina smiled.

'Oh, there is that, too!' Sophia was off again. 'I feel sure he was about to speak to your Papa about paying his addresses to you. Oh, who will now take charge of your future, here in this strange land, with Papa ill and your Uncle Jost at home on the other side of the world, with no Papa or uncle or even cousin to take care of you?'

Wilhelmina stamped her foot. 'Mama! We are able people. We have intelligence. Papa would do what we wanted to make us happy anyway, if he were able. If he is not able, then we will take care of ourselves. We do not need a man to decide our future for us. We will do it ourselves. As far as the old customs of home are concerned in these things, I think we may well find things very different in New South Wales.'

15

The suitor

There were many and long discussions, debates as to which course of action they should take. Sophia had to be assured over and over that she and her daughters would not be disadvantaged socially if they followed one of the suggestions put forward.

It always came back to the same thing. They must first do all in their power to ensure Johann's comfort and possibility of recovery. They must find temporary accommodation, contact Mr Montgomery, then wait for his reaction.

Johann improved slightly and was able to take a little more nourishment. It would be a long slow process, they were coming to accept, for him to regain his speech and some degree of movement.

The days when they rounded Van Diemen's Land and sailed up the east coast of Australia were filled with a mixture of emotions — excitement; anxiety; appreciation of the beautiful beaches and inlets they saw; and fear of the vastness and strangeness of their new country.

It was a never-to-be-forgotten moment when the lookout gave the call 'Land' and they gathered on deck to see the great headlands guarding the entrance to Port Jackson come into view. They hove to, waiting for the safety of light and morning tide to enter the harbour. The spring sunshine sparkled on the water as they dropped anchor. The golden beaches they could see and the strange grey-green trees all enticed and enchanted them, filling the girls with the desire to explore.

Henrietta and Wilhelmina would first go ashore and try to contact Mr Montgomery's agent. He may even come to meet them. Sir Percy had assured them that they would be contacted immediately on arrival — but, of course, Johann had made all those arrangements.

It was late morning by the time they were rowed ashore. Mr Jones had been able to arrange to accompany them. As Wilhelmina stepped aboard, her heart was full of thanks that God had led them safely to dry land again, land they would make their own, land where they would live and their lives develop, possibly for the rest of their lives.

What did the future hold? Where would their lives and circumstances lead them, each of them? She glanced at Etty and Mr Jones.

He was handing Etty onto the beach with great solicitude. What of them? Would anything come of it?

A short, plump man was hurrying down from the building at the edge of the sand. He lifted his hat to the ladies, then addressed Mr Jones. 'I am looking for a Mr Johann Gerhardt,' he said. 'Could you tell me, sir, if he is aboard the ship you have just come from?'

Mr Jones held out his hand. 'Jones, Second Officer of the *S.S.Parland* at your service, sir. These ladies are Mr Gerhardt's daughters. Unfortunately, Mr Gerhardt is ill and unable to come ashore at present. Miss Gerhardt and Miss Wilhelmina Gerhardt have come to conduct his business.'

'Phillips, sir. John Phillips is my name.' He lifted his hat again to the girls. 'Miss Gerhardt. Miss Wilhelmina. I am sorry to hear your father is ill. Not seriously, I hope?' He offered his arm to Henrietta. 'Allow me to escort you to the shade and comfort of our office. Our sun is too strong for such fair complexions. My firm conducts Mr James Montgomery's business in Sydney. He has advised us you were expected and requested us to meet you.'

Jones smiled at Wilhelmina and, with great ostentation, offered her his arm, mimicking

139

Mr Phillips. The little fat agent was rather pompous, wasn't he? Wilhelmina lifted her gloved hand to cover a stifled giggle.

They were led into the office and seated comfortably. Mr Phillips insisted on their partaking of tea. Over the drink, they told him of Johann's illness, the change in their circumstances and their desire to get the unfortunate news to Mr Montgomery as quickly as possible.

'We feel we must wait for Mr Montgomery's reply to our unhappy news, before making any further arrangements,' Henrietta explained.

'But we need to make our arrangements without too long delay,' Wilhelmina added decisively. 'Papa must be settled comfortably and receive medical attention. He has received constant attention from Dr Cartwright since he became ill.'

It was decided a letter must be written to Mr Montgomery, explaining the situation and that a courier be procured to deliver this to 'Llanfylhn' without delay. The two girls were left at the office to write the letter.

Mr Phillips hurried off to find a courier and Mr Jones went to look out the possibilities of suitable temporary accommodation, then to return and escort the girls to inspect the lodgings he had found.

It took some time to word the letter suitably. At last it was complete and sealed. Mr Phillips returned with the news he had hired a courier who would leave within the hour.

'It will take him no less than a week to take the communication and return with a reply,' he told them.

Henrietta was shocked. 'A week, Mr Phillips!' she exclaimed. 'It is so far from Sydney, then?'

'Yes, my dear young lady. And roads are not all good, by any means.'

'And we must take Papa over these roads, all this way?' exclaimed Wilhelmina.

'I would suggest, Miss Wilhelmina, that you and your luggage travel by steamboat from Sydney to Morpeth. That will bring you much closer to 'Llanfylhn' and will be much more comfortable than travelling by coach. It will certainly be much better for your father.'

They were relieved. How helpful the little man was and how kind and thoughtful. They were lucky to have someone like this to guide them in these things. It was more than they had expected.

They set off to view the lodgings in question. What a strange sight Sydney town presented. The old huts of mud and daub were still there, evidence of the first settlement, but further up the hill there were some quite fine buildings. The streets were busy with riders, carts carrying farm produce, people busy about their business on foot and a chain of convicts labouring on the road. There was activity and noise everywhere and a sense of industry and purpose.

Despite the badly rutted streets, the convicts, the urchins playing on the edge of the road, the mud and lack of sophistication, something in the scene stirred Wilhelmina. She found excitement rising in her, a sense of challenge and an urge to accept it.

They found the lodgings Mr Jones recommended. He had enquired at the inn and several business houses and had spent the time inspecting any promising suggestions.

The one he now took Henrietta and Wilhelmina to was a pleasant house set in its own grounds. The gardens were neat and colourful, indications of a careful housekeeper.

They knocked on the door and were admitted by a convict servant. The interior, like the gardens, was pleasant and well cared for. They discovered the landlady was a woman recently widowed who had decided to take temporary lodgers to provide her with income.

Wilhelmina explained their situation and

the need of nursing care for Johann. Mrs Haggety was most sympathetic. They were shown the airy bedrooms and the decision was made.

Sophia was relieved when they returned and told her all that had been arranged. She marvelled at their competence.

Johann was taken ashore and carried up the steps of Mrs Haggety's neat dwelling. He was soon installed in his comfortable bed, looking not too much the worse for the movement.

'We must now go and see to the unloading of our possessions, Mama,' Wilhelmina said. 'You are all right now?'

'Oh yes. Mrs Haggety seems an estimable woman and so kind. We are most fortunate to have found such a place.' She looked around appreciatively. 'But oh dear! How can you see to the unloading of our things? And where can they be put till we know what transpires?'

'Leave it to us, Mama. We will ask Mr Phillips to recommend a warehouse to store our things. There are any number of places for storage. This is the port for such a wide area. Because transport is so poor, there is a great necessity for such places.'

'And do thank Mr Jones for his assistance and finding this comfortable lodging. Oh, if only he had spoken to your papa . . . ' She turned away, leaving the sentence unfinished.

Mr Phillips had abundant knowledge of the storage possibilities, being closely associated in his capacity as shipping agent for many large firms and landholders in the interior. He had soon made the necessary arrangements.

Now the girls watched the unloading of their trunks and the furniture. All was accomplished safely by nightfall and they climbed the hill in company with Mr Jones, with lighter hearts.

They found Sophia sitting on the verandah with Mrs Haggety, enjoying a cup of tea. She was looking much happier. She greeted them brightly. Mrs Haggety bustled off to get more cups and a fresh pot of tea.

When their travelling cases arrived by horse and cart, Henrietta and Wilhelmina went off to unpack. Mr Jones sat on with Sophia. They sat in comfortable silence for a few moments. 'I cannot tell you how much I appreciate your assistance to us in all these arrangements, Mr Jones,' Sophia said, smiling at him.

'It is my great pleasure, Mrs Gerhardt,' he replied. He cleared his throat and looked uncomfortable. 'Er . . . Mrs Gerhardt,' he ventured hesitantly. 'There was a matter about which I wished to speak to your husband.'

Sophia caught her breath. He was going to

speak to her about Etty! Oh, what should she say?

'As Mr Gerhardt is so indisposed, I wonder if I may be so bold as to approach you? I see no other alternative,' he finished lamely.

'Certainly, Mr Jones,' Sophia responded. 'What did you want to say?'

He cleared his throat again and twirled his cap. 'Er. I am sure you cannot fail to have perceived the great admiration I have formed for your daughter, Miss Henrietta.' He coughed. 'She is the most wonderful young lady I have ever met.' He looked at her appealingly.

Sophia smiled. 'I have noticed.'

He relaxed a little. 'I wished to ask your husband's permission to court Miss Henrietta — with a view, of course, to marriage,' he added quickly. He went on, relieving Sophia of the necessity to respond at this stage. 'I realise, of course, that you know nothing of my background, so before you make any decision, I would like to tell you something of myself.' He looked at her for confirmation.

She nodded. 'Please proceed, Mr Jones.'

'My father is Admiral Abel Jones of the British Navy,' he said.

Sophia gasped. Admiral! In the British Navy! And she had been anxious about his family! Mr Jones was speaking. 'He is now retired and lives not far out of London. My mother is the youngest daughter of Sir Peter Cunningham. They have been happily married for forty years. I have a brother in the army and two sisters.'

'Oh, my husband was in the army in Baden,' Sophia hastened to say. 'He resigned his commission to come to Australia.'

'I know it can be lonely as the wife of a sailor, but I do not intend to be on the sea all my life. I have saved and traded. I know the business. I must return to England on the *Parland* and I return in twelve months' time when I hope to resign and settle here.'

'Resign? And what would you propose to do then?'

'I hope when I return to England to persuade my father to join with me in investment, setting up our own shipping line. I believe he would be interested in such a venture. As I said, he has had great experience with ships. I have had some not inconsiderable experience now and I know trading, particularly trading that brings all manner of goods to this new settlement.'

His eyes flashed in excitement. 'It is growing, expanding and more and more goods will need to be brought to the colony for a bigger and bigger market. If my plans go as I hope, I will settle in Sydney, building a handsome dwelling here. I would make frequent buying trips overseas, but would not be away as I would be in my present position.'

Sophia's mind reeled. Son of an admiral of the British Navy and son of the daughter of a knight! At present he was second officer on the *Parland*, but young yet — and with a view to being head of a shipping line. He was such a personable young man! Oh yes. She was sure Johann would approve.

He was still speaking. 'If I could have your permission to approach Miss Henrietta, I should be the happiest man alive.'

Sophia smiled at him. 'Oh, Mr Jones. I think my husband would be most happy to give his permission and, in his inability to do so, I give you mine.'

16

Into the unknown

The week passed quickly for the two girls, who found much in the activity of Sydney town to amuse and interest them. Sophia was happy to rest in the comfort of Mrs Haggety's verandah when not needed to attend to Johann. The doctor had given them hope that he may recover his speech.

As the spring sunshine filled the room one morning when Sophia entered, he turned his head. She hurried to his side, excited by this accomplishment. 'Oh my darling, you are able to move!'

She thought a muscle twitched at the corner of his mouth in his effort to smile. He made a gutteral noise and seemed to be trying to speak. What was he trying to say? His eyes kept turning to the door and back to her. Was he wondering about the girls?

'The girls have gone to inspect the shops,' she said, then added, 'They will be all right. Mr Jones is escorting them.'

Johann's eyes opened wider.

'You are wondering about Mr Jones'

attentions to Henrietta?'

He blinked.

'Then worry no further, my darling,' Sophia said happily. 'He is a most suitable young man. He spoke to me on the matter, since you were unable to receive him, and I have given our permission for him to court her.'

She put her hands together in satisfaction. 'Oh Johann, he is a most worthy suitor. I gave our permission gladly. I was sure you approved of him as far as we knew of him. But when he approached me, I did not need to ask one question. He volunteered all I wanted to know so willingly. Such a straightforward young man.'

She leant towards him and told him of the young man's family. She smiled happily and went on, 'He has such nice manners and is so polite and attentive.'

There was a new expression in Johann's eyes, a glimmer. A tear rolled down his cheek onto the pillow — and was there almost a little smile?

★　★　★

Mr Montgomery's reply to their letter was so sympathetic, so solicitous. He urged them to follow his instructions to Mr Phillips his

149

agent — to travel with their luggage by the steamer to Morpeth, their furniture following later by sailboat.

He would meet them at Morpeth with his carriage and make particular arrangement for Johann's safe journey to the cottage prepared for them at 'Llanfylhn'.

'How very kind and considerate,' Sophia observed when she read the letter aloud.

The girls exchanged glances. What about an income? If 'Llanfylhn' was so remote, probably with no village close by, was there any likelihood at all of finding pupils to teach — music, or anything else? Sophia, however, was now sure of a home — and Mr Montgomery seemed to have everything in hand.

It was an uneasy few days, especially for Wilhelmina. Uncertainty, not knowing, was worse than anything else.

They paid up their account for the lodging and said an amiable farewell to Mrs Haggety, promising when they came to Sydney to enjoy again her hospitable lodging.

Mr Jones saw them onto the boat. He had been most constant in his attendance upon Etty since gaining Sophia's approval. Henrietta blossomed under his wooing. They took a turn around the deck when their luggage was attended to. 'We sail with the tide,' he said as he and Henrietta walked out of sight. 'I shall not see you again for almost a year.' He was silent a moment. 'I don't know how I shall endure that. I am very much in love with you, Henrietta.'

He had stopped and now stood facing her, clasping both her hands in his. 'It is no shipboard fascination. I can't bear to have you out of my sight. But I must accomplish my plans. I am remiss to speak to you like this when I am about to sail out of your life for a whole year. I know I am not being fair to you. Yet my feelings for you force me to speak.'

He lifted her hands to his lips. 'I love you with all my heart, my Henrietta. There, I said it, my Henrietta. And your feelings may not be as mine.' He looked searchingly at her. 'Though I believe I have cause to hope.'

Henrietta's mind was a whirl. If she stated her growing love for him, would he think her forward, an easy conquest? She tightened the pressure of her hands in his.

He smiled. 'Don't say anything now. I want to make you mine right now. But that cannot be. I shall continue my courting by letter and count the days until I can behold your beautiful face again.'

The steamer blew her whistle. 'I must go. Would that I could be carried wherever you go. But the time will come.' He kissed her hands again and they turned and walked quickly to the gangway.

★ ★ ★

At Newcastle, they left their ship and boarded a small vessel to transport them up the Hunter to Morpeth.

Newcastle was a busy port. There were many ships loading and unloading. The coalmines in the immediate vicinity ensured that there would be a continual supply of coal loaded onto a line of vessels in the harbour.

The journey up the Hunter was an idyllic one. The lush pasture dotted with homes, clearly visible from the ship, lifted their spirits. As they passed through the alluvial flats, their picture of the new country as a mysterious and fearsome place was changing rapidly. In spite of this, Wilhelmina was greatly relieved to reach Morpeth.

As the ship pulled into the jetty, they lined the rail, searching for a figure that might prove to be Mr Montgomery.

There was quite a crowd at the jetty and around the shipping office. A line of vehicles was drawn up outside the enclosure. Carts, waggons and an array of passenger vehicles were evidence of the importance of Morpeth as a port.

Wilhelmina's gaze swept over the company assembled below. What would this man be like? It was all very well for Mama to be sanguine about their position now that they were landed in New South Wales and had been instructed to proceed to Morpeth. But they knew nothing about this man personally. Even Papa knew only scanty details of the position for which he had resigned his commission.

If only he could tell them any more details that he might have known. He had now said a few words and hopefully his speech was returning. But it was highly improbable that he knew anything more. They didn't even know if Mr Montgomery was married, if he was old or young — only an idea of the size of his property. Was he a man of integrity? Whatever he was like, they were now very much at his mercy — three women and an invalid man!

Mama was blissfully expecting to go to 'Llanfylhn' and live in the cottage prepared for them. She didn't seem to have a thought beyond that. What of income? How would they survive and keep their own dignity, integrity and independence?

The boat was secured and the gangplank lowered. A well-dressed man with a dark beard and dark curly hair showing beneath his hat detached himself from the waiting crowd and walked briskly up the gangplank. He was perhaps middle-aged.

He reached the top of the gangplank and looked around expectantly, his eyes darting over the passengers at the rail. His eye fell on Sophia and her daughters standing slightly apart. He approached them, raising his hat as he drew near.

'Have I the honour of addressing Mrs Gerhardt?' he asked politely. 'I have come to welcome Colonel and Mrs Gerhardt and their two daughters.'

Sophia smiled. He had called Johann 'Colonel'. How courteous of him. What a nice, upstanding man he appeared. She was sure she had no need to worry now about their future. Wilhelmina had been making all these plans, but now it appeared there was a nice man to take charge.

'I am Mrs Gerhardt,' she said, 'and these are my daughters, Henrietta and Wilhelmina.'

He bowed politely to them.

'My husband, of course, is in the cabin. He is, I am pleased to say, making gradual progress.'

'I am glad to hear it,' he replied brightly. 'Perhaps if he is well enough, I could make his acquaintance now if it is convenient. I assure you I will not tire him. And then, may

I escort you and your charming daughters to a tea room in the town for some refreshment? By the time we are back, your luggage may have been unloaded.'

They moved towards the companionway. 'Of course, your heavier luggage will not arrive for a few days. I have arranged for our bullock waggons to pick that up and bring it to 'Llanfylhn'.

So he must be going to take them to 'Llanfylhn'! And if their furniture was coming, he must be planning they settle in. Then what?

Wilhelmina glanced at him, noting his firm, friendly manner. He already had Mama in the palm of his hand. She herself would wait and see.

They had reached the cabin. Sophia entered and approached Johann lying in the bunk. 'Johann, Mr Montgomery has kindly come himself to welcome us. I have brought him to make your acquaintance.'

She turned, smiling, to Mr Montgomery. He approached Johann, removing his hat as he came into the cabin. 'I am very happy to make your acquaintance, Colonel,' he said, 'though most unhappy that you have been so ill. I sincerely hope our sunny climate may benefit you and your return to health be expedited.'

Johann raised a hand slightly and it was taken in the firm grasp. 'I have the cottage prepared for you,' their visitor continued. 'I believe we have sufficient for you to be tolerably comfortable until your own things arrive in a week or so.'

'So we are going to 'Llanfylhn'?' Sophia asked. 'We have been in turmoil since my husband became ill, not knowing what would happen now he cannot take up the position we have come all this way for.'

'But of course, my dear lady!' Mr Montgomery looked astonished that they could have thought otherwise. 'We could not possibly have you bereft in a strange land like this.' He smiled, a strange little expression crossing his face. 'This is not the civilised, sophisticated world of the grand duke's court that you have known. Many have made a new start and are living decent lives and working hard. But there are others in this country whom, I assure you, your husband would not like you to come across.'

He gave a little laugh. 'Then again, I would not dare disappoint my wife by not bringing you back with me.' So! He had a wife.

Wilhelmina felt a flood of relief. She had heard that the colony was short of women. Men were fighting and hungry for women. And if this man was alone . . . Living in a

156

remote situation . . . And a woman and two young ladies arrived on his doorstep . . . And they were under obligation to him . . .

He was speaking still. 'The prospect of a woman of more her own age and two young unmarried ladies coming to us has filled her with excitement for the past months. We have one family, our convict overseer and his wife and family. But that is all for a considerable distance.

'To have you coming to be close by has been a joyous anticipation for her. I could hardly restrain her from coming with me to meet you. Only the need for comfortable room in the carriage convinced her to await you at home.'

They left the cabin, Johann obviously much relieved on hearing all the plans. He closed his eyes and relaxed against his pillows.

* * *

Mr Montgomery escorted the ladies along the street. It was a tidy little place. They could see a stone church and a large stone residence up on the hill. The spring sun was hot on their backs as they walked.

Mr Montgomery led them to the tea house. It was a pleasant, weatherboard building with windows directly onto the footpath. The

157

tables were set out neatly, covered with starched white cloths.

Mr Montgomery rang the brass bell and the proprietress emerged from the kitchen behind, wiping her hands. Over tea, he described the journey they were to undertake and told them something of his property.

Sophia set her cup down. She had been holding it in both hands. 'Mr Montgomery,' she said hesitantly, 'you are being most wonderfully kind. We are deeply indebted to you. But my husband cannot take up his position. You will be needing the cottage for whoever you appoint to that position.' She swallowed, embarrassed. 'We must not. We do not wish to impose upon your generosity.'

Mama's pride, Wilhelmina thought. She would not accept charity. Really, she felt the same way herself. She did not expect anything for nothing. That was what had been worrying her. She and Etty were able and willing to work. But she wanted it to be respectable, ladylike work.

Mr Montgomery hastened to assure Sophia. 'Please, do not waste another thought upon such a matter, Mrs Gerhardt,' he cried. 'We have a plan. We only await your and Colonel Gerhardt's approval. As I said, my wife feels the lack of female company. You will be fully occupied caring for your husband who no doubt needs a great deal of careful nursing and will probably need assistance.

'Our plan is that, if they are willing, your daughters,' he smiled at the girls, his eyes twinkling, 'take it in turns helping you nurse their father and being companion to my wife. There are many things she would like assistance with that servants do not seem to be able to do to her satisfaction. There is assistance with her correspondence — and helping to entertain our guests when we do entertain.

'Those occasions are rather different from entertaining in the old country. Many guests often stay overnight, because of the long distances it is necessary to travel. At times, we may need both young ladies at the same time if you can possibly manage.'

Sophia's face was a study. Her varying emotions sought for supremacy: companion to Mrs Montgomery — involved in the social life of the family — not having to accept charity.

He was still speaking. 'I shall, of course, recompense them over and above the use of the cottage.' He chuckled. 'Oh, I assure you it is we who will be indebted to you. I understand and now see for myself that your daughters are well versed in the social graces.'

★　★　★

And so it transpired. They returned to the wharf and their luggage, now being available, was laden on the carriage. Johann was carried out and installed with cushions and rugs as comfortably as possible. They climbed in. The door closed. The driver took up the reins and flicked his whip. They were off on the last leg of their journey.

Soon they would see 'Llanfylhn' and begin their new life in Australia.

17

'Llanfylhn'

The journey was accomplished as smoothly as could be expected. The countryside, fresh in the flush of spring growth, gave promise of a plentiful season.

Although it wearied him greatly, Johann's spirits were enormously lifted. His immobility and confinement to the cabin had been depressing in the extreme, adding to the weakness and frustration he had endured since his collapse.

They were impressed with the farming throughout the district. There were well cared-for paddocks and stands of corn and barley — in some places, paddocks of wheat.

Mr Montgomery told them of the rural ventures, the settlers along the Hunter — and of the floods, when the river stretched out right across this rich fertile soil, depositing its silt, with all the nutrients it carried.

As they came to Patterson, he knocked on the roof and had the driver pull up outside the lovely little church. 'We attend here on occasion,' he told them, 'but mostly we worship in the little church at Allynbrook. It is tiny, but I think you will find it quite charming. We are on the Allyn River, of course, that runs into the Hunter.'

What a lot they had to learn about this new land. The old world had the familiar beautiful Rhine, the traditional architecture of the houses and churches and here and there castles or monasteries! Oh, it was different.

Yet Wilhelmina at least felt that rise of excitement and challenge again. In spite of his love of his homeland, his heritage and the trauma of leaving it all, Papa had felt this lure of challenge. It was a fundamental thing to which something deep inside her being responded — the urge to accomplish, to succeed against all odds, to go out, as Papa had said Abraham did, trusting in God to lead him.

Here it was all just beginning. Later times would depend on what was done now. There was a sense of untouched resources. Despite the farms and dwellings, it was obvious they did not extend very far back from the roads. It was all waiting.

It was growing dark by the time they turned in at the gates of 'Llanfylhn'.

'I will not take you to the homestead now, but rather to your home,' Mr Montgomery said. 'Colonel Gerhardt will need your ministrations and rest. No doubt the journey will have been a toll on his strength. There is plenty of time now — though my wife will be anxious to see you. We will send a carriage down for you tomorrow so that Colonel Gerhardt can also come and see us, if that is possible.'

Their luggage was unloaded and he opened the gate and led them up the path to their new home. It was a single-storeyed, commodious, slab timber building, with French doors covered by wooden shutters opening onto the verandahs. The front door gave entrance into a pleasant hall.

A large room — possibly a sitting room — opened off this and, further down the hall, there were doors to what were obviously three bedrooms. A verandah encircled the whole. Behind, but connected by a narrow covered way, was another smaller building which proved to be the kitchen and dining room. A small verandah ran across the front and a wide one at the back.

This house had been the original homestead until the present one was built.

Mr Montgomery ensured that they had lamps lit and the fire burning brightly in the wide fireplace. Then, after seeing Johann settled in his bed, he wished them a sound and comfortable sleep and, promising to send the carriage tomorrow, took his leave.

They sat long by the fire. After the warm day, the night was cool. The warmth of the fire was comforting. There could even be a frost in the morning.

Johann seemed to have settled down and was now asleep. Wilhelmina slipped off her shoes and held out her feet to the fire, wriggling her toes.

'Don't put your feet too close to the fire, Wilhelmina,' her mother warned. 'You'll get chilblains.'

'Oh, but it's such a comfort.' Wilhelmina sighed.

'How strange this house seems,' Henrietta mused. 'It is different from our home in Wiesbaden.' She looked up at the ceiling, the beams of the roof visible.

'It is quite spacious, though,' Sophia said. 'And it has a comfortable atmosphere. When we get our own pieces, I am sure we can make it very comfortable.'

Why was the kitchen and dining room separate from the bedroom block, Wilhelmina wondered. Perhaps for coolness — they said it was very hot in summer. The wide verandahs all around would keep the sun off the bedrooms. They would have to experience all these things to understand all the whys and wherefores. But oh, there was a freedom about the place.

Mr Montgomery was true to his promise. The carriage arrived and a servant to assist with Johann's conveyance to the carriage. However, it was decided Johann should rest after the exertion of the previous day. A female servant was brought to attend to him while the ladies went to make the acquaintance of Mrs Montgomery.

The carriage drive was short. It had been for Johann's benefit that a carriage was employed. It was really only a short pleasant walk's distance between the two houses. They swung into the drive. It was of circular design around a smooth lawn.

The house was a two-storeyed stone building with solid columns along the front and a balcony edged with a wrought-iron balustrade. A wisteria vine winding its way between the columns along the verandah was in full bloom, its soft mauve flower cluster hanging among the new spring green shoots of foliage. Close by and flanking the house were great evergreen trees, with just the roofs of other buildings being glimpsed beyond. Sophia drew her breath in sharply. 'Oh, this is beautiful,' she said softly.

They pulled up at the front door. A small, dainty woman emerged from the house as they alighted.

They mounted the low steps as Mrs

Montgomery came to greet them with outstretched hands. 'Welcome to 'Llanfylhn',' she cried. 'Come along in. I am so anxious to get to know you. I did not wait for you to be announced. We do not stand on ceremony here.' She gave a little laugh. 'Some of our friends think we are too lax in the conventions, but this is not England — or Europe. It is a new world. There is no room for over-attention to the petty conventions.'

Oh, she was liking this lady, Wilhelmina thought. What a freshness and vitality she had! Would Mama approve or would she think she was perhaps a little lacking in formality?

They were led into a large, comfortable room. Skins and rugs were scattered over the wide polished boards. By the large window with a view of the flower gardens, a table was spread for morning tea.

'Please sit down, Mrs Gerhardt,' the mistress of the house said. 'I'll ring for tea.'

She moved to the fireplace and pulled the bell cord hanging there. 'We are very proud of our rose garden,' she said, indicating the garden visible through the window. 'One of our assigned men is a wonderful gardener. He has done wonders with it. I am just hoping that when he finishes his sentence, he is willing to stay on.'

'Some of these assigned people, then, are quite safe to have around the home?' asked Sophia, surprised.

Mrs Montgomery laughed. 'Oh my goodness, yes,' she said. Then sobering, she added, 'That is not always the case, though. This man was convicted and transported to New South Wales for some trifling thing — hardly a crime, one would think. Some of the so-called crimes were so petty. And people were separated from their families and transported out here with extremely little prospect of ever seeing their families again. There are many who are not cutthroats or murderers, I assure you.'

She poured the tea brought by a servant. She handed a beautiful, fine porcelain cup to Sophia, then the girls. The sandwiches were paper thin and the cakes dainty and delicious. She may choose to be unconventional in some respects, but her manners and hospitality were faultless. Sophia thoroughly approved.

'And now I want to hear all about you,' Mrs Montgomery was saying, 'about your journey — and your home in Baden. And oh, all the things you like to do; what you're interested in.' She looked from one to the other.

The next hour was spent in spirited conversation, answering all her questions and asking questions about life in New South Wales and particularly at 'Llanfylhn'.

'Our greatest regret in leaving our homeland — although it wrung our hearts to leave the life we know, the country we love — ' Sophia checked herself. 'Our greatest regret is that our dear Wilhelmina has had to relinquish a great opportunity — although, as her Papa has stated many times, if what he fears comes to be, it would not be possible anyway.'

Mrs Montgomery's gaze was surprised, interested. 'And what was the opportunity?' she asked.

Sophia explained: the offer of the grand duchess; the invitation to study under Mr Chopin; the promise of becoming famous as a concert pianist.

Their hostess' eyes were wide with wonder. 'And you left all this to come to New South Wales?' she marvelled. 'Oh my dear, what a decision!'

Wilhelmina nodded. 'Yes. But as Papa has said, if an uprising occurs as he thinks it will, there will be no concert pianist — and no grand duchess, either.' She shrugged and smiled ruefully. 'The timing of all this is unfortunate.'

'Perhaps it is not God's will for you, my love,' her mother added.

'Well, you will certainly be a wonderful asset to our social gatherings here,' Mrs Montgomery said. 'We have had no such exalted musician in our midst here on the Allyn — or anywhere else I have visited.' She smiled happily. 'I shall be the envy of all our friends.'

Wilhelmina shuffled, embarrassed. 'Oh, I am not an exalted musician, Mrs Montgomery. I am just a student, though I do play a great deal. I love it. I hope I shall be useful to you.'

They proceeded to talk of the arrangement for them to work as companions. They would be required to take over the arranging of flowers, especially when the Montgomerys were entertaining; to take over some of the charitable errands; to help to plan menus and programs; to accompany Mrs Montgomery on many social occasions and visits.

'And a myriad of other things,' Mrs Montgomery finished. 'Your life here will be very different from your life at court. But some of our friends and neighbours hold very close to old ways. Although we are less constrained, we do not wish to offend them.' She grimaced. 'And my patience is sometimes tried. It will be good to have someone by my side.'

She smiled, her eyes twinkling. 'I'm afraid there are those who, although not nobility, like to impress that they are the nobility of New South Wales, and hold court.'

Henrietta glanced at her sister, a little smile playing round her lips. Wilhelmina would have to mind her tongue. They rose to go, all happily anticipating the future association.

As they came out onto the verandah, a young man was leading a horse around the drive. Mrs Montgomery raised her hand and called him. 'Billy, please bring Rosco here.'

She turned to the others. 'This is Rosco, my horse. He is a most intelligent animal.' She reached out her hand and the horse nuzzled her fingers. 'Rosco hurt his right foreleg and Billy has been giving him some extra treatment. We badly need the services of a veterinarian.' She hastened on. 'Billy is the son of our overseer of the convicts. He is almost like the general of an army. We have 120 convicts working here. Billy's family has been with us some years. He has grown up here.

'Billy, these ladies are Mrs Gerhardt and her daughters, Miss Gerhardt and Miss Wilhelmina Gerhardt.'

Billy lifted his hat and bowed slightly to the ladies. What an attractive man he was! He was like a Norse god, Wilhelmina thought — a fine physique and wide, alert, blue eyes.

Interesting.

He smiled at them. The girls' beauty was not lost on him.

18

Billy

The furniture and trunks arrived early the next week. How strange to see everything packed on a bullock-drawn waggon. They heard the crack of the whip and the bullock driver's voice before they came into view.

Would anything be still intact? Yet watching, they realised the slow, stolid pace of the beasts of burden counteracted some of the impact expected from the holes and ruts in the road. The load was packed high, securely tied down and covered.

The bullocks were called to a halt. The driver, refreshed with a cool drink and with the help of two of the assigned men, began the unloading. Trunk after trunk, box after box was unloaded and stacked on the capacious verandahs.

Then came the untying of the furniture. Wilhelmina hovered as the men struggled in with the piano. 'Oh, be careful. Don't bump it. Put it down gently.'

They manoeuvred it safely into the sitting room parlour and set it down carefully.

'Across the corner, please, where the sound is not impeded and where the light from the French doors can fall on the music.'

At last, all was to her satisfaction and the other pieces unloaded. The bullocky, as he was apparently known, roused his beasts again and, proceeding to the unyoking yard, led them to pasture.

Now they set to work on the trunks and boxes. One after another they were opened to check the contents.

By nightfall, the sitting room was looking most comfortable; the rugs they had brought had been lain over the dark, polished boards; the credenza's mirrors shone; and the tapestry-set chairs looked pretty.

We must purchase a couch to match our chairs, Sophia thought. And with the curtains she had brought and a silver dish here, a crystal vase there filled with flowers . . . Oh yes, she could hold her head up. It may not be Wiesbaden, but she could entertain here. It would be comfortable and in good taste.

She smiled as she left the room. Tomorrow she would continue.

★　★　★

Wilhelmina ran her fingers over the keys.

Considering the movement and the journey,

the piano was surprisingly near tune. She found the small tuning instruments in her music case. They had correctly anticipated there would be no piano tuner available and Mr Rhyngold had instructed her in the intricacies of the art of tuning.

Her ear was her greatest asset. She sounded a note firmly, tightening the string fractionally, sounding adjusting. Then she sounded several notes consecutively, then together, then went on to the next note. With a sigh of satisfaction, her fingers moved up and down over the keyboard when she had finished. Then she launched into Chopin's compositions and the world was lost to her. Her mother coming in to call her for lunch broke the spell. She sat for a moment, then rose from the stool with a shaky breath. A tear trickled down her cheek.

★ ★ ★

They woke next morning to the strangest sound. It was coming from the garden. It sounded almost like a maniacal laughter. Whatever could be making that noise? It was so loud. The two girls ran out to the verandah.

There, on a branch in the gum tree by the gate, were four thickset birds — grey and brown with white breast and head. They were throwing back their heads, lifting their beaks and emiting this strange sound. Fascinated, they stood watching.

'What is it, my dears? What is making that noise?' Sophia's voice came to them from her bedroom.

They hurried in. Johann was awake, too, with the noise.

'It is birds laughing at us. It's the strangest sound, isn't it? They put their heads back and open their beaks and laugh. Like this.' Wilhelmina proceeded to imitate the birds.

'The sun isn't even up yet,' Henrietta said. 'Let's go and get dressed. It's lovely outside. We might go for an early walk.'

The morning air was cool and brought colour to their cheeks as they walked briskly along the track. It took them past the yards and the stables. The horses were already being attended to and they could see a team of convicts working in the vineyard. So there were vines established. They must remember to tell Papa.

As they drew level with the stable, a figure emerged leading the horse they had admired at the homestead. It was the same young man. There was no mistaking him. He lifted his cap when he saw them. 'Good morning. You are out early.'

'We were wakened by the strangest sound,' Henrietta explained. 'It was birds, we discovered. But it sounded almost like laughter. Whatever is it?'

Billy laughed. 'Kookaburras. There are quite a few about. They're often called laughing jackasses. They are real Australian birds.'

They chatted for a few minutes.

'How is Rosco?' Wilhelmina enquired.

Billy frowned. 'He's making progress, but not as quickly as I'd like. His leg is still tender. I wish I had someone to ask for advice.'

'Papa would know what to do,' Wilhelmina put in quickly. 'Would you like to come and ask him? He is, as you know, incapacitated, but he is saying some words and may be able to help you. It would do him so much good if he thought he was being helpful.'

Billy listened eagerly. 'I would very much like to do that,' he said with a wide smile. 'It is too early yet to disturb your father, but I will come later in the day. Thankyou very much.'

He went to turn away, then swung round. 'I believe you ladies do ride?'

'Oh yes. Papa taught us to ride when we were small children. Papa is very particular about our riding.'

'Have horses been arranged for you?'

They exchanged glances. They had not thought that far ahead. 'Not that we are aware of.' Henrietta spoke for them both.

Billy smiled broadly. 'Then I will see what I can arrange.' He was gone.

'What a nice, friendly young man,' Henrietta said. 'And so handsome.'

Wilhelmina was unusually quiet. Henrietta glanced quickly at her sister. 'Yes, oh yes,' she agreed quickly. Her eyes were following the receding figure of the young would-be vet.

Sophia had breakfast ready when they returned. Johann was fed and regaled with all they had seen on their walk and the encounter with Billy.

'He is coming to see you later, Papa. Will you like that? He needs to seek your advice in treatment of Rosco.'

Johann grunted assent. It would be so good to be useful. This immobility and dependence on his family was hard to bear.

The morning was busy with unpacking. There seemed to be an interminable number of trunks and boxes. Had they really brought all these things with them?

Late in the morning, they heard a great commotion coming from the fowl yard at the end of the back garden. Hens were cackling, roosters crowing. There was fluttering of wings and knocking.

Wilhelmina ran down the path. Whatever was wrong with the fowls? Was someone frightening them? She pulled the catch of the gate and swung it wide, bursting through and hastily closing it again. She ran to the fowl house, the source of the commotion.

Suddenly she stopped, almost falling in her sudden interruption to her career forward. From the hens' nest box protruded a long striped tail, the like of which she had never seen. She stood transfixed. The hens were still hovering around cackling, their feathers fluffed. The rooster was importantly strutting round and darting ineffectually near the door of the house.

Then a short leg with a large foot emerged as the creature moved backwards. Then another leg appeared. Finally the whole thing — what was it: animal, or what? — emerged. There was a fat body where it widened out in the middle, then two more feet and a small head at the end of the long neck. It had a kind of tongue that darted in and out.

Wilhelmina stared, hypnotised with horror.

In and out, in and out darted the tongue. It was moving cumbersomely slowly towards her. Finding her feet, she turned and, flinging the gate open, ran up the path screaming.

She burst into the kitchen. 'Mama, Etty!

There is something down there attacking the fowls. Oh! Oh! Oh! I don't know what it is. It's like a dragon or something.'

'Whatever are you talking about, Wilhelmina? There are no such things as dragons.'

'No, but . . . but it's like a small kind of dragon. I don't know how else to describe it,' she gasped. 'It's about this long and about this big in the middle and about this high off the ground. And its tongue keeps going in and out, in and out. Oh dear, who can go and frighten it away?'

They looked at each other helplessly. If Wilhelmina was frightened of it . . . ?

A knock sounded at the door. Sophia went to answer it.

'Oh Mr . . . Mr . . . '

'Just call me Billy, Mrs Gerhardt.' The voice came through to Henrietta and Wilhelmina. Oh, thank goodness. He would deal with it, Wilhelmina thought. She was sure nothing would frighten Billy.

'Billy, you are come at a most opportune time. There is something in the fowl yard that has almost frightened Wilhelmina to death. We just don't know what to do.'

He came through quickly. 'Probably just an old goanna,' he said. 'They eat the eggs if they get a chance and the chooks make a terrible fuss.'

He strode down the path. The girls followed fearfully behind. Billy pushed the gate and went to the fowl house. 'Nothing here now,' he called, 'but he's left his trail. See the mark on the ground where his tail has scraped? And there are no eggs. He's probably had a good lunch and gone back up his tree.'

'Gone up his tree!' gasped Wilhelmina.

'Do you mean to say those things are in the trees?'

Billy laughed. 'They won't hurt you — certainly not if you don't touch them. They look clumsy old things when they are just walking along, but they move and climb the tree like a streak of lightning if you scare them.'

They glanced fearfully up the trees around the yard.

'They won't jump down on you or anything like that,' Billy hastened to assure them, becoming aware of the degree of their terror. 'They don't normally bite or attack you in any way — only if they are cornered they might try to defend themselves.'

They were somewhat reassured and ushered Billy into the house to meet their father.

Wilhelmina set about preparing lunch. What a fright that creature had given her! She shuddered again, remembering its clumsy approach, the little beady eye — and the tongue. Thank goodness Billy had come just then.

She considered a moment. Yes. It was nice, she conceded, very nice — and comforting, sometimes, to have a man around. Especially a man like Billy.

19

Settling in

The new pattern of life soon established itself. They had settled comfortably and with little fuss into the house. They discovered that, along with the rest of the workers on the property they were to be supplied with meat and milk. This, together with the fowls that had been given, would provide much of their food.

Each day, the milk was set in wide shallow dishes and the cream later skimmed and churned into delicious fresh butters.

Sophia was much impressed with the generosity of Mr Montgomery towards not only his paid workers but also the assigned convicts. She spoke to him one day regarding this. 'I find if they are well treated, most of them respond better, Mrs Gerhardt. They are well-fed and sheltered, and allowed a good deal of freedom in their work. A man approaching his finishing time is placed in charge of each group and, of course, there is my overseer who manages the whole. He is also responsible for discipline when necessary.'

A grim expression crossed his usually cheerful face. 'However, we do not employ the cat-o'-nine tails here, as is the case in some instances. I do not believe that is the way to treat any human being. These men — and women in some cases — are issued with their ration of rum each day. If there is trouble and disciplinary action needs to be taken, I find that the withholding of that ration has far more effect than flogging.'

He looked towards a gang working on the track in from the road. 'I hope that when a man leaves here, he may be ready to make a life for himself in this country and not have a grudge and hatred for all his fellow men.'

★ ★ ★

Johann recovered a degree of slow, laboured speech, but his paralysis did not improve further and his general condition was poor. His weight and inability to help himself were a severe burden to him and his nurses.

As suggested, the girls alternated their activities helping Sophia with the running of their home and care of their father and being companion to Mrs Montgomery. It was pleasant working at the big house and Mrs

Montgomery easy to please. Though uncon-ventional in her views, she still required a high standard from her staff. But then, this was what they were used to, so they fitted in comfortably.

Mrs Montgomery was most interested in their life at the palace when the grand duke and duchess were in residence. She asked endless questions about it. Having been born in New South Wales, she had no experience of such things.

'And you played for the grand duchess, Wilhelmina?' she asked one day.

'I played on the piano in the music room and she heard me. And then, when I played for Mr Chopin, she was there,' she replied. She was arranging flowers in a high epergne on a table in the main hall. The mingled perfume of the roses and jasmine was heady.

'You must play for us at our next gathering. We will have a party for New Year and you must play for us. There will be several families coming. I have asked Georgina Dalhunty to favour us on the piano and her aunt Mrs Jessica Hamilton to sing. We shall have quite a concert. Then we shall have some singing and a midnight supper to welcome the new year — and perhaps some dancing. It will be quite gay.'

What would she wear, Wilhelmina thought.

Her court clothes would be too grand for a home party. She would have to go through the clothes trunk.

Etty and Mama would have to, too. They would be excited by this news.

When she arrived home, they were just setting the table for tea.

'What do you think? We are going to have a party for New Year,' she called.

There were questions and excited chatter. 'What shall we wear? We'll have to look through the trunks.'

'I'm sure we can find something suitable,' Sophia said. 'We may need to alter something, but I'm sure we can manage. We are all right now. We have our home and we dine quite well, but we must be careful. We do not know how long Papa may be ill. We may need money for medical attention for him. We must keep some in reserve. I do not want to spend anything unnecessarily.'

Henrietta put her arm around her mother's shoulder. Wilhelmina looked at her with love in her eyes. 'Of course we'll manage, Mama — and you will be the best dressed lady in the room. Who else there will have been at a palace reception as we have been?'

After they had settled Johann for the night, they sat in the cane chairs on the front verandah.

It was a clear night, pleasantly cool after a hot day. The soft, velvety darkness enfolded them. A crescent moon cast a soft light from the star-studded sky and the shadows under the trees were deep. It was a peaceful moment, the day's work done.

The distant sound of voices drifted to them from the assigned men's quarters and the rise and fall of music of an accordion.

'God has been good to bring us to this place,' Sophia said softly. 'We have come to be with good people — and we are free and need not live in fear of our lives.' Their thoughts turned to their homeland.

★　★　★

The head gardener — Frobisher, as Wilhelmina discovered his name to be — came into the conservatory, his arms laden with roses. The perfume filled the room.

She turned quickly from her task of arranging. 'Oh, Mr Frobisher! How beautiful! You have brought me a great deal of pleasant work. Have we any roses left in the garden?' she asked laughing.

'Aye. There's plenty more, miss.'

'Why so many this morning? I had already started on these flowers here.'

The man glanced around, then leant

forward conspiratorially. 'Mr Montgomery told me it's the Mrs' birthday today and he'd like roses everywhere,' he waved his hand, 'them bein' 'er favourite flowers.'

He put them down carefully. 'Very proud of 'er roses, she is — says I do a good job with 'em.'

'You do, too, Mr Frobisher.'

'Ye can do it when ye know what to do,' he said confidently.

'How do you come to know what to do with plants, Mr Frobisher?'

He glanced at her, assessing her expression. He drew himself up. 'I was head gardener for Lady Penelope McMillan back home. My father was head gardener before me. I learned from him when I was a young 'en.' He wiped his face with his handkerchief. 'Knows all the tricks I do.'

Head gardener to Lady McMillan! What a mixture there must be if one knew the stories of each of the convicts. He was proud of it, too, you could see — his position, his skill and training.

Could she ask him how he came to be in New South Wales, serving time as a convict?

She glanced furtively at him. He was inspecting the plants in the conservatory. 'You must have been very sorry to be forced to leave such a position,' she ventured.

His eyes swept up, on guard, trying to read her expression. On meeting her calm gaze and slight smile, he relaxed. 'Aye. Very sorry.' He smiled ruefully. 'Had no choice, though. Seven years beyond the sea.'

'And what brought that sentence?'

'Sold some plants I'd grown in the glass house. The estate manager came when I was goin' out with 'em in me 'ands. Said they were 'Er Ladyship's property and I was usin' 'er time to grow 'em when I should a been doin' me work. S'pose they was 'er property. But they was growed from seed I collected from the garden. She wouldn't a minded, but 'e charged me. Said I was betrayin' a position o' trust, an' a bad example to the men under me care. It was too late when 'Er Ladyship found out. She didn't like me leavin' at all.'

Have you got a family, Mr Frobisher?'

'Aye. I was married. But me wife died soon after I landed 'ere. Terrible shame she felt. Broke 'er 'eart.' He was silent a moment. 'Me son an' me daughter Polly are both married now. Maybe I'll see 'em one day.' He gave a short laugh. 'Maybe they'll come to New South Wales.'

Poor man. Fancy being transported for such a thing. And his family — what they must have suffered. And you could see he was proud of the position he had held.

He roused himself to speak again. 'I be lucky, lucky to be workin' 'ere. Me time will soon be up. The Mrs wants me to stay on. Maybe I will.' He mused a moment. 'Be nice to 'ave a place o' me own, though. Reckon I could 'ave a place p'raps close to Sydney, or some big town, an' grow flowers and vegetables to sell. I be thinkin' about it. Might stay 'ere a while, though.'

So he had dreams still. After all the turmoil of prison and transport to Australia on a convict ship, he still had dreams.

'Mrs Montgomery values your work — your knowledge — very much,' she said. 'She would be very sad to lose you. Perhaps when you are free if you decide to stay on, they may find, or build a house for you. As a free man and head gardener on 'Llanfylhn', you would not live with the convicts. You'd have your own house, I feel sure.'

He stood tall, looking at her with surprise. 'Ye think they might do that?' he asked incredulously.

'Yes. I know Mrs Montgomery wants you to stay. Why don't you mention it some time?'

He nodded thoughtfully. 'Aye. I might do that. Me own 'ouse an' all again. Aye.' He went out, still murmuring under his breath.

So it was Mrs Montgomery's birthday. She put the flowers quickly in a large bucket of water and, slipping unobserved out the door of the conservatory, ran the short distance to their house. She was back in the conservatory when Mrs Montgomery came down the stairs.

'Good morning, Wilhelmina. You are early at your task this morning.'

'Mr Frobisher has brought in such a lovely lot of roses. Come and see them,' she called gaily. She would not mention the birthday yet.

When the opportunity afforded itself, Wilhelmina went to the kitchen. Mrs Duff, the cook, was kneading the bread. 'Can I have a word with you, Mrs Duff?' she said, moving across the kitchen to the table. 'No, don't stop kneading.'

Mrs Duff had taken her hands from the dough and was wiping the flour away.

'I only want to speak to you for a minute.' There was a brief quiet exchange.

Sally, one of the kitchen maids, lifted her head curiously. Wilhelmina went quickly back to the drawing room.

★ ★ ★

It was a hot day. The weather was really warming up. What was it going to be like when summer really came — December,

190

January? Fancy thinking of December and January being excessively hot. It was all upside down. There would be no white Christmas for them now.

★ ★ ★

After lunch, the household settled for a rest. Mrs Montgomery had gone to her room. Wilhelmina donned her broad hat and made her way down the path.

At three forty-five she emerged, now carrying a large deep box in her arms. She followed the path this time to the kitchen entrance and, opening the kitchen door, disappeared inside.

20

Unfamiliar feelings

Wilhelmina removed her hat and, hanging it on the stand in the hall, entered the sitting room. The table had been set for afternoon tea with the lace cloth and the good china and silver service. She lifted the covers. Cook had done well.

A sound behind her made her turn. Mr Montgomery entered the room. 'Ah Wilhelmina, you are here. My wife is not down yet?'

He looked around the room with satisfaction. 'Thankyou. You have done well with all the roses. Lizzy loves her roses.' He smiled. 'It is her birthday today.' His eyes twinkled. 'Rather an important one in a woman's life. I wanted to make it somewhat special. One doesn't have many ways of making an occasion special here in New South Wales — in a small, intimate way, I mean.' What a lovely man he was. They were ideally matched.

'I hope it is all right,' she said softly. 'Mr Frobisher confided it was her birthday. I have a little surprise, too.'

He looked up questioning.

'Oh James, you are back already.' She was coming down the stairs. 'Wilhelmina, ring for tea, please.'

Wilhelmina pulled the cord and moved back to the table. In a few minutes, the door opened and Betty, one of the maids entered, carrying the tea tray. She was followed by Mrs Duff, tidy now with a clean apron and cuffs, bearing a large, circular tray with a high silver cover.

'Mrs Duff! What is this?'

The cook smiled and glanced towards Wilhelmina.

'Happy birthday from Mama, Etty and me,' Wilhelmina cried. 'Here is something of our tradition.'

She lifted the cover to reveal a high cake smothered with cream and chocolate and surmounted with cherries. 'Oh, how wonderful! Oh James, look! Have you ever seen such a cake?' She kissed Wilhelmina on her cheeks, her eyes shining. 'Oh, what a birthday cake! Thankyou, Betty. Thankyou, Mrs Duff.'

Mrs Duff and Betty moved towards the door.

'We'll leave a taste for you,' Mrs Montgomery called to them both, laughing.

The cake was cut and lifted carefully onto

the plates with the silver trowel. Mrs Montgomery cut a piece with her fork and lifted it to her mouth. 'Mmm! Delicious!' she enthused, savouring the moist chocolate cake, the cherry-filled cream. 'What is it called?'

'It is blackforest cake. Mama made it. I ran home and told her it was your birthday when a little bird told me this morning. We decided to make it a surprise. It is our very favourite cake for special occasions. We wish you a very happy birthday.'

'It is delicious. Mrs Duff is a good plain cook and manages very well really. But oh, she couldn't produce something like this. Your mother must be a very good cook, Wilhelmina.'

'Yes, indeed she is. All the women in her family are good cooks. They are very proud of their cooking.'

'And she has taught you?'

'Oh yes. We can both cook well, too. There are many recipes which are family treasures.'

Mrs Montgomery was thoughtful as she relished a second slice of the cake. 'Wilhelmina,' she said hesitantly. 'Do you suppose your mother would give Mrs Duff some instruction in some more fancy cooking? As I say, she is a good plain cook. I think she would be amenable, possibly excited, by an opportunity to expand her skills.'

'Mama is proud of her skills. She enjoys it. I feel sure she would not only be willing, but thoroughly enjoy herself. Someone would have to stay with Papa, of course.'

Mrs Duff, when approached, was quite willing, though doubting her ability to ever produce something like the blackforest cake. Ginger biscuits, fruit cake or patty cakes were more her line.

Sophia when consulted was delighted. Again, it would be a way of repaying Mr and Mrs Montgomery for their kindness and generosity.

★　★　★

Sunday was a day of quiet activity at 'Llanfylhn'. The weekday routine was suspended for the day and only the necessary work attended to. The bulk of the property population — the Montgomery family, the overseers, paid staff and the convicts — all attended church, usually at Allynbrook.

The girls were up early, dressed and prepared for the ride to church. Billy had been entrusted to escort them, driving them in the sulky. They tied their hats on as they heard the hoofbeats of the horse approaching.

Sophia saw them out the door. 'I do not have to remind you to be circumspect,' she said quietly as they kissed her goodbye.

'Mama!' exclaimed Wilhelmina. 'Really! You know we always behave as ladies.'

'Yes, well . . . ' said Henrietta, remembering the sailor on their voyage to the colony.

'Remember to whom you belong,' Sophia called as they walked down the path.

Billy drew up and fastened the reins. 'Good morning,' he greeted, lifting his hat. His eyes roved appreciatively over the young ladies he was to escort. He handed them gallantly up as they climbed into the sulky. He bounded up himself and took up the reins.

What a pity. Miss Henrietta had climbed up first, so was now sitting next to him. He'd have to manage that better when they were coming home. Henrietta was very nice, but . . .

They moved off, the horse breaking into a trot.

It was a pleasant morning, clear and warm. The sun was not so hot yet, though it was mid morning. Perhaps today would not reach yesterday's high temperature.

'Oh, it's not hot yet,' Billy informed them. 'This is not midsummer yet. You will no doubt feel the heat this year, but you will soon become acclimatised.' He glanced at their dresses, at the material. 'You may have to see how to lighten some of your clothing.'

He hoped he had said that without seeming forward.

Wilhelmina watched, noticing his firm, confident hands on the reins, his manoeuvring of the sulky.

They could see the Montgomerys ahead of them. Mr Montgomery liked to drive himself in his buggy. This was a new acquisition — a stylish, light, fast vehicle, where the roads permitted.

A dray laden with the older women convicts and another with the paid staff made their way more slowly. Most of the convicts walked, some stolidly tramping. The others enjoyed the respite from work and the chance of talking to members of the opposite sex.

The overseer of convicts, Billy's father, brought up the rear of the cavalcade in an open phaeton, his wife and younger members of his family accompanying him. Although some communication between the women and the men convicts was overlooked, from this vantage point he was able to see all was decent and in order.

They drew up outside the church grounds. The little stone church was built in the valley. It was a picturesque spot, the hills rising steeply on either side, the Allyn River winding its way, meandering between the folds of the hills.

They filed into church. Henrietta led the way. She turned in to an empty pew. Wilhelmina followed. Billy brought up the rear. This was better. Now he could sit alongside Wilhelmina all through church. The Montgomery family sat in the front seat on one side and the Lindsays, landholders from farther up the valley, the other. The free staff sat at the rear and the convicts stood at the back.

The church was very small compared with their homeland places of worship, but it had an intimate feel. The timber pews shone with polish.

The first hymn was announced. They stood to sing as the little organ played the tune.

Wilhelmina opened her mouth to sing, then a strong full voice was lifted beside her. Her breath stopped in shock. The voice continued, full, round and mellow — a deep voice, echoing from the walls of the small enclosure, leading the congregation. Billy was singing. What a beautiful voice he had! What strength! What volume! Yet he wasn't shouting. It was just full and free and . . . glorious! She recollected herself and joined the singing.

The nearness of this Norse god man beside her was decidedly distracting. It was hard to keep her mind on her prayers. He was so tall

— and muscly — and oh! He had such a presence about him.

She glanced at Etty. Her eyes were closed. She must be intent on her prayers. As though feeling her sister's gaze on her, Etty's eyes opened. She frowned slightly, indicating more attention was required.

The rector's sermon was rather dreary. He had lots of quotes, lots of references, chapter this and verse that. Wilhelmina's attention wandered. The noise of the convicts shuffling on the stone floor was becoming more noticeable.

'Have you ever done something wrong?' thundered the rector's voice. Silly man. Why did he think all the people standing at the back of the church were here?

'If we say we have no sin we deceive ourselves and the truth is not in us.' His voice cut through her thoughts. 'But if we confess our sins he is faithful and just to forgive us our sins and cleanse us from all unrighteousness.'

Was he talking to her? Of course. He was talking to each one present. It wasn't only the convicts at all. It was everyone. Yes, she had sinned, because sin was any thought, word or deed that was against the will of God. Papa had said that. Along with everyone else, she needed forgiveness.

He was talking now about the way the Lord said to pray: 'Forgive us our trespasses as we forgive them that trespass against us. For if ye forgive men their trespasses, your heavenly Father will also forgive you. But if ye forgive not men their trespasses neither will your Father forgive your trespasses.'

She had been like the man in the story Jesus told. He was trying to pull out a speck from his brother's eye when he had a beam in his own eye. She had been judging, setting herself above the convicts.

What was that other thing about saying you loved God, then holding bad feelings towards anyone? Papa had told her that many times. Your brother was anyone else, he said. That was it. 'If a man say I love God, and hateth his brother, he is a liar. For he that loveth not his brother whom he hath seen, how can he love God whom he hath not seen?'

And Papa had always added, 'He who loves God, loves his brother also.'

★　★　★

At last, they were out and on their way home. It was a bright, happy party that headed home.

Billy set the horse at a brisk pace. Suddenly he started to sing: 'Onward Christian soldiers, marching as to war.'

His voice boomed out. Wilhelmina joined in.

Henrietta looked at her. She caught her glance and hesitated. Etty was looking decidedly uncomfortable. What was wrong? Billy was singing a hymn. Henrietta shook her head. Wasn't this a ladylike thing to do?

She glanced over the convicts trudging along the side of the road. Heads turned with the sound of Billy's voice. Most just smiled. Probably Mama would say it was drawing attention to themselves.

She held her hat with her gloved hand and smiled sweetly. She would act like a lady. Mama would be proud of her decorum. She must remember she was a Gerhardt of Wiesbaden, even if she was now in New South Wales and she had no career in front of her.

But this man beside her made her forget other things around her. When he had helped her up into the sulky, had his hand lingered over her fingers? Had he held them more tightly than was really necessary?

And it was not just the touch of his hand. It was his eyes, that blue of his eyes, searching hers, asking unspoken questions. She just had to lower her eyes, wrench her gaze from his.

Oh, she had never felt like this with anyone

before. Why was he so disrupting to her? He was just the overseer's son. She knew nothing at all about his family beyond that.

Her pulse quickened as he handed them down and opened the gate, lifting his hat in farewell. Her ear followed the sound of the hoofbeats as they receded towards the carriage shed.

21

What might have been

Christmas had come and gone. What a strange Christmas! No log fires, no mistletoe in the hall, no snow, no carol singers in the streets (no streets!), no midnight service.

But it was such a hot day. The thermometer had reached 100 degrees Fahrenheit. How to bear it? They had roasted a rooster from their own flock and the cake and pudding had been cooked weeks ago as always. At least that was familiar.

The whole company had gone to church at Allynbrook. There were many carriages, sulkies, buggies — all manner of horse-drawn vehicles outside the church grounds.

For this festival, people had come from far and wide. There was no hope of everyone fitting inside the church. The convicts and many servants crowded around the open windows and doors, or stood and sat on the ground outside. Oh, the joy of the service, the singing. Even the convicts seemed to feel the wonder of the festival.

And the rector had spoken simply and

fluently of the birth of the Christ Child: of God coming to earth in the person of Jesus, the baby of Bethlehem, to show his people how to live and to die for them on the cross, all because he loves them. She mused on the wonder of it. 'He came for each one of us, as a helpless baby dependent on his mother.' The rector's voice was warm with feeling. 'Love. That was the reason. Love.'

Wilhelmina felt the rise of emotion, of wonder. She felt the glow of love around her. She closed her eyes to be more intensely aware of this intangible presence. She could feel the harmony flowing among the congregation, convicts and all. She looked around, her heart full. Then she glanced at Billy sitting beside her and her heart gave a little leap. Oh, God's world was wonderful.

One shadow hung over them. Johann was not so well. He seemed to be deteriorating. Poor Papa, dear Papa: he was suffering.

★ ★ ★

But now it was almost New Year and preparations were in full swing for the New Year's Eve party. The dining room and adjoining drawing room, both large rooms, had been opened up, making a very large area for the many guests invited. Decorations were being hung, supports being erected for garlands of fresh flowers planned for the hall and reception rooms. Mrs Montgomery darted about, delighted with the suggestions being offered by Henrietta and Wilhelmina.

Sophia was called in to supervise the catering preparations. She and Mrs Duff had taken to each other quickly, Sophia encouraging Mrs Duff and convincing her of her ability to add the extra touches which demonstrated the flair she herself possessed.

Wilhelmina had offered rather tentatively to test the piano and adjust the tuning, if necessary. Her offer was accepted with alacrity. It was a beautiful piano. Her fingers lingered lovingly over it.

At last, all was ready. The guests who would be staying overnight were expected soon. The flowers had been sprayed with water to maintain their beauty in the heat.

'Oh, it all looks beautiful,' Mrs Montgomery enthused. 'Now, off you go. We must all make ourselves look beautiful.'

They had been through the trunks weeks before Christmas. Each had decided on a dress that with some modifications would suit admirably.

Etty's was a satin gown of emerald green. The colour highlighted her soft golden hair and her grandmother's pearl necklace glowed with a soft lustre on the creamy skin of her throat and shoulders.

There had been much discussion about Wilhelmina's dress. She had not yet made her debut into society. She was not yet out. Yet she was now of age.

'But there will not be any 'coming out' for me, Mama!' Wilhelmina had said, looking rather crestfallen.

'Oh, my poor darling,' Sophia had cried. 'Oh, have we done the right thing? Where would you make your debut here in these wilds?' She was close to tears.

'Mama, could we make this party Will's coming out? There is nowhere else. Could we not make this it? We could dress her hair in a grown-up style and arrange her dress so. Oh, we could do it. And she would be included in the ladies!' Henrietta waxed enthusiastic as she spoke. 'It will be a new beginning, a new year — and an entrance into full adult society for Wilhelmina.'

The idea was accepted wholeheartedly. Then the search began for just the right dress. At last, they decided on a deep red taffeta gown trimmed with lace and ribbons.

★ ★ ★

The guests began arriving soon after they had entered the house by the French doors.

There was the sound of carriages coming up the road and sweeping round the drive; the voices raised in greeting; the wishes for New Year; more guests following. Oh, the excitement of it! The babble chatter and laughter! It was the most exciting thing that had happened since before the whole turmoil of their emigration had begun.

How grown-up Wilhelmina looks, Sophia thought. She is very beautiful, with her dark hair dressed softly around her face, and gathered in a cluster of curls, the dress emphasising her tiny waist — and the bouffant full skirt. Johann had been so proud of her when she twirled before him for his approval. It would be the best 'coming out' they could have.

The guests were all moving into the big room, greeting friends infrequently seen. It was going to be a lovely party.

There were trays of drinks balanced carefully by the maids as they moved among the guests. Two of the younger convict men had been carefully instructed and now acted as waiters, resplendent in new uniforms. It was a grand evening for the servants, too.

At last, everyone had arrived. Mrs Montgomery, standing by the piano, called for attention. How pretty she was. Her gown was a bright sky blue and made her eyes seem bluer than ever. She clapped her hands. The chatter of voices subsided and she announced that Mrs Jessica Hamilton had consented to entertain them with a vocal solo. She would be accompanied by her niece, Miss Georgiana Dulhunty, who would then favour them with a rendition on the piano.

There was a polite round of clapping and the soloist moved to the piano. She was a woman of perhaps thirty-five, a pleasant-faced lady, tall and slim. Her accompanist — a plump, self-assured girl, seated herself with a self-conscious air of importance. It was a pleasant enough performance. Mrs Hamilton had a sweet voice; untrained, but mellow.

Now it was Georgiana's turn. Wilhelmina watched with some trepidation. What would it be like? Oh, she wished she could slip outside so she didn't have to endure the agony if her suspicions were right regarding this performer.

She began. The sound echoed through the room. Wilhelmina shuffled. There was no escaping it. She could hardly cover her ears.

The first choice was finished and the guests applauded politely. The girl seated herself again to favour with an encore, taking this as a sign of approval.

It was almost more than Wilhelmina in her excited mood could bear. She cringed. She looked around for a way of escape, but she was hemmed in at each turn.

Georgiana finished her encore and the little wave of applause was repeated. She bowed low, a prima donna receiving the adulation of her public.

Mrs Lindsay sitting near Wilhelmina leant towards her. 'That was very nice, was it not Wilhelmina?' she asked.

Wilhelmina's pent-up feelings burst out, her voice louder than she had intended. 'She may have been note perfect, but her touch was like a clockwork sledgehammer.'

There was a split second of stunned silence, then a great hubbub of voices as everyone tried to cover the words with more words.

Mrs Hamilton flushed, but Georgiana was making a great show of replacing her music in her case. Sophia looked with horror towards Mrs Hamilton.

Henrietta caught Mrs Montgomery's eyes. That impish lady's eyes were laughing. She turned hurriedly from Henrietta's gaze and was quickly deeply in conversation with the Lindsay's nephew Phillip Drinkwater who had come to visit them.

Henrietta made her way to Wilhelmina's side. 'Will, however could you be so rude?' she demanded softly. 'To speak so of an artist who has consented to favour us with her music!'

'Artist! Music!' she scoffed under her breath.

Henrietta turned away. It would do no good to reprimand her sister now. There were more drinks and dainty savouries circulated.

Then Mrs Montgomery took her place again beside the piano and again called attention. 'My dear friends,' she called, 'I now have a very special treat for you. We now have living with us here on 'Llanfylhn' a family lately come to us from Germany. Colonel Gerhardt was to have been our veterinary officer and overseer of our vineyards and winery. The Gerhardt wines of the Rhine valley are famous. Unfortunately, he is ill. However, his younger daughter Wilhelmina has relinquished a most promising career as a concert pianist to come to New South Wales. I have asked her to favour us. She is now going to entertain us with a collection of Chopin waltzes.'

Wilhelmina rose. She had regained some of her composure, but she dared not seek Mama's eyes. Oh, how could she have burst out like that? It was unpardonable. The girl had not had her opportunities. But oh, she was so self-important. That made it much worse. Even so, it did not excuse Wilhelmina.

She wended her way to the piano and seated herself quietly. Her hands lay for a moment on her lap. Then she touched the keys and, as always, nothing else existed. Her fingers caressed, lingered, tripped over the keys and danced with the lightness of thistledown. She held the last note till it died away, her wrists lifting and finally her fingers leaving the keys. There was another deathly silence, another silence of shock.

She lifted her head, looking swiftly around.

And suddenly it broke. The thunderous applause and babble of voices broke over her. 'Wherever did you find that girl?' Mrs Lindsay was beside Mrs Montgomery. 'Oh Lizzy, her music! What can one say?' She gave a little laugh. 'One cannot say quite the same about her manners. But oh, Georgiana is such a self-important little miss, isn't she?'

Elizabeth Montgomery hushed her friend. 'I'm hoping her mother didn't hear. I don't think she did.' She rolled her eyes skywards. 'It was so embarrassing.' Then she added, 'The trials of the truly talented!'

The chairs were now moved back to make way for dancing. Two of the convicts proficient on the accordion and the violin soon had their feet tapping; sets were made up and the reels commenced with a will.

Wilhelmina slipped out through the French doors across the verandah and out into the garden. She was quiet now. But the

211

enjoyment, the party mood had gone. She walked across the lawn and leant against the big Moreton Bay Fig tree. She would have to 'face the music'. She smiled ruefully at the expression. Mama would be ashamed of her. Etty would be embarrassed. Oh, if only she were still in Heidelberg and under Mr Chopin's instruction! Why, oh why did it all have to be happening just now?

It wasn't Papa's fault. Poor Papa, he was trying to protect them, trying to keep them safe. They were safe. It wasn't his fault that her promised fame had been snatched away from her.

Then whose was it? It had all happened because of the upheaval in Baden, the danger of an uprising. It all happened at the same time: her opportunity, the grand duchess' offer, Mr Chopin's acceptance of her as a pupil, the danger.

Who was she blaming then? Who was she feeling resentful against? Not Papa; not the grand duchess. Who was it? Who was responsible?

With shock she thought, was it God? Was she blaming God, fighting against God?

She leant her head on her arm against the trunk of the tree. The great wave of grief that she had held at bay ever since Papa had resigned and they had declined the grand duchess' offer of patronage flooded through her.

Why did it have to happen like this? Why God, why? Her mother's voice came into her mind. 'Perhaps it is not God's will for you, my darling. Perhaps God has other plans for you. Trust him.'

The torrent of tears flowed unchecked.

22

The eventful ride

'How could you do it? However could you be so rude, so impolite? I could not believe my ears! My daughter, who has been brought up in polite society, who has lived in the grand duke's palace, who has spoken with the grand duchess! One would think you had never had any training in the way to behave!'

Sophia looked with frustration and disbelief at her daughter. Wilhelmina was certainly looking very demure and repentant now, but that didn't erase what had happened.

Sophia turned away, in her agitation wringing her hands. 'We can say 'goodbye' to any invitations now. It will soon be all through the district that our daughter is completely ignorant of the social graces.'

'Mama, I'm sorry. I've said I'm sorry. But my ears couldn't believe that clock-like one, two, three, four of that girl's playing. Wind her up and she'll go until she runs down: that's what it sounded like. And if she hadn't put on such airs and graces, I might have been able to bear it and keep my mouth shut.

'But when Mrs Lindsay said, 'That was nice, wasn't it Wilhelmina?', I couldn't hold it. I couldn't tell a lie and agree. So many things in polite society are so false.'

'But that is to preserve people's pride and self-esteem.'

'Hmmph! Georgiana didn't need her pride to be preserved. She has plenty.'

'Two wrongs don't make a right. As well, you have been told many times. You are most fortunate to have studied under such a teacher as Mr Rhyngold. You should be gracious enough to be patient with those who have not had such a privilege.'

Wilhelmina dropped her eyes. And where had such privilege got her? She had the training, the potential for great things. She had the ability, the talent, the gift, the dedication. And there it all now stopped. She swallowed hard, blinking back the tears.

Henrietta had not spoken. No doubt she, too, had been most embarrassed. Looking up, she caught her sister's eyes on her. Henrietta gave a little smile.

'It isn't always easy being a grown-up, Will. You have to remember you are grown up and you can't be quite as free as when you were a child,' Sophia said, looking with compassion at Wilhelmina.

Her daughter was such an honest, straightforward little person and yet so intuitive and with such dreams. It must be hard for her. And having to renounce the promise of fame she could have attained! 'Oh, I can understand how you feel,' Sophia said, turning back to her, 'but nothing excuses your rudeness. You must learn to consider other people's feelings, their situation — and their point of view — sometimes, at the expense of your own feelings. There is no need to tell a lie. You can learn to choose your words kindly without that.'

Sophia moved over to Wilhelmina. 'There, there. You have said you are sorry. We will say no more about it. Time will tell whether or not anyone includes us in their invitations to social occasions.' She patted Wilhelmina's shoulder and walked out of the room.

Lunch was a quiet meal. Papa had been fed some soup. He was now sleeping.

Wilhelmina gathered up the dishes, stacking them on the tray. 'I'll wash these up, Mama. You go and rest. You look tired.'

Sophia watched her daughter as she went towards the kitchen. She could be so thoughtful, so kind. She stood up with a sigh, deciding to follow Wilhelmina's suggestion.

★　★　★

They heard the sound of the gate and footsteps coming up the path. Wilhelmina went to answer the door.

'Hullo.' Billy stood on the step, lifting his hat when she appeared. 'I've got a letter for Miss Henrietta.'

'A letter for Etty!' Wilhelmina's eyes flew open wide in surprise. 'Whoever can it be from? And who brought it?'

'The mailman has just been. He left it all up at the house. I called in for Mrs Montgomery to see Rosco and she asked me to bring it straight down.'

'But I didn't know there was a mailman!' Wilhelmina exclaimed.

'The steamer comes to Morpeth every week. Jack Hale the mailman picks up the mail. But he has a very large area to cover. I suppose this is the first letter that has come for any of you since you arrived. He doesn't always have cause to call here, of course.'

Wilhelmina recollected her manners. 'Oh, I am so remiss!' she exclaimed. 'I have left you standing here on the step. And you have been so kind to bring this down to us. Do come in and I'll get you a cool drink.'

Billy's face brightened at the invitation. 'Thankyou. It is hot. Can always do with a drink.'

He followed her into the hall. 'Come

217

through onto the other verandah. It's cooler there. I'll just take this to Etty, if you will excuse me.'

She left him sipping a cool lime water. 'Etty, Etty,' she called softly when she reached their bedroom. 'There's a letter for you.' She waved the letter aloft.

Henrietta sprang up from the bed where she had been resting. 'A letter for me?' It could only be from one person. A letter from anyone at home wouldn't have time to reach her yet. She took the letter, her heart thumping hard. She slit the envelope and withdrew the bulky letter. Yes. It was from him. Wilhelmina watched the flush suffuse Etty's face.

'Who is it from?' she asked.

Henrietta lifted her eyes. 'It's from Mr Jones.'

Mr Jones had written to Etty! So he was really serious about her! Where had he posted the letter? Was Etty going to read it to her? No. No. She mustn't ask. Etty would tell her what she wanted to tell her of what he had to say. They had always shared everything. Although so different, they were real confidantes. They understood each other. But this was different. You are growing up, Wilhelmina, she told herself.

'I'll leave you to it, then,' she said,

remembering Billy sitting alone on the verandah. He had finished his drink.

'Could I speak to your father later about one of the horses? There is so much I want to learn from him. He has such a store of knowledge.'

'I'll see if he is awake now,' Wilhelmina answered. 'If he is, he will have heard you come and will no doubt be hoping you come in for a word.'

Johann was awake. His face brightened at the request.

'I have a horse I can allot for your use if you would like me to bring him down later,' Billy said as she showed him into her father's room. 'Perhaps I could accompany you on a ride to see if you like him?'

Wilhelmina gladly agreed. That would be wonderful — a ride with Billy Foster. Everyone called him Billy. She hadn't yet heard him called Mr Foster. His *father* was Mr Foster. She hugged the thought of the ride to herself. His eyes said so much more than his lips.

★ ★ ★

It was such fun! She hadn't enjoyed herself so much for months. Billy had brought Bright Eyes as soon as he had returned to the stables and attended to the sick horse. He was a lovely animal — sixteen hands and well formed. She ran her hands over him, talking to him, patting his neck and smoothing his nose. He nuzzled her hand. Oh, he was lovely.

'Mr Montgomery says he's to be kept for you. We've got a lot of horses here,' Billy had told her.

They'd started out slowly, then progressed into a canter along the river. Now the wind blew through her hair, her hat flying off her head and hanging by the cord, as they galloped across the paddock. Oh, the freedom of it, the freshness. She felt cleared of all the emotions of the last few days. Life was wonderful, after all.

More than wonderful. Billy was such an exciting man.

They drew rein under the big gum overlooking the creek and dismounted. The horses nibbled the grass. There was a beautiful view from their vantage point — the winding creek lined with willows in their full summer dress, the clear bright sky dotted here and there with cloud lazily floating over the hill. It was a peaceful scene.

'I'm thirsty,' Wilhelmina said. Then her eyes sparkling, she grabbed up her skirt and cried, 'Race you to the creek,' and set off running down the hill, laughing gleefully.

Billy followed in hot pursuit. He caught her just before she reached the creek. Grasping her by the shoulders, his arms went round her and, crushing her to him, kissed her full on the lips.

The world reeled around her. Unknown emotions raced through her. Momentarily, she responded. Then suddenly she recollected herself. She put her hands on his chest and pushed him from her. 'You forget yourself, Mr Foster,' she gasped. They stood panting with the strength of their emotions. Wilhelmina turned to the creek. 'Anyway, I was coming to get a drink,' she said.

Billy was beside her in an instant. His hands gripped her and turned her to him. 'Look me straight in the eye and tell me you didn't want me to do that,' he challenged.

She glanced up at him. His piercing eyes seemed to see right through her. And that wave of . . . what? seemed to be about to engulf her again.

'You are being very forward,' she ventured, not looking at him.

'Look at me,' demanded Billy. 'Tell me you don't want me to be.'

She tried to look at him. But oh, it was too much. She couldn't tell a lie for the sake of polite society here. And there were no other words in her head. Not a single one would come. She twisted and slipped from his grasp and went running up the hill. 'We must go home,' she called. 'The horses will be straying.'

Billy watched her go. A satisfied little smile played around his lips.

23

Henrietta and Alister

Henrietta read and reread the letter. Alister — she could call him that now: they were formally courting. He had posted the letter in Hong Kong where he had made many contacts in preparation for his plans regarding the shipping line he hoped to establish.

He hoped to be in England by April and to be back in Australia, this time for good, before Christmas and, if all his plans went well, contract builders for construction of his house. 'I shall certainly need your views on that matter, darling Henrietta if, as I hope, you consent to be my wife.' There was much in the same vein that Henrietta, closing her eyes, hugged to herself.

★ ★ ★

There seemed to be many things that brought Billy to the house in the next few months — a letter; a message; some flowers Frobisher had given him; a joey found on the road; some flowering gum blossoms for their interest;

some wild cherries, or lilly pilly as they were called; or some information, guidance he required from Johann.

Johann had taken to him. Their mutual interest and love of horses was a bond, but it was more than that. In spite of his own formality, Billy's freshness and lack of ceremony amused and appealed to him.

'Good man,' he said to Sophia. 'Honest.' He lifted his brows. 'Wild,' he said and held up his clenched hand, drawing it to him as though he was reining in a horse.

'You think he needs reins to keep him in check?' Sophia asked.

He smiled and nodded slowly.

'He has eyes for Wilhelmina,' she said quietly. 'He has spoken nothing to me about addressing her.'

Johann lifted amused eyes to hers.

'You think he will not think of such a thing? It probably will never occur to him. Oh Johann, times are changing. Our old customs of protection are breaking down. Where will it all lead to? Oh well, they are little more than children yet.'

Johann shook his head slowly and lifted his hand in a motion of disagreement. 'Take care,' he said.

★ ★ ★

They walked down the track together, the reins of the horses looped over their arms, gazing across the paddocks. 'This is what I want to do, Will,' he said.

'What? Lead your horse down the track? I thought you liked to ride,' she teased.

'You know what I mean. I want to be able to stand on a hill and look out over the valleys and know 'This land is mine'. There's something about it, owning your own place — and managing it; working out what you want to do without having to ask anyone, or be told to do what someone else wants.

'There are lots of new things happening. There are machines to do the work that takes three or four or more men now. Someone was telling me at the cattle sale at Patterson last week about a machine that cuts lucerne. Imagine! And there'll be others. I want to try out these things.

'We're not standing still. Things are moving, changing on the land, just as your mother was saying about in factories.

'I suppose it's good and bad. But it will be bad for those who don't go with it. They'll be left behind. You've got to think ahead, Will.'

She nodded. Billy was right. She always said you had to think ahead.

Billy turned and looked to the mountains bordering 'Llanfylhn' land. 'Over those mountains there is land just as good as this, if not better. The Williams River runs through there; it starts in those mountains.'

'Have you been there? Do you like it?'

'I went over the track. It's hardly more than that — pretty steep in parts. Have to watch your step. We rode over to pick up cattle Mr Montgomery bought. We brought them back that way. Would be a job to take a load on a dray or bullock team over there yet, though.

'It's good country. The river is as clear as crystal. Stony bottom. And the further up you go, the colder it gets. Actually starts up on what they call the Barrington Tops. Rough country there, though — wouldn't be hard to get lost up there. Plenty dingoes.'

'Do you think you might buy land there some time?' Wilhelmina didn't doubt he would make it possible if he wanted to.

'Mmm. It's just opening up, really.' He laughed. 'I haven't got enough money yet. I'm saving. But the government's got a scheme of selecting. I'm getting the information about that. Don't know how much you can select, but Mr Montgomery says that's the way to go. You have to do certain things on the land and show you know what you're about.'

Oh, Billy would know what he was about. It would open up yet another world. They mounted their horses and turned their heads for home.

★　★　★

Their first year had almost gone. The seasons had come full cycle. The winter that had caused local people to complain of the cold had to them been so mild. There was no snow and no ice — except on the fowls' water trough and the dish under the tap on the tank when there was a frost. They were almost old timers now, knowing what to expect.

Henrietta had received more letters from Alister Jones, he having posted them at every available place. He had spoken of his schemes to his father and he had agreed to invest. He was accompanying him to Gravesend, London and Portsmouth to search for a suitable vessel for sale, a good seaworthy vessel with all the necessities for the kind of cargo to be undertaken and the ports it would be necessary to visit.

So his dreams were being realised.

When would he be back in New South Wales? Each letter was more loving. His longing to be with her was becoming unbearable. After they were married and his venture underway, she must accompany him to England so that he could bring her to his mother and father. He knew they would just love her. This was, of course, if she accepted him and they did marry.

If her answer was no . . . ? He could not bear to think of it. But he was full of hope.

Sophia watched Henrietta as each letter came. Alister Jones would be an admirable husband for her. He would be courteous and thoughtful. His social position was exemplary and it appeared he was in a financial position to provide well for her. She would most likely have a beautiful home in Sydney. But oh, Sydney was a long way away. When she married, they might be lucky to see her once a year, if that.

And Wilhelmina was growing up. She and Billy, it was obvious, were forming a very strong attachment for each other. Still, he had said nothing about asking their permission to address her. Johann was probably right. He never would. She must be vigilant. They were both young people of strong emotions and it would be her responsibility.

Poor Johann. Her heart lurched. Johann was slowly slipping from her.

What if Wilhelmina married before long? She was of age to marry now. She would have to care for Johann on her own. And when he left her . . . where would she live?

Just as they were putting the last dishes

away after lunch, the dogs along the way set up a barking. A horse's hoofs were heard and the sound of a vehicle drawing up outside. Wilhelmina ran to the hall door and peered through.

A tall, slim man jumped down from the smart vehicle and tied the horse to the hitching rail. He turned and looked towards the front door, then opened the gate and started up the path. Whoever could he be?

She took a few steps down the hall then, realising the identity of their visitor, turned and ran back to the kitchen. 'Etty, Etty,' she cried. 'There's a visitor for you coming up the front path.' The heavy door knocker fell.

Henrietta, looking mystified, left the kitchen and crossed the verandah. Then she saw the visitor. She gave a little high-pitched cry and ran down the hall, throwing her arms around his neck.

Amid laughter and tears, he finally held her at arm's length. 'Does that mean 'Yes'?' he asked, beaming at her.

'Yes. Oh yes, Alister.' She wiped her eyes with one hand, still holding his other hand.

'Really Henrietta, how very undignified. You must restrain yourself and act with more decorum.' Wilhelmina advanced down the hall with mock severity.

Sophia, coming to see what all the fuss was

about, added her welcome to the commotion.

He was brought in and taken to see Johann. Alister was shocked at his condition, although Johann was able to speak a little. He was just growing weaker and weaker.

'Colonel Gerhardt, I wish to speak to you on a matter of vital importance to me,' Alister said.

Johann nodded and looked at him questioningly.

'When you were so very ill and unable to speak, I asked your permission through Mrs Gerhardt to court your daughter Henrietta. That permission was given. I now ask for her hand in marriage. I love her very much and I believe she returns that sentiment.' He looked expectantly at Henrietta's father.

Johann smiled and lifted his hand in blessing. 'Gladly,' he murmured. 'Be good to her,' he said slowly, pausing between the words.

Now the excitement was beyond words. When would the wedding be? What were the plans?

Alister could not bear to be parted from his love again after the long separation. Would Mrs Gerhardt consent to their marriage as soon as possible so that they might return to Sydney together? There, Alister would find temporary lodging while their house was built. Then they must all come and visit.

'But a wedding dress,' cried Sophia. 'Where shall we get a wedding dress? Oh, how can these things be done in a short time?'

'Mama,' Henrietta interrupted. 'I know what I want to do. I shall wear my coming-out dress. It is white. It is beautiful. And I have worn it only the once. We will make a bonnet and veil and it will be lovely.'

Sophia looked uncertain, but was soon talked into agreement. It was a beautiful dress.

The date was eventually set for a month's time. This would allow for marriage banns to be read and the wedding to be arranged. It would be a small wedding, seeing they had no family of either bride or groom, other than themselves, to attend. There would just be the Montgomerys, the Lindsays, the closest neighbours and Billy and his family. The wedding would be at Allynbrook and, at Mrs Montgomery's insistence, the reception would be at the big house.

The rector was contacted and the arrangement decided upon.

The days flew by. Then the morning dawned clear and bright, Henrietta's wedding day.

Alister had accepted Mrs Montgomery's invitation to stay with them that last night so

231

he did not see his bride until they met at the church.

'Etty, you look beautiful,' whispered Wilhelmina as Henrietta turned from the mirror. 'You are a sight to behold.'

The beautiful, soft, muslin dress was trimmed with garlands of tiny roses, the waist emphasising Henrietta's slim figure. Henrietta's glowing face was proof of her overwhelming happiness.

Johann insisted on being present, so Billy had offered to carry him to the carriage and, taking the greatest care of him, to take him to the church and back to 'Llanfylhn'. He had a wheelchair in the carriage for his comfort in church.

Wilhelmina as bridesmaid, wearing a soft pink taffeta dress, modified from a former court model, helped Henrietta to the door of the church. Mr Montgomery was to give her away in place of her father.

They stood for a moment, then the organ began the bridal march. The ceremony had begun.

★ ★ ★

The return to 'Llanfylhn' was a joyous affair. Johann, still insisting on being present, was carried into the sitting room. Mrs Duff excelled herself and the grand wedding cake was proof of Sophia's tutoring. The happy couple were toasted and wishes for a long, happy life expressed. At last they were on their way. They waved them off after much hugging and kissing and admonitions to write often.

The time came for them to go home. Billy again, carrying Johann and with great gentleness, helped to settle him in his bed. 'A drink of spirit, rum, whisky?' he said as he turned to Sophia. 'It may help him after such a big day.' He looked at Johann, concerned. 'He is a brave man,' he said solemnly.

Sophia went to get the suggested pick-me-up. Billy found Wilhelmina in the kitchen. 'Well?' he said, looking into her eyes, taking her hands in his.

'Well what?' she asked.

'When are we going to do this?'

'Do what?'

'You provoking little creature. You know perfectly well what I'm talking about. When are we going to get married?' He looked at her half-laughing, but his eyes serious.

'Are we going to get married? You haven't asked me yet.'

'You know we are,' he whispered. 'I love you, Wilhelmina.'

She lifted her eyes to his. There was a different expression in his eyes. They were not piercing now. They were serious, filled with love. 'Oh Billy, I love you, too,' she whispered. 'But how can I leave Mama now?'

24

Permission granted

It was lonely without Henrietta. Though the quiet member of the family, her leaving was a great loss. They all realised how much they depended on her gentle tolerance and patience.

Wilhelmina had no-one in whom to confide. She could talk to Mama, but that was different. She turned more and more to Billy for companionship. Now that their love had been stated, their conversation was more relaxed, more open. Now it was 'when we are married . . .'

'You know, you have never spoken to Mama or Papa about addressing me,' Wilhelmina said as they sat on the kitchen steps in the evening.

'A bit late for that!' exclaimed Billy. 'I've been addressing you ever since the day you arrived!'

'I don't mean just talking to me; I mean courting.'

Billy considered a few minutes. 'Don't see that's necessary,' he stated. 'I'll ask if I can marry you — soon, when you say so.' He looked at her with a grin. 'If they say no, I'll just pick you up and put you on my horse and gallop away with you, like those knights of old you tell me about.' He was quiet a moment. 'It's how you feel that matters.

'Do you know, one of the fellows up there,' he indicated the convicts' quarters, 'was telling me that at the female factory in Sydney, they line the women and girls up, all the ones that are not married that is, and men looking for a wife go there and make their choice. They look them over like cattle they may be buying. And the girl has no choice! She just has to marry whoever picks her.'

'I suppose anything is better than where they are,' Wilhelmina responded. She thought of girls she had known. 'Of course, sometimes marriages are still arranged. There again, the girl hasn't much choice. She just has to do what her father says. Thank goodness, Papa is not like that. He has always said he wants us to marry for love, true love — to last till the end of our lives. He approved of Alister right from when we first met him on the ship.'

Billy stared out into the night. 'Does he approve of me?' he asked, trying to make it sound nonchalant.

Wilhelmina smiled at him. 'He hasn't said. But I think he is fond of you. He always brightens up when you come to see him. You cheer him up.'

'Do you think he will say 'Yes'?'

'Oh Billy, he is fading away. I can see it happening. How long do you think we will have him?' There was a catch in her voice. 'And what of Mama?'

★ ★ ★

The winter was hard on Johann. His immobility made it hard to keep him warm. As the second anniversary of their arrival approached, his departure from them seemed imminent. The doctor from Patterson called periodically, but there was nothing he could do. They could only keep him as comfortable as possible and watch and wait.

The sun was just rising over the mountain on a clear Spring morning when Sophia, going to see if he was awake, found he had slipped quietly away. She put her hand on his arm. It was quite cold. He must have died some hours before.

She could not realise he had gone. She stood for some time just looking at him. He just looked to be asleep, quite peaceful. In fact, some of the lines of suffering in his face seemed to be gone. Dear Johann. He had wanted to protect them. He had thought of them. He had wanted so desperately for them to be safe.

At last the tears came. She knelt beside the bed, her hand on his. Gradually she calmed. He would be with God now. He would not be in pain. She must think of that.

But what of her? What of Wilhelmina? What would Johann say? The reply flashed into her head as though he were speaking to her: 'Pray. Ask God. He will make it known to you.'

She rose and went to tell Wilhelmina.

Johann was buried on the little promontory near the river. It was a tiny graveyard. They had not known of its existence. Mrs Montgomery had suggested he be buried there. It was the 'Llanfylhn' cemetery. They had found the grave of a baby, Joseph Montgomery, born 15 March, died 10 April 1845. There was only one other grave, that of a convict, Arthur Richards, who had died while serving his term.

They gathered for the service on the little point. The water gurgled over the stones at the edge of the river, the young, green shoots on the weeping willows swaying in the breeze.

The rector was reading. 'Some men will say, How are the dead raised up? And with what body do they come? Thou fool, that which thou sowest is not quickened, except it die. And that which thou sowest, thou sowest not that body that shall be, but bare grain, it may chance of wheat, or of some other grain. But God giveth it a body, as it hath pleased him, and to every seed his own body.'

Dear Papa. God would give him his true body. The old one he had would be gone. It had been a burden to him ever since the stroke. He had always said, 'As you sow, so shall you reap.' He had sown love and goodness; trust in God. He had been faithful. God would hold him in his care.

★ ★ ★

Sophia removed her black bonnet and laid it on the end of the bed. She tidied her hair at the mirror and smoothed her hands over the skirt of her black dress.

They had not had a black dress for Wilhelmina, but Johann would know it was no lack of respect when it was decided she must wear grey. She had wept torrents when told of her father's death, but she was a sensible person and knew he was released from his pain. He would have a better life.

What now of Billy? He had been very solicitous and kind throughout all this. It seemed inevitable that they would eventually marry. Would Billy ask for her hand? Surely

239

he would succumb to this courtesy?

It was impossible not to like him — and to depend on him. Johann had been fond of him. He was certainly intelligent, in spite of his lack of education. She turned away and went towards the kitchen for a cup of tea.

Wilhelmina looked up as her mother entered the kitchen. She poured a cup of tea and passed the plate of biscuits. 'I miss Etty.'

Sophia nodded. 'It seems so strange to have her so far away. She will be so sorry she could not be here.' Sophia sipped her tea. 'She should have the word tomorrow. I don't know whether Alister is at home at present or not.'

Billy and Wilhelmina exchanged glances. 'Mrs Gerhardt,' he began diffidently. 'This is probably not the time to talk about this, but what you just said makes me think it is.' He looked at her, unsure.

What was he talking about?

'You just said Alister may not be at home. I've been thinking about that.' He cleared his throat. 'I'm sure you know how I feel about Wilhelmina, how we feel about each other.' He glanced up, looking directly at Sophia. 'I love her very much, Mrs Gerhardt. I was going to ask your husband's permission to marry her at the end of the year. There are some plans being made here in the management of the place. But what you just said about Alister being away . . . And anyway, Sydney is so far away . . . You have no man to care for you or help you now.

'I'm asking for your permission, now, to marry Wilhelmina. I'm asking now so that our betrothal can be official. Then I can perhaps have the right to look after you both.' He paused. 'Will you please say 'Yes'?' he finished with a half smile.

'Oh Billy! What can I say?' Sophia swallowed. This was the second time she had been approached on these grounds. It had been easy when Alister spoke to her. Now Billy. Well, was there any real difficulty? Billy's family background, other than his immediate family, was a closed book to her. She certainly hadn't heard anything about a high military position or a knight in his fore-bears. It was the strength and the magnetism of the man himself that caught your attention.

Johann had eagerly looked for his visits. He was fond of him, in quite a different way from his regard for Alister. But yes, fond of him. Billy would go far, he had said. But who would hold the reins Johann had suggested he needed? Was Wilhelmina strong enough? She thought of the New Year's Eve party and Wilhelmina's never-to-be forgotten gaffe, of her outspokenness and honesty.

She smiled. 'As you say, Billy, I certainly

did not expect this today. However, I appreciate your thought in wanting to help care for us as your reason for speaking now.'

She looked across at Wilhelmina and back to the young man looking so earnestly at her. 'You are right, I am aware of your feelings for each other and I expected this question sooner or later. As it is sooner, I shall say 'Yes'.'

Wilhelmina jumped up from her chair and ran around to her mother, throwing her arms around her neck. Billy, too, had risen and was smiling broadly.

Sophia held up her hand. 'Provided,' she stated, 'you can convince me of your plans for provision for her welfare and happiness. Marriage does not end with the honeymoon, you know. It is a lifelong affair.'

There was much chatter and excitement. Billy shook her hand and then, gaining courage, kissed her cheek. They talked on, sitting casually at the kitchen table.

It was as though Johann was there. So many times as Sophia thought, 'What would Johann think?', the thought had flashed into her head.

There was the aloneness she felt, especially before this glowing young couple — and yet she felt Johann close. Perhaps it was the right time for Billy to speak. It lessened the thought of the parting.

And he had spoken, very well, the kindness of his heart bound up in the choice of the time. He was not devoid of all the niceties of the conventions. As Wilhelmina said, some of the customs in polite society were false or unnecessary — so long as the important things were observed and the heart in the right place. That was what really mattered.

*   *   *

Once again, the trunks must be gone through. They searched. There were dresses Sophia could use as mother of the bride, but nothing promising for the wedding dress.

The last trunk was filled with things that had not been disturbed for a long time. As they neared the bottom, Wilhelmina gave a little cry. 'Here, Mama! I can see a white or cream dress right at the bottom!' She hastily removed everything and lifted out the lace from the trunk.

'Oh, my wedding dress!' cried Sophia. 'I have not taken it out for years.'

Wilhelmina held it up. 'But Mama! It is beautiful! Do you suppose it will fit me?'

'You mean you would like to wear my wedding dress?' asked Sophia incredulously.

'Yes. Why not? It is beautiful.' She was

quickly undressing and reached for the dress. She slipped it over her head. 'Can you do the buttons up, Mama?'

Sophia's hands shook as her fingers fumbled with the tiny buttons.

'Easily,' Sophia said happily, her heart thumping against her ribs. 'Oh, if you are happy, it will do beautifully.'

It was getting on towards Christmas when Mr Montgomery announced that he would be making Billy head stockman. The number of cattle had greatly increased in the last few years. 'Llanfylhn' now had its own stud of Hereford cattle and were breeding not only to build up their own numbers, but to supply the growing demand in the market.

Mr Montgomery still bought stores cattle for fattening. Billy had for some time been given the responsibility of attending the cattle sales and buying on his behalf. His experience and eye for weight, beasts likely to fatten well and quickly, had developed.

He was particularly interested in the stud herd. There was the fascination of selecting bulls with particular characteristics, then waiting to see their effect on the next season's progeny.

This new position would give him more freedom and authority to use his now considerable expertise and judgment.

He had spoken with Mr Montgomery of his plans to marry Wilhelmina. They must have their own house, Mr Montgomery had said, and had commenced plans for this. Sophia listened to all the arrangements. It seemed all would be well with the young couple. Wilhelmina would be provided for.

She had assumed that they may live in the house with her and had been thinking of ways to give them privacy. She would have moved into the girls' room and rearranged her own bedroom for them. But if Mr Montgomery was going to provide accommodation for his head stockman, what of her — and this house?

25

Nuptials

Wilhelmina wakened with the sound of the kookaburras in the garden: her wedding day. Today, she would marry Billy. How she loved him. They would make a good life together. Billy had dreams. If he was really keen about them, he'd make them come about.

He was so strong, yet so gentle and loving, so kind and thoughtful. But he wasn't dull; not at all. And he wasn't afraid to say what he thought. He wouldn't do something just for the sake of it being the 'right' thing to do. It would be because he thought it was the right thing to do.

Oh, he was the most wonderful, exciting man she had ever met. And today he would be her husband.

She sat up, throwing back the sheet. It was hot already. She glanced out of the window. The sky was clear except for a few high clouds drifting over. But it felt like there could be a storm later.

She looked at her wedding dress hanging from the wardrobe. Fancy! She had never thought of wearing Mama's wedding dress. If she had still been in Baden, she would no doubt have had a new dress made for her wedding. But here, Mama's dress was perfect — and no-one had seen it.

But then, if she had still been in Baden, she would never have met Billy. She wouldn't be marrying him. Most likely she wouldn't be getting married for years. She might have just been coming to the height of her career. It was a sobering thought. Just think: she might not have met Billy! How terrible not to know this love for him and be surrounded by his love, by the prospect of their life together.

God had brought her to a different life: he had brought her to Billy and the wonder of their love. She wasn't in Baden; she was here — and Billy was here.

What would it be like never to have known him? Life would be so dull. Oh, life was very complicated — and contradictory. She swung her feet onto the floor. She would dress and run up to the big house and see how the flowers were. Some had been arranged last night. They would need spraying. The others would have to be done this morning.

Etty and Alister had arrived three days ago and were helping with arrangements. The reception was again to be at 'Llanfylhn' at Mrs Montgomery's insistence. Mrs Duff had made the wedding cake and all the catering was in hand.

This time, there would be Billy's family and some of his friends and friends of his family. The rest of his relatives were still in Wales. With the Montgomerys, the Lindsays and the new overseer of the vineyard and winery, there would be a larger gathering than for Etty's wedding.

She was not so sure about some of Billy's friends. They seemed a little wild — uncouth, she thought. They weren't the sort of people she would want to associate with.

★ ★ ★

The time went quickly. The flowers were all finished. The reception room looked beautiful. Sophia was very proud and happy with the arrangement. But the lingering thought of her future persisted. She placed the last little posy beside the guests' place cards. She stood back to admire.

'It all looks very nice, Mrs Gerhardt.' Mr Montgomery had come into the room unnoticed. 'And our little Wilhelmina is getting married.' He smiled. 'Well, well. They have to grow up and leave us, I suppose.'

Sophia came to a decision. 'Mr Montgomery, I have been thinking a great deal of my position now. You were so kind as to arrange positions for the girls when we arrived here in such straits. Now, not only has Johann gone, but today my last daughter leaves home. I cannot expect to remain in the house you have so generously provided for us.'

She paused. 'I . . . I have not come to any decision about my future. I do not know quite what to do. Perhaps I could be a live-in companion, or nurse to some elderly person. I am rather at a loss to know where to start. I have a little money and Johann's brother Jost has been very kind and sent me some periodically. But I have not enough to set myself up in another establishment and have enough to live on. I wondered if you could advise me.

'Billy wants to 'look after me', he says. But they are so young. I do not want to be a burden on them. And I am not old yet. There must be something I can do.'

Mr Montgomery smiled. He had been fiddling with a serving-spoon from the table while she spoke. He put it down firmly and looked at her directly. 'You are happy here with us, are you not Mrs Gerhardt?'

'Oh yes. It is not that, or that I want to leave 'Llanfylhn'. Not at all. It is just I do not wish to impose. Besides, it would not be

249

correct to live in your house when I cannot pay for it.'

'We, too, have been thinking of your future,' he said, putting his hands in his pockets and strolling up and down. 'Lizzy, we both, have become very fond of you and your family. We feel we have gained an extended family. We think of you as family. We would feel utterly bereft if you, too, left us.

'However, we understand your feelings. We have a plan. Next year, we want to travel overseas for some months. We want to spend more time away from 'Llanyfylhn' for one reason or another — the children at school in Sydney, Lizzy's parents in Melbourne.

'We had been wondering what we could do about someone suitable to keep an eye on the house, on the garden — all the things Lizzy particularly does. It is a beautiful home and we want to keep it that way.

'Then we had an inspiration. We put the two needs together. Would you consider taking the position of caretaker of 'Llanfylhn' on a permanent basis? Now that you no longer have Colonel Gerhardt to care for, your time would be your own. If you feel you could consent to this, we should be greatly in your debt. It would mean we could come home to this lovely place and it would be as though we had never been away.

'There are plenty of people to do the gardening, Frobisher has agreed to stay on and the house staff would remain. You would really be mistress of 'Llanfylhn' in our absence.

'It would take a great load off our shoulders to have you, whom we trust implicitly, in charge. We could come and go with light hearts. What do you say?'

Sophia's eyes filled: not to have to leave these dear friends; not to have to leave this house she had come to love, even though it was not grand; not to have to leave her last home with Johann, where she could see him in every room; to retain her independence; and to act as mistress of 'Llanfylhn' in their absence; to manage the big house as though it was her own!

'Oh Mr Montgomery, I do not know what to say,' she said softly.

'Then just say yes and we'll call it arranged. We'll talk more about the details later.'

'Thankyou, then. Yes. It is beyond anything I could have hoped for.'

★ ★ ★

The bridal party had arrived. Henrietta was fussing around Wilhelmina, adjusting her veil, straightening her dress. Alister was to give the bride away, now being the man of the family.

Wilhelmina peeped in the door. There was Billy standing up at the chancel step. Her heart gave a leap of joy.

The music started and, her hand on Alister's arm, they proceeded up the aisle, followed by Henrietta. The service proceeded in a daze. They made their vows, their promises 'till death us do part'. Billy placed the ring on her finger. The minister pronounced the blessing. They were married.

There was kissing and slapping on the back for Billy when they came out of the church. The bell rang out joyfully. Billy's excited voice and laughter could be heard above the buzz of voices.

The sky overhead looked as though the morning's prediction of storms could be realised. The clouds were building up. The air was hot and tense.

They drove back to 'Llanfylhn' and the drinks flowed liberally. The speeches were appropriate and amusing and the health and long life of the young couple was toasted enthusiastically.

One of Billy's friends, a short, stocky fellow, came over to them with two glasses. 'Here we are, Billy. Have a last drink with your old mate. You'll have petticoat government now. No more time for us.' He put one glass down heavily and rather unsteadily on the table. Raising the other he said loudly, 'A toast to the boys!' He drank greedily.

Billy, smiling foolishly, looked decidedly uncomfortable. He lifted the glass and, holding it, looked at Wilhelmina. Her expression told her opinion of his friend — and the toast.

'Come on, Billy. Drink it up. Aren't ya goin' to drink with yer ol' mate? A drop more won't hurt! For ol' times' sake!' He swayed slightly.

Avoiding Wilhelmina's eyes, Billy drained the glass. Wilhelmina looked away from him. He reached for her hand, but she snatched it away. How could he drink that stuff? Rum. And for a toast like that? And that oaf — 'friend', he called him!

Henrietta leaned over and whispered in her ear.

'I don't care,' Wilhelmina hissed. 'That is disgusting.'

They rose to speak to each of the guests. Billy's friends crowded round him, separating them. Henrietta ushered her on, chatting, guiding her to the other end of the room.

Through a gap in the crowd, she saw Billy being plied with drinks. Why didn't he refuse them? This was their wedding day!

At last, it was time to change and leave. Their valise had already been stowed in the buggy they were to use to go to Patterson and a room reserved at the hotel. Billy had trouble with his shirt buttons, but eventually they were ready and waved goodbye.

Sophia's brow was creased with concern as Billy whisked the reins and they set off at a brisk trot. It was a quiet journey except for Billy's voice booming out, song after song, and his urging of the horse. Wilhelmina clung to the seat and the hand hold. Whatever had happened to Billy? She had never seen him like this. Had she mistaken the kind of man he was? What had she married?

The storm that had been gathering all day broke as they drove into the hotel yard. They clambered down and ran for shelter. Wilhelmina was shown to their room. Billy remained at the office to settle their details and then to bring their valise.

Great streaks of forked lightning rent the sky, the thunder deafening overhead. The heavens opened and the rain poured down. Gutters overflowed and the road was soon awash. Wilhelmina watched. It all reflected some of the turmoil in herself.

The air at least was fresh. It was a relief to breathe it in after the tension of the day.

She took off her bonnet and laid it on the chest of drawers. Billy was a long time coming. She walked around the room, looking at the pictures on the walls, the furniture, the washstand with jug and basin.

The rain seemed to be easing. There were voices. 'For he's a jolly good fellow, for he's a jolly good fellow, for he's a jolly good fellow and so say all of us. Hip hip hooray, hip hip hooray, hip hip hooray!' Men's voices — and it sounded as though they had imbibed very freely. Drunk. Ughh!

Where had Billy got to? It couldn't take this long to fix up at the desk and get the valise. She couldn't change till he brought it. Heavy footsteps and a thud sounded outside the door. There was some murmuring, then the door knob turned and Billy, a dishevelled Billy, appeared, dragging the valise. His necktie was askew, his hair hanging over his eyes.

'Got detained, Will,' he said very carefully, not looking at her. 'Boys wanted to wish us well!' He closed the door, turning unsteadily. 'Great fellas. Friendly, very friendly — 'specially when I said we were just married today.'

Wilhelmina watched him with fascinated horror. He was drunk! He had been drinking with those louts downstairs while she waited up here for him. She strode over to him and took the valise. 'Sorry, Will,' he said with great

255

dignity. 'Couldn't be rude and leave the boys when they were wishing us well.'

Wilhelmina did not reply. Opening the valise, she took out her nightgown, then proceeded to unbutton her dress. She poured some water from the jug into the basin and washed her face and arms.

Billy traced an unsteady path to the washstand and put his hands on her shoulders. 'Take your hands off me, Billy Foster,' she hissed.

'Whatsh wrong, Will? This our wedding night!' He smiled foolishly at her. He came towards her again, putting out his arms to go around her.

Putting her hands against his chest, she pushed with all her might. He stumbled back and collapsed onto the couch behind him. Wilhelmina grabbed a pillow and flung it at him. The eiderdown followed suit. 'If you think you're going to share my bed in that condition, you are very much mistaken. I am not a harlot. And I will not have a drunken sot near me, husband or no husband.' She pulled her nightgown on, blew out the light and climbed into bed.

There was silence after her outburst. Then she heard him shuffling and his shoes drop, one by one, and silence. Before her pulse had steadied, the silence was broken by his snores.

26

Billy's ambitions

Billy untied his boots and dropped them on the verandah. It was hot. Summer was really hanging on. The leaves of the wisteria and Virginia creeper were already colouring and the long grass in the paddocks held the seed heads high.

He'd had a good morning. The acres along the creek flats were being ploughed. He'd plant oats there and Mr Montgomery had agreed to his plan to establish lucerne.

He'd plant it with a cover crop of wheat. It should do well there. Lucerne roots went down deeply and would find the water. It would be great to have the oats for late winter. They'd harvest the wheat and the lucerne would be good feed in late summer. They could even make hay to have in reserve.

Mr Montgomery was a good boss — gave him a fairly free hand and would listen to suggestions he made and give them fair consideration.

But what it would be to have land of his own! He'd had a good deal of experience now. He'd be capable of making his own decisions — and running the place. What it would be to climb a hill and look down over a valley and think, 'This place is mine'; to look out over the cattle in the paddock around the hills and think, 'I own all these'.

Of course, he'd have to start off in a small way. But you could build up. Cattle multiplied very quickly over a few years. It would probably be a good idea to have a few irons in the fire and not just depend on cattle — to start with, anyway.

Perhaps dairying could be a good way to start. But for that he'd have to buy land close to town to get milk and cream to market while still fresh. Then again, you could set the milk and make butter from the cream and use the skimmed milk for pigs. Pigs were a quick return enterprise if you had plenty of milk as well as other feed. There were lots of possibilities, depending on where you had your land.

'That you, Billy?' Wilhelmina called, appearing in the kitchen doorway. 'Ready for a cup of tea?'

He followed her into the kitchen. She poured his tea and passed the apple tarts and fruit cake across the table. He munched the tart appreciatively. No doubt, Will was a good cook.

'Had a good morning?' she asked.

'Yes. All going well.' He took another tart. 'Hot out there, though.'

Wilhelmina poured another cup of tea.

'I've been thinking about land of our own again. We'll never get very rich till we get something of our own.'

She looked at him, considering. He was working hard and saving. They were getting ahead. 'Do you think we've got enough put by to set ourselves up yet? There's not just the price of the land, is there? There's the cost of a house and everything.'

'I know, but I'm thinking about this scheme of selecting. I'll have to get the information about it.'

'So long as we don't lose what we've got.'

'Well, it's only growing by what we save from my wages now. Can't get interest if you haven't got it invested somewhere. And I'm not trying any banks after what happened with the Bank of Australia. I like to know I've got what I've worked for.'

★ ★ ★

The idea filled Wilhelmina's mind all afternoon. Billy had gone to the northern paddocks and would not be back till late. She lay down for a rest on the lounge under the

259

grapevine after lunch. She really needed the rest. If her suspicions were true, she may be needing more rest through the day soon.

Billy arrived home just on dark. She had tea ready and went to meet him. He was just setting his saddle up on the verandah. What was that smell? She kissed him and pulled back. 'You smell like rum!' she said accusingly, her thoughts racing to the night of their wedding.

'Yes.' He laughed a trifle self-consciously. 'I went right up to the end of the place and I met Bert Rapson from over the other side. He came over the Tops looking for some strays.' He put his arm around her waist. 'He had a flask in his hip pocket and shared it before we left for home. Wasn't much,' he added, as though an afterthought.

'I wish you wouldn't have it at all. I hate it.' She turned towards the door. 'Come on, hurry and wash. Tea's ready.'

After tea, they sat on the verandah. The night air was cool and fresh and a little breeze came up from the dam. 'I went right up and looked over into the Williams valley this afternoon.'

Wilhelmina looked up. She had been thinking of telling him of her suspicions.

'It's just as good country as this. Water's just as good, too. Bert tells me there is land over there been opened up for selection. If we select, there'll be so much less outlay.' He paused. 'Think about how we can build the house when we do get land. There'll be a dairy and shed and blacksmith's shop and saddle room, too, of course. We could probably build a storeroom on the house. We could always add to the house later if we plan it out properly first.'

They talked on into the evening. As the moon rose, Billy yawned and stretched. 'Better turn in. I've got an early start in the morning.

★ ★ ★

They were in bed. Wilhelmina snuggled down, her head on Billy's shoulder. 'I wish you wouldn't drink rum, Billy,' she said softly. 'It will form a habit, a desire for it. And besides, it's an old man's drink for the winter, to warm him up. It's just good as medicine.'

'You worry too much,' he responded drowsily. 'I'm not drunk, am I?'

'No. But you'd better not be, either.'

He chuckled.

'You might have responsibilities soon.'

Billy's head jerked up. 'What do you mean?'

'You might have more to provide for than

261

just me,' she answered.

'Your mother's all right?' he asked instantly, concerned.

'Oh yes. Mama's very well. And happy. I mean someone very small — and very new.'

She heard him draw his breath in. 'You don't mean . . . ?'

'Yes,' she cried, laughing.

His arms came round her, crushing her to him.

★   ★   ★

He was gone at first light. She could hear the men calling to each other and the pound of the horses' hoofs.

They were bringing the cattle into the yards today, separating the bigger calves from their mothers. There were some that had missed being branded, so there would be plenty of activity and noise: calves bellowing, anxious mothers trying to get to their offspring.

She had dressed and was setting the table for breakfast, the pan of hominy simmering over the fire. Someone was coming. 'Are you there, Mrs Foster?'

She hurried to the verandah. One of the boys was at the fence. 'Billy says would you get some bandages and splints ready. Glad

Girl put her foot in a hole and we think her leg is broken.'

'Oh no. Poor Glad Girl.' Billy was very attached to his mare. She had given them some good foals as well as being a good stockhorse.

'They're over at the yards,' the boy called. 'Can you bring them as soon as possible?' He was off, back to the action.

She hurried to the cupboard where rolled bandages were always kept ready for emergencies. What about splints? There were some pieces of timber in the shed. She went quickly down and selected some that might be appropriate. With the bandages in a basket and the timber pieces under her arm, she made her way as quickly as she could to the yards.

Work had ceased. The boys were grouped around the horse. They had somehow got her onto the slide and managed to tie her down securely.

Billy was examining her leg while two of the boys held her head. His hands searched the leg, probing to line up the bone. It appeared to be a clean break. It should mend. She may not do stock work again, but she was a good mare and, if it did mend, they could still get a few more foals from her.

Wilhelmina watched as he splinted and

bandaged the leg. How strong and sure his hands were. She loved his hands, kind hands. He had a real empathy with animals.

★ ★ ★

The steers were in the yard ready. This mob was to be taken to Patterson for sale. Billy was going with the boys. He wanted to make enquiries about selecting land. If he could get a block over the mountain on the Williams, it would be handy and would be accessible to cattle sale centres.

Wilhelmina stood at the gate and waved as they moved off in clouds of dust. It was a routine sale. Prices were still up for good cattle.

When they arrived in Patterson, Billy collected the papers and attended to the office work. Then he headed for the court house. He pushed the door open and strode to the counter. A clerk answered his bell call. 'I'm looking for information about selecting land,' he said.

'Are you a landholder already, sir?'

'No. I work for Mr James Montgomery of 'Llanfylhn',' he replied.

'Did you come to the colony as a free settler or . . . ' the clerk coughed, 'some other way, sir?'

'I'm not an ex-convict, if that's what you're getting at,' Billy responded briskly. 'I've been here since I was seven years old.'

'I just asked, sir, because there is a scheme to assist ex-convicts to make a new start.'

He riffled through his papers. 'Now here, sir, for agricultural selectors of from forty to three hundred and twenty acres, the only conditions required are an advance payment of ten pounds and the signing of a declaration that you will reside on the land.' He closed the folder.

So if that was all there was to it, he would soon be a landholder. Billy's heart leapt. The clerk was speaking again. 'That means, of course sir, that the land is to be used for agricultural pursuits. That means felling trees, clearing the land and using it for crops. However, all is in a state of confusion. The scheme is not working out satisfactorily. It is highly probable this Act will be repealed. Other Acts are foreshadowed. It is impossible at this moment in time to give you accurate information that will be lasting, so there is no security of tenure.'

The clerk looked at him, his pince-nez glasses on the end of his nose, his eyebrows raised.

'What sort of state is that to be in?' Billy asked. 'I thought we wanted this country to be populated and developed.'

'I'm sorry, sir, but perhaps in a few months it will all be sorted out and a fair and just sharing of land be made for everyone.'

Billy walked out in disgust. What an inefficient, bungling way to handle things! A man ought to stand for parliament and show them how to run the country. No hope of that, though, with the little bit of education he'd had — and there'd be no chance against the big landholders that made things suit their own ends, anyway.

Will ought to have been a man. (Perish the thought!) She would have shown them a thing or two. But how could a person go ahead with plans to select, get out on his own, when things were in such chaos?

He made his way back to the sale yards, chafing with frustration. He collected his horse and was leading him out of the paddock when a familiar figure appeared in the last pen in the sale yards. He lifted his hand in greeting. Billy led his horse over to the rails of the yard. 'How are you, Erny? Did you make some good purchases?'

'Not bad. Good cows. I'd have been happier if I could have bought them cheaper. But they're good stock.'

They stood talking for a few minutes. 'Well, better go. It's a good ride home.'

'I thought you'd gone. Saw you while the sale was on, then you disappeared.'

Billy gave a disgusted grunt. 'I went down to the courthouse to get some information about selecting land,' he said.

'What? Looking to go out on your own?'

'Yes. But things are in such a mess. You know, they couldn't tell me anything definite at the moment. What was may not apply for long. Several new Acts foreshadowed. Makes me sick. This cursed government! They're a lot of bunglers.'

Erny agreed. 'Have you got any money to invest in land?' he asked. 'There's a good little place coming up for sale over our way on the Williams. It hasn't gone up yet. I was talking to Jack Taylor the other day and he wants to sell. It's on the river.' He nodded his head. 'Good little place — just a bit small for most people wanting land, but you could always add to it when you get underway. The price is right, too. Hasn't had a lot done to it yet — lot of clearing to do — and no cultivation yet. But a good basic place to start for someone not afraid of work.'

'I'll think about it.' They parted; and Billy turned his horse's head for home.

The homestead was his first stop when he reached 'Llanfylhn'. Mr Montgomery came to meet him. Billy handed him the papers. He went through them as they talked.

'You've done well, Billy,' he said approvingly. 'The cattle are doing well under your management.' He paused. 'I have a few changes in mind. As you know, I bought another place, smaller than 'Llanfylhn' certainly, but with a view towards my son taking it over when he is of age. I have asked your father if he would take it on as manager. I want to keep the two places quite separate.'

He looked searchingly at Billy. 'How would you feel about taking on the job of overseer of 'Llanfylhn'?'

27

A difficult decision

Overseer at 'Llanfylhn'! Why, he wasn't thirty yet! What an offer! Will would like the house, too; his old home where he had grown up; his parents' home. It was a nice house, much bigger and more imposing than their present cottage.

He'd really be 'Mr Foster'. But things like that didn't matter to him. They all knew him as 'Billy'; he liked it that way. He was one of them. He'd have to keep authority, though. That mightn't always be easy when he'd been 'one of them'.

What would Will say? Three servants went with the overseer's job, too — a gardener and two house staff. What would she say?

But what a choice to have to make!

This block that Erny had talked about sounded just what he was looking for. He'd said the price was right, too — because it wasn't developed, probably. He wondered what the price was. His mind had been full of that. How he'd tell Will about it when he got home. Now Mr Montgomery had taken the wind clean out of his sails.

He dug his heels into his horse and rode to the horse paddock.

Wilhelmina had seen him go to the big house. She stirred the fire, inspected the food cooking, then sat on the verandah waiting for him. As he opened the gate and walked up the path, she called, 'You've had a long day.'

There was a strange expression on his face. He smiled. But there was something.

'Mmm,' he said, enjoying the long drink she had placed beside his chair. 'Yes. Been a long day.'

'Did you get a good price for the cattle?'

'Yes. Not bad. Not bad at all.'

He put the glass down. 'I went to the courthouse. Oh, they are a lot of imbeciles, this government. Couldn't get any sense out of the fellow there. The Act they brought in not long ago is being superseded. There's nothing definite at the moment. Come back in a few months, I was told. Hopeless,' he said in disgust.

'Oh well. I suppose there's no hurry.'

'I don't think I want to be in it — this selecting, I mean. Even if they do get it sorted out as the fellow said, they could change the conditions, it seems to me. You'd never know where you were.'

He paused, then told her of Erny's

information. 'I saw Erny Taylor after the sale. He says there's a place over near him for sale. Says the price is good. It's not developed very far yet; that's why it's cheap. Only small, but with lots of potential, he seems to think.'

Wilhelmina's heart gave a jump.

'It might be worth looking at it. Just over the mountain here. On the river, too.'

'Do you know what the price is?'

'No. But I think I'll find out.'

Wilhelmina rose. 'You must be hungry. I'll serve up,' she said.

Billy patted the chair. 'Sit down another minute.'

She sat down again, looking at him in surprise. 'You like Mother's place, don't you? The house, I mean. The overseer's house.'

Wilhelmina bent a mystified look on him. 'Yes. It's a lovely house. Why ever do you ask me that?'

'Well, Mr Montgomery just asked me how I'd feel about taking on the job of overseer of 'Llanfylhn'.' There, he'd told her. He watched her reaction.

Wilhelmina's eyes flew wide open. Her mouth dropped as she looked at him stupidly. 'Overseer of 'Llanfylhn'?' she exclaimed. 'Why, that would mean you would be in charge of the whole place when they go away just like Mama is up at the house!'

He nodded. 'Yes. I know. I can't believe it.'

'You're sure you didn't misunderstand him?'

He looked at her with disgust. 'Do you think I would misunderstand a thing like that?' he asked, then added with a glint in his eye, 'And I haven't had a drink either. I'm not drunk.'

They talked as Billy carved and Wilhelmina served up the meal. They talked over dinner. They sat on the verandah and talked as the moon came up and rose high and the chucking of the ducks on the dam gave way to the croaking of frogs and the chirps of the crickets.

They went to bed and talked as the wind sighed through the willows along the creek, the curlews shrieked their eerie call and a mopoke called somewhere away off. The clock in the dining room had struck twelve before their eyes closed and they slept.

★ ★ ★

'Mama. Mama. Where are you?' Wilhelmina called next morning as she went through the house. She found Sophia in the fowl yard, searching for eggs.

'I'm racing that old goanna,' she called. 'I

272

got there first this time. I want to make some sponges.'

'Oh, are you having a party?' Wilhelmina asked.

'Just Mrs Montgomery and Mrs Lindsay for afternoon tea,' her mother replied.

They entered the kitchen, Sophia putting her eggs on the safe.

'Mama, just think!' Wilhelmina said excitedly. 'Mr Montgomery has offered Billy the position of overseer!'

'Overseer?' gasped Sophia. 'What about his father?' She sat down at the table. Whatever was going on?

'He's to go to the new place Mr Montgomery has bought — and he wants Billy to take over here!'

Sophia's surprise showed clearly in her expression. 'Billy is very young for such a position,' she said carefully. 'I know he is very able, but to have authority over so many men — and men he has known for some years. Some of them would have been here for years and seen him grow up. It will not be easy for him.' She paused. 'Or them.'

'That is true.' Wilhelmina looked at her mother. 'And let us be honest, Mama. Billy does not stand on ceremony. It will be hard for him to assert his authority, if he accepts.'

'It is not definite then?'

'No. Mr Montgomery asked him and he has to decide. But Mama, that is not all.' Sophia glanced up quickly. What more could there be? 'As you know, Billy has talked for a long time about wanting to have land of his own. He keeps saying, 'I want to stand on a hill and look out and be able to say, 'All this land I see is mine.''''

Sophia nodded.

'He saw a man yesterday at the cattle sale who told him of land for sale over the mountain, on the Williams River.'

'And he wants to buy it?' Sophia asked, smiling.

'He was all excited about it. Then, when he got back to 'Llanfylhn', Mr Montgomery was telling him how pleased he was with what he has achieved with the cattle and offered him the position of overseer when his father goes. Now he doesn't know what to do.'

Sophia's eyes dropped to the table between them. Then she lifted them to her daughter. 'What do you suppose Papa would say?'

Wilhelmina smiled. 'He would say, 'Pray about it. Ask God to guide you. And an answer will come.''

Sophia smiled, nodding. 'That is what you must do.'

'Yes,' Wilhelmina said softly. 'I have come to know that for myself, more and more

— not just on Papa's belief, but my own.'

Still she sat looking at her mother. 'And Mama,' she said softly.

Sophia raised questioning eyes. What else?

'Mama. I think I am going to have a baby.'

* * *

Billy could hear the piano before he got to the house. The music poured out, filling the air with the wonder of its sound. How did Will feel about her music? She didn't talk about it, but she must feel sometimes that she had been robbed of a great deal. Still, she seemed happy. No doubt she was releasing her feelings now with this question of whether or not to take the position Mr Montgomery offered.

There would certainly be more social life of the kind she was used to — the gatherings at 'Llanfylhn', the dinners, musical evenings; that was what she liked — providing the music was of a reasonable standard.

He didn't think there would be much of that kind of thing over the mountain if they bought this land he was thinking about.

He put his saddle down and walked along to the sitting room door. Wilhelmina had just finished. She smiled at him. 'Have you

275

come any further in your decision-making?' she asked.

Billy sat down. 'I'm afraid I go round in circles,' he said ruefully.

Wilhelmina told him of her conversation with her mother.

'We'll do that. We'll pray. But we've got to put our minds into it, too,' he said. 'The other thing I have to do is weigh up having land of my own, being out on my own, independent, standing on my own feet with the possibility of making good, perhaps ending up quite well off. Or with the possibility of losing what I have if I have bad luck with seasons or disease in cattle or crops. Against this, there is the security of a good job, well paid, good conditions, but working for someone else — his stock on his property, not mine. That's the other thing I have to think about.'

He must make his own decisions, Wilhelmina thought. She would suggest and help him consider, but he must make the decision.

'I have a few days to think about it,' Billy said, 'but I can't settle to anything till I do decide. They talked on over the next two days, round and round, covering all the aspects they could think of in both propositions.

At last, after breakfast one morning, Billy stood up purposefully. 'I think I have thought enough. I'm a man of action. I keep coming back to the same thing. As your father would say, I think that is the answer: it all depends on this place being as attractive as Erny says.'

He picked up his hat and looked around the kitchen where they had been sitting. 'This has been a good little home, hasn't it, Will? You've been comfortable here?'

She nodded. 'This has been home,' she said.

'Home is where we are together,' she said simply. 'I'll go with you, wherever you want to go, Billy, whatever your decision.'

He smiled broadly at her, an excited light in his eyes. 'I'll be back for lunch,' he said as he went out the door. She watched as he opened the gate and pulled it shut, then he turned and strode up the hill to the big house.

28

A warm welcome

They halted their horses when they were halfway down the mountain and a turn of the track gave a long view down the valley.

It was not so different from the 'Llanfylhn' side. The land fell away sharply here in the headwaters. The glint of the sun on the river that snaked its way down the valley gave promise of a plentiful supply of water. It was a wide river further down the valley — wide for these parts, anyway.

'That's Jack Taylor's place, down there where the timber comes right down to the river. Erny was saying most of the settlers have cleared the river flats and got cultivation going, but Taylor hadn't got that far.'

He was thoughtful a moment. 'I can see that now. A bit of clearing and there'd be some good crop land there, just as good as any of the other blocks.'

Billy obviously was impressed with what he saw. It certainly did look promising. They moved off again and reached the Taylor place at mid morning.

The house stood on a knoll well back from the river. To Wilhelmina's surprise, it was somewhat like her mother's house — a good slab construction with a detached kitchen.

The Taylors took them over the place. It was as Erny had said — a good small place, undeveloped, but with lots of potential. Now what was the price? That was the deciding factor. Billy was keen about it, but the price would decide the matter.

Jack Taylor named his price.

'Is that with the existing implements? The plough, slide, the dray? That sort of thing?'

Jack agreed this was so.

'Then if I have the option on the place, I'll get back in touch with you in a couple of days.'

The sun was dropping low in the sky when they set out for home. 'It's just too good to miss, Will,' Billy said as they climbed the gap. 'I can see all sorts of things I can do on that place.'

'The house is quite comfortable, too, and it could be added to quite easily when we need to.' Wilhelmina had been planning a garden and could see the difference some attention and imagination could make. It could really be quite a dignified home.

'The view is just so beautiful from up there on the hill.' She looked at him with a twinkle.

'And can you sit on that verandah and look out over your kingdom, do you think?'

It was a late, but happy homecoming. Now Mr Montgomery must be told.

★ ★ ★

'Whatever shall I do without you? Oh my dear Wilhelmina, I am bereft! I am so sorry you are leaving us. Oh, I can understand. Billy is an ambitious young man. He is lured by the fascination of owning his own land. But oh, what shall we do?' Mrs Montgomery looked beseechingly at Wilhelmina.

'He was very gratified and flattered by Mr Montgomery's offer of the position as overseer,' Wilhelmina said apologetically. 'It was a hard decision to make. He is so attracted by the prospect of having his own place. But I also think it may have been hard for him to assert authority here where he has grown up.'

'I can see that. In fact, James did wonder about that. But he has done so well with the cattle management, he decided to offer it to him. But however shall I entertain my guests now with you gone? Your reputation has gone far and wide. I am sure at least half my guests accept my invitations in the hope they will have the opportunity to enjoy your music.'

And so it continued.

Billy again rode over the mountain pass and the transaction was agreed upon, the formalities eventually completed in the Lands Office in Dungog.

★ ★ ★

The air was rent with the crack of the whip and the shouts of the bullocky as he urged his team. The bullocks strained. Great beasts of burden, what strength they had. Straining together, the harness creaked under the pressure.

It was steep, too steep for a bullock waggon; the load too great; yet they strained. It would be risky going down the other side. They'd have to weight the waggon with a log to break the descent.

They chocked the wheels, rested the bullocks, then tried again. At last, inch by inch, they reached the top and rested. Here the valley of their new home spread out before them. There were settlers, huts and houses and one or two tents dotted along the river. Eventually, the descent was safely negotiated and the little cavalcade was on easier ground.

They made good time and before dark the bullocks were unyoked and freed. The few pieces of furniture and the trunks were unloaded. They were home. It was a beginning.

★ ★ ★

The leaves of the apple tree beside the house filtered the moonlight shining in the window. The changing silhouettes of the branches and leaves was like moving lace. It was a soft glow of moonlight. The moon was not yet at the full.

Wilhelmina listened to the night sounds. They were different from the ones at home — at 'Llanfylhn', she corrected herself. This was home now.

There were still the birds settling, but no ducks on the dam — there was no dam. A frog croaked close by. Was it in the well?

She could hear the wind in the trees. But it was not the hush of the wind in the willows she was used to. They were close to the creek there. This was the movement of wind high in the leaves of the tall trees; a different symphony. Here the house stood above the willows, looking out over the river flats, the river and down the valley, almost as the palace in Heidelberg looked out over the town.

How were things there now? Had the

uprising Papa feared come about? What of the grand duke and duchess? How different life was now, how very different. She sighed and turned over, resolutely closing her eyes.

★ ★ ★

Billy was up first. He was dressed by the time Wilhelmina woke. 'I'm going down now to go over that flat to see just where I'm going to fence. There are trees there that I can use for posts and rails for the fence. I don't want the cattle getting in when I've got it ploughed up and a crop in.'

'You'll have a lot of work with the clearing first, won't you?' Wilhelmina asked. 'Where are you going to start?'

'I'll go over the place this next few days and make out my plan. One of the first things I want to do is dig over the vegetable garden. There's a bit of a garden out the back. We'll do more later, but we'll make a start with what's there. Then I want to plough that little bit of cultivation that Jack had started. We need to get some wheat and barley in now for our own use. I hope by the time the Spring comes I'll have more cultivation ready for corn, so we can have our own hominy.'

Wilhelmina's mind was starting to whirl. What a lot there was to think about. She had learned a lot at 'Llanfylhn', but it was a large, established place. Here they were not actually starting from scratch, but not far from it.

The part that the Taylors had established most was the house and the well. How wonderful to have such a good supply of water! And the house was quite roomy, though, as their family grew, they would add to it. That was in the future, though. For now, she must make a comfortable home with what she had.

★ ★ ★

Their pieces of furniture were few. There was their bed, which Billy's family had given them, two sitting room chairs that were gifts from Mr and Mrs Montgomery, a small table. And her piano. She ran her hands lovingly over it. It looked rather incongruous with a wooden box placed in front of it for a seat.

She had a few pieces of material for curtains, but these things would come later. For the present, their cupboards would be boxes piled on top of each other and a rod and curtain across the corner of a room would make a wardrobe.

Over a hearty breakfast, they talked excitedly of their plans, so excitedly that they didn't hear the rider pull up at the gate. The first they heard was footsteps on the verandah.

'Anyone home?' a voice called.

Wilhelmina hurried to the door. A tall, broad-shouldered man stood there. 'Bert Goodwin, Mrs Foster,' he said smiling, holding out his hand. 'Just called to welcome you. We live up the track a bit.'

He held out a parcel he was carrying. 'We thought you might find a shoulder of bacon handy. Always a lot to do when you're trying to settle in. My wife Beth will be over to see you later on, but she sent me over with this now.'

How wonderful to be welcomed with such a thoughtful gesture! 'Thankyou very much, Mr Goodwin,' Wilhelmina cried.

Billy had followed her and now added his thanks. 'Do sit down with us and have a cup of tea. Have you had breakfast?'

He accepted the tea and the two men were soon deep in conversation on farming. 'We work in together here along the river,' Bert told them. 'A sort of barter system, I suppose. I helped Ab Nolan put up his fences and he helped me ringbark trees up at the back of my block. We can all get on a lot better and a lot quicker that way. We'll do the same with you if you want it that way.'

Billy agreed wholeheartedly with the

suggestion. He had been thinking he would have to pay workers if he wanted to get the clearing and ploughing done before winter. Now this would make a great difference.

'We're a mixed lot along here,' Bert said. 'Got some English free settlers, a couple of Scotsmen and a German. He came out to fill the job of a shepherd. There were quite a few of them came — shepherds, that is. He got a bit of cash together. Now he's got his own little place and doing well. He still has a bit of trouble with the language, but he makes himself understood.'

He looked at Wilhelmina. 'You are German, too, aren't you Mrs Foster? I thought your accent was German. You don't have trouble with the language, though. Then we have a couple of ex-convicts. They've done their time. Now they are making good. They weren't really criminals, you know — trifling things really. Quite respectable now.'

Bert was the first of their many callers that first day. Each one came bearing gifts to help with the settling in and to make their acquaintance — a bottle of jam, a dozen eggs, a bottle of milk, a pat of butter, a loaf of bread, a pie or a cake. What a wonderful welcome!

They had learned the names of all their neighbours, the number of children, what each of their blocks was like and where they had their community gatherings.

The large shed behind Bert's house was where they gathered for dances and parties. Coppers were set up over fires outside for tea and the cakes supplied by the wives provided a feast for supper. They danced their toes off to the music of Tot Kenny and his fiddle.

As she snuggled down in bed at the end of the day, Wilhelmina's heart was full. Thank God for this happy day, for the wonderful people who had come and welcomed them so generously.

It may not be the life she had known at 'Llanfylhn'; it certainly was not what she had known in Heidelberg or Wiesbaden; but it was going to be very interesting.

29

The business side

Little by little, the clearing was done. Billy had ploughed the small cultivation area and planted his wheat and barley. There was a nice drop of rain soon after and the green shoots soon appeared. Wilhelmina had watched the green tinge thicken as the days passed. It was fascinating to see it come like this.

Now the clearing was going on in earnest. Most of the big trees had been felled, then sawn into lengths, the two men, one on each end of the long cross cut saw pulling and pushing alternately, rhythmically. Then there was the laborious digging out of the stumps when the sawn logs were pulled aside and the saplings and the scrub dug and pulled.

Billy decided there was enough timber for his fence. The logs were split with the wedge and sledge-hammer. Each night he was dirty, tired and happy, the glow of his achievements shining in his eyes.

Wilhelmina watched all the activity from her vantage point on the verandah.

As the warm sun of autumn gave way to winter, the frosts began. But then there were the beautiful clear sunny days. She moved with the sun, following it around the verandah, sitting in the cane chair, sewing, preparing for the baby. If it was a boy they would call him Edward after Billy's father. But a girl? They hadn't decided yet.

By spring, the clearing was finished and the long post and rail fence erected. Billy now went over the paddock ploughing, breaking up the soil, working it well in preparation for planting his crops.

He had planted oats in the first part already. It was getting a bit late, but it might be worthwhile. They were already reaping the benefit of the early start on the vegetable garden.

He planned next autumn to sow lucerne with the cover crop of wheat as he had done at 'Llanfylhn'. Soon they would have their first drop of calves from the cows he had bought to begin his herd. It had been a good season this first few months, but you had to prepare in case of drought. A shed full of hay was a great stand-by.

★ ★ ★

The baby was born in the first week in October. He made his entrance with a lusty cry of protest. 'He's got his father's voice, all right,' cried Beth Goodwin. 'Oh, he's beautiful, Wilhelmina! Just look at him.' She held the baby aloft.

Wilhelmina lifted a weary but excited head. Oh, he was like Billy! He'd be so proud, so excited.

Sophia had come over two days ago to be with her. Beth Goodwin and Josie Nolan — Josie had a tribe of ten children — had come when Billy came with the call, 'the time has come'.

Sophia took her grandson in her arms. What would Johann have thought of this little fellow? If only he could see him. She wrapped him in the cloth and laid him gently beside his mother.

'I'll call Billy,' Josie said. 'He's trying to occupy himself down at the shed.'

The news soon went down the valley. All afternoon, men were calling down to Billy at the farm, slapping him on the back, congratulating him. 'Have to wet his head tonight,' they said. 'Come up to Bert's place after tea and we'll celebrate.

A son, eh? Isn't it marvellous?' And they went away, shaking their heads and smiling.

★ ★ ★

Wilhelmina lay in bed. The baby was asleep. He had sucked well and seemed a strong little fellow. Billy had glowed with pride as he held him. He had gone up to Bert's for a while now. The boys wanted to drink a toast to the boy and wish him well. 'Congratulate me, too, of course. Nice of them to come down and see me and want to wet the head of this boy of ours, isn't it?' He had kissed her and gone out whistling.

Now she was listening for his return. It was getting late. Surely he'd soon be home. At last she dozed.

★ ★ ★

She came up groggily from the depths of sleep. What was that noise? Someone singing! Suddenly, she was wide awake. There was no mistaking that voice. Billy was singing, at the top of his voice. He was well up the road yet, but his voice carried clearly.

She got out of bed and closed the door, turning the key, then got back into bed and pulled the covers up. She must sleep. The baby would be awake to be fed soon. She closed her eyes.

★ ★ ★

The seasons followed in quick succession. The cultivation paddock was ploughed and sown. The crops grew tall and plentiful. Hay was made and stored in sheds, or stacked. Other crops were harvested and the grain sold, their own needs for hominy and flour milled in Dungog and stacked in the storeroom. The herds increased. They were established. And the babies came in quick succession.

★   ★   ★

Billy had for some time talked of the cedar in the forest. 'Great trees like you've never seen, Will,' he'd say. It's beautiful timber. It would be wonderful for furniture.' Now he was talking about it again. 'Joe Thompson's got a bullock team. He's cutting a track up into the forest. He's suggested if I have a team, too, we could work together and cut cedar and sell it in Maitland. That's where the sale for it is. He says they can't get enough. People are crying out for it for furniture and doors and lining in houses. There's some big houses round Maitland now, he says.'

'But do you know anything about getting it or how it's sold?'

Billy looked directly at her. 'I've got some commonsense,' he said. 'I can fell trees. We'd work together on that, anyway. Joe's done it for years.' He hesitated. 'The part that bothers me is the business side of it. It's paid for by superfeet or something. I'm not clear about that.

'There's good money in it, that's the thing. But the business side . . . ' He shook his head. 'You know what I'd be like reading contracts and all that sort of thing.'

'You say there's really good money in it?'

'Yes. Joe was telling me. He's thinking of getting another team of bullocks and training one of his boys to handle it. It's good business.'

'What about bullocks? What would they cost? And where could you get them?'

'Oh, I'd soon fix that up. There's plenty available round about. That part would be all right.'

'In that case, I could do the business side of it.'

Billy looked up. 'You could do it?' he said incredulously. 'You could do it? A woman? With a team of bullocks and waggon loaded with cedar?'

'Yes. Why not?' Wilhelmina stated definitely. 'I wouldn't travel with you, of course. I'd let you head off for a couple of days and then follow on horseback. I could stay somewhere on the way, then ride into Maitland and do the business with the buyers. I could do any shopping and place our order at Cappers, then come home again. You could pick up the order and come home with the waggon.'

'But a woman doing business! I'd look a bit of a fool,' he said doubtfully.

'I can't see why,' Wilhelmina replied. 'You'll have plenty to do delivering and unloading and checking your load without having to go into the office. The timber will all have to be measured, I suppose. It seems to me it's a good idea for me to take over that side of it whether you could do the business or not.'

'Blessed if I know, Will,' he said, rubbing the back of his neck. 'You make it sound all right.'

'Of course it's all right.' She put the tarts she had been making into the oven. 'You make enquiries about the bullocks and get all the details of how it's sold. All that I would need to know. Perhaps Joe and Minnie would come down one day for dinner and we could talk about it together.'

There was a light in Billy's eye now. This would be something that could build up. He could get experience with this first team, then buy more teams, like Joe, when his boys were old enough to handle them.

They were bright lads, keen on the farm and liked to try their hand at new things. Eddy was twelve now and Oliver eleven.

Another year or two and they could both manage teams providing they travelled together with him. To have his boys working with him — what a thrill that would be! They could do it. They handled the horses well and already helped with the cultivation.

Another year or two would make a big difference. They were growing fast — tall, well-built boys they were for their age. Will would probably say they continue with their schooling, but they could fit that in between. A week off every so often wouldn't matter.

His mind turned to the new governess Wilhelmina had engaged. No doubt she was a very educated lady. Will enjoyed talking to her. She was a bit stand-offish, though. 'Yes, Mr Foster. No, Mr Foster. The children are doing nicely. But the boys must concentrate. They must put their minds on their work in the school room.'

They'd rather be out with him, ploughing or sowing or around the cattle, or shoeing a horse. He chuckled. It was good to have your own boy around you. There they were, bringing the calf up to the cow bale to shut it away for the night. They knew the jobs to be done. They were reliable.

He looked at the sky. Might just have time to ride up and see Joe before dark. Nothing like striking while the iron was hot and getting all the details.

What would Joe think about Will doing the business, though? Oh well, she made it all sound sensible. They'd find out the details. His bridle over his arm, he went to the horse paddock and caught his mare. Saddling her, he waved to the boys and cantered up the road.

30

A shrewd businesswoman

The bullocks heaved stolidly into place. Wilhelmina watched from the verandah. Billy was busily yoking them together in order. He was very proud of this team. Sixteen huge, sturdy Devons; they should prove a good investment. He had returned from the bush with his first load of cedar lashed to the waggon.

Wilhelmina could see the colour of the sawn timber. What lovely furniture it would make. The beautiful red colour would be deepened and enhanced with polish. Billy came over the verandah. 'I'll just have a bite to eat, then I'll head off,' he said. Then, looking at the sky he added, 'Looks as though it's going to be a good day.'

'You've got everything? The food bag? And the water cask? Did you fill a couple of water bags for drinks along the way?'

He followed her in. 'You're sure you will be all right?' he asked.

'Quite sure. I'll give you three days start. Then I'll ride over the mountain and stay with Mama the night. Then I'll leave early and go straight to Maitland. Mr Fry I have to see, isn't it?'

He nodded.

'I'll do the business and I'll see if he will give us a contract for a regular order.'

'You sure you can manage all that on your own?' Billy was still anxious.

'Of course I am. It's new for me. But I'll soon learn. I'm looking forward to it.'

Reassured, he rose and, clapping his hat on his head, kissed her. 'I'll be off then. Joe was starting out about now. Be careful. I'll be looking for you to catch us up when you're on your way to Maitland.'

She waved him goodbye as he set off amidst a cracking of the whip and shouts to start the bullocks moving. Slowly, the wheels began to turn. Their first load of cedar was on its way.

Now where were those girls? They had been working in the kitchen block, Polly scrubbing the verandah and Sarah cleaning the stove.

She looked into the schoolroom. Miss Richardson was hearing the children read. Edward was not as fluent as she would like. He had to be frequently prompted. She listened, just out of sight. Oliver, too, made hard work of it.

How was it that a child of hers could be like this? She had always loved to read and revelled in reading aloud to the children. Billy was slow at reading. But then he had so little instruction. No. It was just a matter of application, she was sure of that. They were all intelligent children. They all had the ability.

Eliza and Etty were somewhat better. They were younger, of course. But they, too, left much to be desired. She may be bringing up a family in an unsophisticated country, but there were certain things she expected of her children. To be literate was high on her list.

She went on to find the two girls she had employed as maids. They were quite satisfactory on the cleaning and washing, but she preferred to do the cooking herself. They would have to do it while she was away on the trip to Maitland. She'd only be away two nights. Surely they could manage that.

They would just have to, she decided. And Miss Richardson would look after the children. She was quite confident in that quarter.

What would she need to take with her? A clean blouse and underwear, stockings, handkerchief. She spread the things on her bed.

What was that noise? Glancing up, she

could see through the window. A horse-drawn dray was turning in their gate. Whoever could be coming? She didn't recognise the dray or the driver perched up on the front. The dray was covered with a tarpaulin. It pulled up at the garden gate. Wilhelmina hurried to the verandah. 'Good morning,' she called.

The driver climbed down and tied his horses to the rail. 'I am Karl Grosser, Mrs Foster, maker of fine furniture. I call to ask if you are interested to look at the furniture I make. I do not have shop. I have sample pieces on waggon. You maybe have cedar wood here? I make from your timber.'

A German furniture maker! She would recognise that anywhere. 'Oh, I would very much like to see your samples, Mr Grosser. My husband is on his way to Maitland with some cedar. It is beautiful for furniture.'

The man smiled and undid the tarpaulin. He turned it back carefully. Then, removing the packing, he lifted down chairs and a small table. Now she could see a small chiffonier. Oh, they were beautiful. She clasped her hands in delight. They could cut their own timber and have this man make it up.

By now the children, Miss Richardson, Polly and Sarah were all gathered around the waggon. Karl Grosser explained that he was making a trip through the region now to get possible orders and would return later to start work.

If they had no cedar ready, it would have to be cut and left to season before it could be made up. 'We do not want it to warp and doors not close properly,' he said, then added with a degree of pride, 'That does not happen with my furniture.' He left them to go on down the valley.

Wilhelmina returned to her preparations. She packed the few clothing pieces into a saddle bag, checked she had Billy's lists of timber measurements, the lists with the food order and the extra things she wanted to buy: a few yards of calico; some embroidery cotton; oh, and needles; a new pair of shoes for Eliza — Etty could have the ones Eliza had grown out of. (That was the trouble being the younger one: the eldest always got the new things!) She packed a flask of water, a few dates and some nuts.

In the morning, she would make a sandwich — that would do till she got to 'Llanfylhn'. Mama would be glad to see her.

A fine, fresh morning greeted her when she woke. She dressed eagerly, the thrill of anticipation urging her along. The sun was just peeping over the mountain as she waved goodbye.

They were over the mountain and down on

the Allyn side, heading towards Maitland. It was easier going now. The ascent had been slow, but with the bigger team of sixteen bullocks, they had done it. It meant resting them, of course. But slowly does it, they had reached the top without mishap.

Then Billy had taken the precaution of cutting a small tree and tying it to the back axle of the waggon to steady the descent. There had been no trouble.

Billy looked back. He could see Joe coming. Now they were out of the thicker timber, down among the farms along the Allyn. They'd camp here tonight.

'Thirsty work this,' Joe called as he unyoked his team. 'I've got a thirst to quench when we get to Maitland, but have to deliver this load first.' They made camp and boiled their billy over a fire. It was a good place, with good farming land around here. 'If we make the river the other side of Tocal by Thursday night, it will be a short run in next morning to the timber yards,' Joe said. 'We'll get rid of the load and then head for the old Swan pub for a drink to wash down all this dust.'

Billy nodded. That would be good. But what about Wilhelmina? How was she going? And would she catch them up tomorrow?

★ ★ ★

At Bolwarra, Wilhelmina caught up with the teams. They checked the loads and set off for the timber yard. They had worked out their measurements, calculated the cost. Now it only remained for this to be checked at the yard and she would see Mr Fry. Would she be able to get him to sign a contract for a regular supply?

They reached the yard early in the day. The logs were unloaded and checked by Mr Fry's men. It was agreed their calculations were correct. Wilhelmina knocked on the office door. A tall, thin man opened it.

'Mr Fry?' she asked.

The man nodded.

'I am Wilhelmina Foster,' she said. 'We have just delivered the load of cedar as we arranged with you.'

'Come in, Mrs Foster, come in.' He stood aside to allow her to enter. It was a small office. There was a desk cluttered with papers, a cabinet, a wall of shelves littered with pamphlets and papers and a board covered with papers held together with clips hung on nails.

He took the paper she handed him. 'Ah. I see our men have signed it as correct,' he said, running his eye down the page.

'Of course, Mr Fry. We are accurate in our business. It is well checked before we come this far. You will find no mistakes.'

He looked up. An unusual lady, this Mrs Foster. 'I am glad to hear it, Mrs Foster. That, however, is not always the case in dealing with our suppliers.'

'Then some people must run very ineffi-cient businesses.' Wilhelmina smiled at him. She was a very confident lady, very well spoken — very attractive, too — lovely eyes. They were sparkling at him now. What was her husband doing? Why was she doing the business?

'Er. Your husband, Mrs Foster. Is he well?' he asked diffidently.

'Quite well, thankyou.' Wilhelmina smiled. 'You are not used to doing business with a woman?' she asked, raising her brows.

'Well no, ma'am. It is not usual.'

'I realise that. However, my husband is fully occupied with the unloading and care of the bullocks. I am quite capable of looking after this part of our enterprise, I assure you,' she stated, looking him straight in the eye.

He smiled. 'I believe you are, Mrs Foster, I believe you are.' He counted out the payment for the load. 'All present and correct, Mrs Foster. I do not make mistakes either.' His eyes laughed at her.

Gathering up the payment and putting it in her purse, Wilhelmina said, 'Mr Fry. I had a visit from a travelling furniture maker. He tells me that there is great demand for cedar for furniture and lining of houses and ships — and tobacco boxes. In fact, he said there is a demand that is not being met. You cannot supply the demand.'

He nodded.

'We are just beginning in this industry. We mean to expand. We have a plentiful resource of cedar. I should think you would be glad to have a reputable, efficient, reliable supplier. We, in our turn, to expedite our expansion, would welcome a secure buyer for our cedar. If you were willing to sign a contract to receive a certain amount of cedar every six to eight weeks (we must have a little leeway in the event of bad weather), we would guarantee to supply that timber on time and in good condition at the right price. Would it not be profitable to us both?' She had been looking at him, trying to gauge his reaction.

He rubbed his chin. 'You say every six to eight weeks?' he mused. 'You make it sound reasonable and attractive.' He considered, then put his hands down on the desk. 'I will have our solicitor draw up a contract agreeable to us both. You, of course, will approve of it before we sign.'

So he was agreeable to a contract! What an achievement! Billy would be pleased. This would be regular income. 'Cash on delivery as today, Mr Fry,' she said.

'You are a hard businesswoman, Mrs Foster. Must it be cash if it is a regular transaction?'

'Cash, Mr Fry. We do not trust the banks.'

'Very well, then, cash it is. I will get that contract to you as soon a possible.'

He rose and moved towards the door. 'Thankyou, Mr Fry,' Wilhelmina said with a little smile. 'It is a pleasure to do business with you.'

'My pleasure also, Mrs Foster,' he rejoined, bowing as she passed him and stepped down from the office. Now to find Billy and tell him all her news.

31

Cause for disquiet

The return trip was accomplished more quickly. She had left the food order and farm needs for Billy to pick up and made the other purchases on her list. Now she was anxious to get home and assure herself the children were well.

Billy had been very elated by her news. Here was a regular income, not dependent upon the seasons as the crops were. And not subject to the sort of price fluctuations in the cattle market. He'd still have both of those in his farm, of course, but would not be so dependent upon that income.

And it would be cash. She smiled to herself. She was glad she had thought of that just then.

Her welcome home was enthusiastic. Eliza was thrilled with her shoes — and they fitted. There was some little thing for each of the children.

They all went to bed happy. When was Mother going to Maitland again? the children wondered.

It was Sunday again. They might reasonably expect Billy home today, but this morning there was church.

The minister from Dungog made regular monthly visits now and everyone in the valley came. There was no other church service and no other clergyman came. They took it in turns to have the service in their homes. Everyone brought food and they made a social occasion of it as well, sometimes even playing a game of cricket afterwards.

Wilhelmina gathered the children together. She brushed and plaited the girls' hair. Yes, they all looked very nice. Had the boys polished their boots? At last, they all passed inspection and they, with Polly, Sarah and Miss Richardson, climbed into the phaeton.

'I can drive, Mother. Really I can,' Edward pleaded. Was he capable? Strong enough? He was only twelve. Perhaps it would be all right if she sat beside him. They climbed in and set off.

The service today was to be at Josie Nolan's home. There would be a crowd! Josie and Ab and their ten children made a good start. Josie was waiting on the verandah. 'Wilhelmina,' she called. 'Come and look what we've bought.' She led her to the sitting room, which had been arranged for the service. The doors opened onto the verandah where the overflow was to be accommodated.

'There!' Josie said, her face beaming. 'What do you think of that?' Across the corner of the room in pride of place was an organ. 'It didn't seem right having church with no organ to sing to,' Josie swept on, 'so we bought it. When we build a church, which Mr Ruskin is talking about, we'll give it to the church. I knew you'd be able to play it. Come and have a look at it.'

Josie wanted her to play an organ! She'd never played an organ in her life! 'But I'm a pianist, not an organist, Josie,' she protested.

'It looks just like a piano. The keys are the same, aren't they?' Josie proudly led her across the room and drew back the seat. 'Give us a tune, there's a dear,' she urged.

Wilhelmina pressed a key. No sound. Of course! She hadn't pulled out any stops. What were the stops? Flute? Dulciana? Diapason? That would do for a start.

'Don't forget to pump with your feet,' Josie reminded. 'The man told us how. He showed us, actually. It sounded lovely when he played.' She was looking at Wilhelmina with such big, excited eyes, confident in her ability to produce the required tune. There was no getting out of it. She seated herself firmly and began to pump. It was energetic work. She pressed the keys and the sound burst forth.

'Oh, those little levers here beside your knees are the things that make it go louder. Did you have your knees against them?' Josie hastened to say.

She realised she had been bracing her knees against the 'little levers'. She released her pressure and tried again. This time a reasonable note sounded.

'There you are. I knew you could do it,' cried Josie happily. 'Here's the hymn book. You just get a little more acquainted with it while I go and welcome the other folk coming.'

So! It looked like she was the organist for church services in the Nolan place, at any rate. And when a church was built . . . ?

Like a piano, Josie said. It was *so* unlike a piano! Would she ever get through this service with a reasonable amount of her reputation as a musician intact?

The service began. The responses were enthusiastic and prayers devout.

Then the first hymn was announced. Wilhelmina pumped the bellows full of air, then, making sure she wasn't pressing the 'little levers', put her hands on the keys. The sound swelled forth and the congregation sang. She was realising the touch had to be quite different; not like a clockwork sledge-hammer, she thought to herself, smiling inwardly — more like something sliding over the keys: one going down as one came up.

Suddenly, the sound wheezed and faded. Panicking, she took her hands off the keys. Silence. The congregation continued singing. Then she realised that in her concentration on getting the right touch, she had quite forgotten to keep pumping.

She pumped madly for a minute, then began the next verse. The chord boomed out, ricocheting from the walls of the room. She had forgotten those wretched 'little levers' and now realised she was pushing them to their full extent.

Mercifully the hymn finished, accompanied by the ill-concealed amusement of the less controlled. Flushed with mortification, her heart hammering and close to tears, Wilhelmina searched for her handkerchief.

'Don't worry, Wilhelmina, don't worry. You'll get the hang of it.' Josie wasn't in the least perturbed. 'It was lovely to have it to accompany the singing. It sounded so much better.'

What could she do? She would just have to come up here and practice, to remember all these things, to get hands and feet going at the same time, and that the feet are not always in time with the music. Oh, what was she letting herself in for?

They drove home. The children and the girls and even Miss Richardson had had a most enjoyable time.

They were aware of her quietness. 'Never mind, Mother. I know you were upset about the organ. But no-one else could play at all, so you still did better than anyone else could have done,' Eddy said, trying to comfort her.

What a dear he was — and getting so grown up. She was too sensitive where her music was concerned, even if it was an organ she was trying to play. 'I suppose it was funny,' she admitted, trying to divorce herself from her embarrassment.

'I thought something was wrong with you when it stopped. And Mr Ruskin kept singing loud, so everyone would keep going!' laughed Oliver. 'It was funny, Mother!'

'Yes, and then it went *Boom!* on the next verse and we all jumped. We couldn't hear ourselves above that!'

They were all rolling about convulsed with laughter as they trotted along. Miss Richardson looked apologetically at her and, losing her composure also gasped, 'It really was very funny, Mrs Foster.' Finally, forgetting her own embarrassment, Wilhelmina saw the funny side and joined the hilarity.

★ ★ ★

It was nearly dark when the boys ran in to tell her they could see a waggon coming down the hill away up the road. Billy would be just in time for tea. She set the table and stirred the thick soup.

As she was cutting the bread, she heard it: A full strong voice, singing at full volume to the accompaniment of the turn of the wheels and the plod of the bullocks' hoofs. Billy came in the back door. The boys had helped him unyoke the bullocks. He'd unload the waggon in the morning. Another night on the waggon wouldn't matter.

He opened the kitchen door and peered in. There was Will bending over at the stove. What a lovely round rear she had! He took two quick steps forward and, taking between his finger and thumb a good soft bite of that part of the anatomy so displayed for him, gave it a good hard pinch.

There was a scream. A body backed from the stove. Even in his drunken state, he realised it was not Wilhelmina, but Polly, the plump little maid. She was incensed.

Wilhelmina came running into the kitchen. 'He pinched me!' she screamed. 'He put his hand on me and pinched me! I'm not a girl like that, Mrs Foster, I'm not a girl like that. I work for you, but I won't take that.' Her face flushed. She was beside herself.

'Polly, for goodness sake. Whatever is wrong? Who pinched you?'

'Mr Foster! He crept up behind me when I was bent over the stove and he pinched me!'

Now Wilhelmina's face was flushed. Billy pinched Polly? Surely not. 'Oh Polly, I'm sure you are mistaken. Mr Foster wouldn't pinch you. He's only just home.'

'He did. He did. I screamed and turned round and saw him. He went right out that door very quickly. I'm not a girl to take that, Mrs Foster. I'm leaving. I'm goin' now.' She untied her apron and threw it on the chair.

'Polly. Polly. There's some mistake,' Wilhelmina called ineffectually. The girl was gone to her room to pack her things.

Billy was mortified. 'It was the rum, I tell you, Will. I thought it was you at the stove.'

'Me at the stove? Do you mean to tell me I'm as broad in the beam as Polly? Thankyou very much. And why on earth did you start drinking rum anyway? You know it always leads to trouble.'

She was really upset. It was just as well she had done the business and collected the payment. Otherwise they would probably have had nothing out of that load.

He was very crestfallen. It was all very well

314

to blame his mistake on rum, but if he couldn't resist it, where would it lead them? Joe had wanted to celebrate a successful first trip after they had picked up the orders. They'd gone to the pub and met some other great fellows. And so it had gone. They'd each bought a bottle to 'wash the dust down' on the way home.

He had a headache next morning, but he was unloading the waggon and carrying things to the store when a sulky turned in their gate.

It pulled up and Ab Nolan jumped down. 'I need your help, Billy,' he called. 'Young Roy has broken his arm, I think. You can fix horses' breaks, so I reckon you'd be the best one to set this for us.' He lifted the child gently down and carried him into the house.

Wilhelmina was hovering over the poor little fellow.

Billy washed his hands and came to examine it. 'I've never set a person's bone before, Ab,' he said doubtfully.

'Well, have a go. It's a long way to Dungog and the poor little chap's in pain. Doctor might be away out the other side if I did take him in.' It was true and, in the meantime, the arm would be swelling.

Billy felt it gently, the little boy crying out in pain. His father held him firmly. 'Seems to be a clean break,' he said. 'Suppose I can try. Do it the same as an animal.' He splinted and bound it and gave the child a calming draught. Before long, he slept in his father's arms.

It was not long after the bone-setting incident that Billy heard of a block of land for sale further down the valley. It was a good grazing block. A settler, starting out with too little capital and too little experience, had decided to sell before he lost too much on it.

Billy was interested. He and Wilhelmina had talked about it. With the money they would now make from the cedar, he would buy another bullock team and maybe they could expand this way, too. He was excited about the prospect.

★   ★   ★

Wilhelmina had found another maid to take Polly's place. She was all right, but was she a bit forward? Her eyes were a bit too flirty if there was a man around. As Wilhelmina came across the verandah to the kitchen, Billy was laughing. The girl looked guilty when she saw Wilhelmina. And did Billy look embarrassed? What had they been saying when she walked in?

She went back to call the children from the

316

schoolroom. She wasn't a jealous or suspicious wife. But there had been something. And what had really happened the night Polly had claimed Billy had been too familiar with her?

32

A busy pregnancy

'We're what?' exclaimed Billy. 'Are you serious?'

'Of course I'm serious,' Wilhelmina laughed. 'It is possible, you know.' She lifted her brow at him.

'Yes. Yes. I know. But I thought we'd finished having our family.'

'Whatever made you think that?' she asked in surprise.

'Well, we've got these regular trips to Maitland with the cedar.'

'Mmm?' she questioned. 'And what has that got to do with it?'

'How will we manage now if you're having a baby and later when the baby is born? We'll have to go out of that business.' He sighed heavily.

'Nothing of the kind. I'll manage. You'll see. We'll work the loads so that the baby comes between trips.'

They argued for some time, but eventually Billy allowed himself to be convinced. It would be all right for some months yet. Then they would have to time the loads according to the baby's arrival. She would arrange it with Mr Fry. They were good friends now.

Billy's acreage under cultivation had grown in the last few years. The acquisition of the property downriver had enabled this to happen.

He had hired men for the fencing and had planted a crop of wheat. This would be much more than their own family needs; this was a commercial crop. A new mill had been set up in Dungog and he intended to transport the grain by waggon or dray and sell the grain to the mill.

There was one unresolved difficulty: threshing the wheat. It would be a long, slow business to thresh so much. The only thing to do so far as he could see would be to pay men to do the work.

He had made another purchase of land over on the Allyn. It was a newly opened-up area, high up at the headwaters, heavily timbered. It had to be fenced and some of the trees ring-barked. He would get to it in time. There was no hurry. It wasn't eating any bread.

★   ★   ★

There was a flurry among the ladies in the valley. Wilhelmina Foster was having another baby. The other children were growing up. There'd be quite a gap between the last one and this new one.

'Whoever said I had finished having babies?' Wilhelmina cried when they spoke to her about it. 'The other children will have a wonderful time with a new baby to play with.'

She was sitting on the verandah sewing, as she did in preparation for the arrival of each baby, when she noticed a man walking down the road. He turned in and, as he came closer, she could see his clothes were the worse for wear. He had a little bundle slung across his back with a billy can tied to one end. He came up to the fence.

Wilhelmina stood up. 'Can I see the boss, please?' he asked when he saw her.

'He's down at that shed over there,' she answered, pointing. The man lifted his hat and trudged towards the shed.

What did he want? Probably a good meal more than anything else. She watched and presently Billy emerged and, with the man in tow, made his way to the back gate.

He appeared behind her. 'This man is looking for work. He says he can't get any — walked for miles. Terrible thing when a man can't find work and wants to work. I've told Sarah to give him a meal. I'm going to send him over to the block on the Allyn to start ring-barking. Could you find him some food to last him a while and put it together? I'll get him an axe and a couple of blankets.'

He turned to go. 'Better see if you can find some boots to fit him, too. His are falling to bits.' He went towards the store.

Wilhelmina rose and went to the kitchen to find and pack food for a couple of weeks at least.

★   ★   ★

The months passed quickly and, before she was ready for it, the last trip to Maitland before the baby was due was upon her. Had she been foolish to say she could make this trip?

Mr Fry had joked with her when she had asked for flexibility in this arrival date. 'What? Not get the cedar here on the due date, Mrs Foster? Is that efficient, reliable business?' They had laughed together.

Their cedar was becoming famous around Maitland. There were many homes which prominently displayed furniture made from 'Foster's cedar'. The German furniture-maker Karl Grosser was well-known now, using only their timber unless people provided their own. Her own dining table and chairs and chiffonier were evidence of his skill and craftsmanship.

Billy had prospered. He had managed well and worked hard. If only he wouldn't drink that rum when he was with his friends! She sighed. She was tired, more tired this time than she had been with any of the other babies. Getting old, I suppose, she mused.

★   ★   ★

The waggons had gone. The fine spring weather still held a nip in the breeze and mornings and nights were cold. She would take this trip in easy stages. She didn't want to bring on a premature birth. She set out early and reached 'Llanfylhn' in good time.

Sophia welcomed her. Mother was aging. You could see it in the way she moved. 'Welcome, my darling,' she cried when Wilhelmina alighted. 'Oh, you should not be taking this long journey at this time.' She hugged Wilhelmina lovingly.

'I must, Mother. I'll be all right. I'll take it steadily.'

They talked long into the evening. What was happening at 'Llanfylhn'?

There had been a letter from Etty. Alister had bought another ship and extended his line. And when could they all come to Sydney to spend some time with her? And how surprised she was about Wilhelmina having another baby. She hoped and prayed that all would be well. It was lovely to get her news. It was so long since they had seen each other.

The next stage of the journey would be lighter. Beth Goodwin had insisted she stay with her sister at Tocal. There, she could have a good night's rest and go on into Maitland to do the business, fresh.

She had protested she would be all right, but Beth was adamant. She must on this occasion let discretion be the better part of valour. She had the baby to think of, as well as herself.

At last, she gave in. Beth had contacted her sister. She would be delighted to have a visit from Mrs Foster. Though they had not met, Beth had talked so much about her that she felt she knew her already.

It was pleasant riding at this time of day. The paddocks on both sides of the road were showing the signs of spring. There was good clover in the paddocks and the cultivation strips were green with the growing crops.

Wilhelmina reached 'Glenview' by midday. She was welcomed by the barking of half a dozen dogs and the screech of a cockatoo. 'Be quiet, Cocky,' a woman's voice cried. 'Lie down there.' Goodness! It could almost be Beth talking.

Wilhelmina alighted and was met by Annie. 'They won't hurt you. They don't bite,' she called, waving at the dogs. 'They are noisy, though. Leave your horse there. Just put the bridle round the post. I'll get the boys to look after him.'

She ushered Wilhelmina inside. 'My goodness, you are a brave lady, riding this far at this stage. Beth said you only have a month to go?' She looked enquiringly at her visitor.

'Yes. But I'm quite all right, I assure you. I ride a lot, so I'm quite used to it.'

'Well, come along in. I'll show you your room. Then you'll be feeling like a cup of tea.'

It was a comfortable house — quite new and built of stone. It was much more imposing than the settlers' houses along the Williams. But then this area had been settled much earlier and was now quite established.

It was wonderful farming land and the cattle were sleek and fat. Everywhere in the paddocks near the house there were cows and calves. It was lovely to watch the little things frisking about, playing like children.

Lunch was a pleasant, informal meal. Annie was so like Beth, Wilhelmina took to her immediately. She left them next morning, refreshed and ready for the business of the day.

There was much more business to be done

now. The extra teams Billy had bought now brought so much more cedar each load. It all had to be checked again at Fry Bros and unloaded and stacked.

Billy was watching anxiously for her when she came upon them at Bolwarra. He was eager to get to Maitland. 'Bert has been telling me about a new machine he has seen, a threshing machine. Does the work of several men in half the time. I want to have a look at one,' he said.

The business was completed satisfactorily as usual. 'Remember, we may be a little late coming with the next load,' Wilhelmina reminded Mr Fry.

'I will remember, Mrs Foster — and my very best wishes that all will go well with you and the new member of your family.' He smiled kindly at her.

They left the boys attending the bullocks and rode into Maitland. There were crowds around the sale yards when they passed there. Carriages of all kinds lined the side of the road and saddle horses were tied to the hitching rail. 'Big sale here today,' Billy commented. 'All the good spring feed has created a big demand. Did you notice all the clover as you came along?'

'Yes. Their season here is a bit ahead of ours.'

They reached the rural supplies firm: now for Billy's threshing machine.

The salesman was enthusiastic. He showed them the prize exhibit. 'Does the work of many men, in half the time — and not the waste. There's always waste in threshing. With this, the stalks and husk are blown off and caught here. See?' He stood back, letting them see all its features.

'It seems a very good thing to have if you have much grain,' Billy commented.

'You'll never be sorry with this one,' the salesman said, patting the machine. 'Just look after it and it will last you for years.'

Billy was soon convinced. It would solve the one problem about his big crop. Now he would be able to reap the wheat and, when it had dried, take it back to the sheds and thresh the grain. It would be more efficient. They paid for the machine and arranged for one of the waggons to pick it up.

They parted, Billy to go back to the boys and Wilhelmina to leave her orders. She was glad when all was done and she was able to set out for home.

33

A close thing

The baby was born just a week after Wilhelmina got home from the trip. Beth and Josie were again with her. Close friends, they always supported each other. 'Just a little bit more. Yes. Yes. Here he comes!' Beth cried. 'And it's another beautiful boy.'

Josie took the baby, wrapping him up. 'Here he is, Wilhelmina. And he's none the worse for your trip to Maitland last week.' She held him for Wilhelmina to see. 'You were cutting it a bit fine though, my girl. He might have been born on the road. Just think!'

'But he wasn't. My children wouldn't arrive without you two in attendance.'

There was rejoicing. What love and joy a new baby always brought.

Billy's thresher arrived and was the topic of conversation throughout the valley. One by one, all the men came to see it and to marvel at its wonders. Billy was the envy of more than one man.

After one neighbour had been viewing the

thresher and wishing he could afford such a machine, Wilhelmina saw Billy coming in, his hands thrust in his pockets and hat on the back of his head, always a sign there was something going on underneath the hat.

'You know, Will,' he commenced as he reached her, 'that machine could be an asset in another way.'

She looked at him enquiringly.

'All the neighbours are wishing they had one. Threshing takes so long, even for your own use.' He paused. 'I can't see any reason why we couldn't do the threshing for them and they pay us for the service. I put the dried wheat on the dray and bring it here to thresh. There's no reason why they couldn't do the same with theirs. We'd charge so much a dray load or something like that. I'd have to work that out. It would save them a lot of time and be cheaper than wages for help for the ones working on their own.'

'That does sound a good idea,' Wilhelmina agreed. 'But if you are tied up with that, who's going to do the work you are doing now?'

'The boys can do the farming now. That's it, you see. If we go into this, it will all have to be done while the weather lasts. So it will be whoever's wheat is ready first. Generally I'd say ours would be first, so we could reap that and stack it to dry. Then, when we bring it up to thresh, the boys can go over the paddock again and plough the stalks and husks back into the ground while I go on threshing the neighbours' wheat.'

She nodded. It sounded a good idea.

'That's if they take to the idea. I'll let it be known. And they can come and have a look when I start on our crop.'

What a pity Billy hadn't had the opportunity of a good education. He had a good brain. He was progressive — always interested and anxious to try out new developments. He would have gone far. She looked at him lovingly.

$\star$ $\quad$ $\star$ $\quad$ $\star$

The next trip to Maitland was due. They had put it back a week, but now it must be undertaken. The teams left, Billy, Edward and the other drivers all travelling together.

Wilhelmina packed her bag. There would be nappies and clothes for the baby this time. The weather was unusually warm for early summer. She must wear a very wide hat to try to protect little Arthur from the sun. Perhaps she should not travel in the middle of the day. Stopping to feed and change him would make it a long, slow trip.

And so she set out.

She stopped and rested in the shade of a big tree when the sun became too hot. The baby lay on his rug on the ground and surveyed the moving leaves above him with wondering eyes. He was doing well — only a small baby. But small babies grew into big men.

As the sting went out of the sun, she again mounted, carrying her little bundle. She reached her mother's home just on sundown.

Sophia revelled in the delights of her grandson. 'But Wilhelmina, I do not think you should be riding a horse and carrying him like this. So young he is,' she said, worry in her voice.

'I can manage, Mother. You know I am as happy on a horse as sitting in a chair. Papa had us on horses before we could walk. It will be all right.'

She set out again very early, following the same routine. She was getting tired holding the baby. But not long now. She was to again stay with Beth's sister.

The heat was getting very oppressive. All day she watched the sky as clouds gathered on the horizon. Storm clouds! What would she do if it started to rain? She'd just have to shelter little Arthur as well as she could. She urged her horse along.

The clouds gathered thicker and moved

across the sky — great, burgeoning clouds. The sun was blocked out. Was it going to follow around the mountains or sweep across the whole valley?

A great fork of lightning hurtled earthwards ahead of her, followed quickly by a deafening explosion of thunder. The horse started. Steady boy, steady. She drew the reins tight. She had no free hand to pat him, to soothe him. 'Steady boy. Come on now, just take us quietly. It's all right now.'

He settled down. The baby was asleep. Only another mile to Glenview.

As the first drops of rain fell, she turned onto the track to the house. Annie came running, taking the baby, helping Wilhelmina down, calling the men to unstrap her roll, bring the saddlebag, unsaddle the horse and let him go. It was hard to make herself heard between the claps of thunder and the rising wind.

Now the heavens opened and a torrent of rain fell. It pounded on the roof. The wind swept it across the verandahs. The garden was soon awash and rivers of water ran down the track to the house.

'Oh Wilhelmina, look what you were nearly caught in. You and this little bundle might have been drenched. As it is, you must be damp. You change the baby and I'll find you some dry clothes.'

They were so thoughtful, so concerned for her welfare and for little Arthur. But she would have to go on in the morning. The teams would be at Bolwarra tonight and would be moving off early into Maitland. She must get to them before they got to the timber yards.

The rain had eased by morning. Against the advice of Annie and her husband, Wilhelmina mounted her horse and, with the baby, set off. The clouds were building up ominously again, great black-grey clouds with a tinge of green.

She urged the horse along. What would she do if there was hail? Those green tinges in the clouds indicated hail.

The road and the paddocks were awash — not a speck of dry anywhere. Water ran down the gutters in the road and all the potholes were full. There must have been inches in that downpour, she thought.

She could see the waggon as she approached the camp site. Why were they not yoked and making ready? She had feared she might be running late and they would already have left.

Billy greeted her. 'Can't go any further,' he called.

'Why not?'

'Just look over there.' He pointed.

She had been so intent on the road and the baby she had not looked across the paddocks to the river. Now she looked. To her horror, she saw it had burst its banks and was covering the low-lying farm land.

'It's rising fast,' Billy said. 'There's no hope of getting across there.' Billy took the baby. She dismounted and stretched.

'Whatever can you do,' she asked, 'with all this timber on?'

'Nothing we can do except wait till it goes down. We couldn't take this load back anyway if we wanted to. We'd be bogged before we got a couple of miles.'

What could she do with little Arthur? They didn't even have a tent. The men camped around the fire or under the waggon.

'Perhaps I should go back to Annie,' she suggested.

'The way that river has been rising in the last hour you wouldn't get there, love,' Billy said gently. 'There must have been even more rain up river. This isn't all local water. It's rising fast. Lucky we are on a bit of a knoll here. But I don't think any of us will be going anywhere for a while.'

They made a fire and boiled the billy. There was enough food for a few days if they rationed it out. They'd buy more for the return journey when they got to Maitland.

'There's nothing for it but to camp under the waggons, Will,' Billy said as darkness settled over them.

They lifted the tarpaulin and crawled under the waggon. The ground was wet, slushy. Billy found a piece of tarpaulin and laid it on the ground for her and the baby. Then the rain started again.

'Sounds like it's developing into good general rain,' Billy said. 'It'll do wonders for the country. Not so good for the people in the low-lying part along the river. But even they will benefit by the top dressing their farms get.'

Wilhelmina was silent. Why, oh why hadn't she stayed with Annie? She had to get the baby to somewhere dry.

When morning came, she had made up her mind to try to get to a house just up the road. If she could get there, surely they'd take a woman and a baby in. She'd have to cross the water in the gully — if it was too deep she'd swim the horse across.

Billy objected to her plan, but eventually gave in. He caught the horse and helped her up. 'There's a real gully there, Will — and it's wide. It will be too deep,' he protested.

'I must try,' she said. 'I've got to get him to somewhere dry or he'll be sick.' She was close to tears. She gathered the baby firmly to her and took the reins, turning the horse towards the gully.

'Come on, boy,' she said softly, 'come on. You've got to get us across that gully.'

She urged him towards the water. He turned, shying away from it. 'Come on. You've got to swim.' She turned his head again, determinedly making him face the water.

Again he shied away. Wilhelmina slapped his neck with the reins and dug her heels in. He advanced into the water. It was rushing, the centre of the stream afloat with sticks and leaves.

He floundered, lost his footing and plunged into deep water. Then, throwing up his head, he thrashed around out of her control. The little group at the waggons watched in fascinated horror. She hung on, grasping the baby.

The horse, now facing the bank from which it had come, touched ground and, scrambling up, reached safety. It stood shaking. Billy caught the rein and led it further away from its terror. 'Give the baby to me,' he said.

Wilhelmina handed him down. 'I couldn't get him to swim it,' she choked.

'No. Never mind now.' Billy put his hand out to help her.

She leant against him and cried. 'It's all right,' he comforted. 'You're safe and Arthur's safe. I told you it was too dangerous. You'd need plenty of strength and strong control to get a horse across there. No hope with a baby in your arms.'

The rain came on again and continued for most of the next few days. Everything was wet now: their clothes, the food; they were drenched themselves.

Billy had turned the tarpaulin down to shelter them from the winds. Even so it was cold, with water all around and underfoot and no sign of it abating.

At long last, the rain stopped; the river and the gully began to fall and reached a point where she was able to ride safely across to the house up the road. By this time, little Arthur had developed a horrible cough. The family took them in to the comfort of warmth and dry clothes.

It was another week before they could get into Maitland. But the tarpaulins had been taken from over the load to shelter mother and baby and the cedar had been soaked. It all had to be unloaded, racked against fences to dry out and then reloaded.

★　★　★

Boys, girls, maids, governess all came running as she rode down the road.

'Oh Mother, where have you been? We've been so worried,' Eliza called.

Etty put her hands up to take Arthur. A fit of coughing struck him and he started to cry. 'Oh Mother, he has got a nasty cough. Poor little fellow,' she cried.

They plied her with questions, fussing over her when they heard of her ordeal. 'We could have lost you,' Oliver said solemnly. 'And Arthur.' He looked gravely at his little brother.

'It was to try to get him somewhere dry, out of the rain so he wouldn't get sick that I tried to cross the gully,' Wilhelmina explained. 'He's so little I wanted to protect him.'

'Why did Father let you do it?' Eddy asked.

Wilhelmina pretended not to hear.

34

Children of their father

Summer came with a vengeance in late November. In the hot, dry conditions, the wheat ripened. Each day, the crops were inspected and readiness for harvesting estimated.

At last, the wheat was considered ready.

There were no schoolroom lessons for the boys now. Every morning, they were up early to do the chores until the sun had dried the dew. Then the reaping hooks were brought and they set off for the farm. They cut and tied the stalks into sheaves and stood them to dry. It was hard work, especially for young boys, but they revelled in it. Here was where their hearts were.

Then came the day when they brought the first load in to be threshed. Billy started the machine. It was a wonder of wonders. The wheat flowed into the bin. A farmer up the valley came in to look. Those who had taken up Billy's offer to thresh watched their crops closely.

No-one else had wheat to sell. Those who

brought their wheat to Billy just wanted it threshed and bagged and taken to the mill to be ground into their year's supply of flour.

Throughout the summer, there were few school lessons for the boys. 'I'm fourteen now anyway, Mother. It's time I left off school lessons. I can read enough. And I know my sums,' Eddy had said.

Wilhelmina watched in frustration. It was all very well this being farmers with their father, but would it give them all they needed for life as the years went on?

They all had a smattering of music. It was too much to expect the 'farmers' to sit at the piano and practice. But they could all sing and all loved to have a party and gather around the piano.

I suppose their life is so different from my early years, Wilhelmina thought. But it would be nice to have one, at least, who would love to make music as I have; to excel. It would be something of a salve for the wound of the lost career.

Perhaps she would persevere with the girls. She must tell Miss Richardson that the boys would not be coming to the schoolroom until the harvesting and ploughing was finished.

She walked along the hall. Miss Richardson was sitting at her desk with her head in her hands, her elbows on the table. 'Meg, is something wrong?' She hurried to her side.

The teacher lifted her head. 'Mrs Foster, I don't think I am being very effective. Eddy and Oliver have not been in the schoolroom all week. And now Eliza and Etty are gone. They have worked well this morning, but since lunch they haven't had their minds on anything I say. All they want to do is get outside and watch that threshing machine or ride horses around the cows, or anything totally devoid of academic advancement. They seem to have no aspirations at all in that regard.' She slapped her hand on the desk.

Wilhelmina sat down. 'I know,' she agreed. 'I have just been considering the same problem. You and I know the advantage of education. But here in this wilderness, beautiful as it is, it is hard to instill a vision of the benefit of such things. Only today, Eddy told me he could 'read enough now, and knew his sums'.

'They read what they have to, not for the love of it, not as a means to gain, to absorb so much knowledge, to appreciate the beauty and wonder of words, to open a door on a limitless world.' She sighed. 'I'm afraid we will have to let Eddy go. I think his father will support him in this. We will persevere with Oliver another year. The girls we will certainly persevere with.'

She stood up. 'I shall go and relieve my feelings on the piano. Perhaps it will inspire those young ladies. Inspire or not, they will find they must continue with their music also. If I do not insist, they will regret it in years to come.'

Dear piano. She opened the lid and ran her fingers over the keys. Here was her solace, her joy. She played for an hour, moving from one composition into another. Miss Richardson came in and sat unobserved in the corner. As Wilhelmina stood to close the piano, she slipped quietly out.

★ ★ ★

'Round your fingers, Eliza.' Wilhelmina put her hand over her daughter's fingers. 'Up on the tips. You need to use the tips of your fingers to press the keys. It gives you so much more control.'

Eliza tried again.

'That's better. Now try this passage again.'

She persevered for half an hour. The clock struck the hour. 'Can I go now, Mother? We've been half an hour. That's time, isn't it?'

Wilhelmina sighed. 'Yes. Off you go. Don't forget to practise as I have shown you tomorrow.'

'All right, Mother.' She was all smiles now; released from labour.

341

'Billy, you can't take the boys with you. They are not men yet,' Wilhelmina objected.

'Of course they can come.' Billy was adamant. 'Those cows and calves didn't just disappear. Someone has taken them off. And those prime bullocks just about fit for market didn't just walk off, either. They were driven. I tell you, we've got to go after them — and the boys are good stockmen, even if they are only lads.'

'But if you catch up with the people responsible, they could be dangerous. The boys are not old enough to defend themselves,' Wilhelmina replied, wringing her hands. Whatever she said fell on deaf ears. Billy had made up his mind. If they went well up the mountain, that could be dangerous, too, in this weather. The ground was wet and a horse could slip on those stony ledges.

Oliver ran back to say goodbye. 'Don't worry, Mother. We'll be all right. We've got to find those cattle. The rustlers have got to realise they can't just go off with our stock,' he said very importantly.

They rode through the paddock to the foot of the hills. The ground was muddy, the heavy rain softening it here at the edge of the thick timber.

'Here, Father!' It was Eddy calling. 'Here. Look!' He pointed to the tracks clearly visible.

Billy spurred his horse across to where Eddy had been searching. He was right. There were tracks of cows and calves — and a couple of horses. 'That's them, all right,' Billy agreed. 'We'll follow them and see where they lead.'

The tracks led to the top of the range. They looked down over Chads Creek and followed along the ridge. 'Here, boys. Look here,' Billy called. He pointed to a track coming from the other side. They were beside him in an instant. More cattle tracks showed in the soft soil, joining up with the ones they had been following.

'These jokers have been taking small numbers from different places — probably in the hope it won't be noticed until it's too late. I'll bet we find tracks joining in all along the ridge.'

They must have a yard or holding paddock of some kind up here. But where? He'd probably need help if he came on them. The tracks were fairly fresh, but there was no sound of cattle. They must not be close yet.

'Eddy, do you think you can ride to Maitland and get the police?' he asked.

'Yes, Father. I can go. But what are you

going to do?' He was excited at the prospect of going for the police, but then, he might miss out on the excitement of catching the rustlers. Maybe they needed the police, though. He'd go.

'I'll follow along further and see where they go. Call in and tell Mother what's happening. But don't delay. This is the best trail we've had. And I want to get them this time. Be as quick as you can. Bring them back with you. Off you go.'

Eddy wheeled his horse round and let him have his head down the steep descent. When he reached home, Edward called, 'Mother! Mother! Where are you?' He flung himself off his horse and came running onto the verandah.

Wilhelmina hurried out. Whatever was wrong? Had someone had an accident? Oh, she knew Billy shouldn't have taken the boys.

'Mother, we've found the rustlers' tracks and Father and Oliver have gone on following them and Father sent me back. I've to go to Maitland and bring the police back.'

'Oh my goodness! Can you go all that way on your own?'

Edward gave her a withering look. He swallowed a drink of water and was about to go. 'Father said to call in and tell you, but not to delay — so I'm off.'

'Wait a minute. You'll be hungry.' Wilhelmina grabbed a bag and hurriedly put some thick slices of bread and cheese into it, then included a big slice of fruit cake. Edward slung it over his shoulder and was gone out the door. They heard the sound of his horse galloping down the road.

Billy and Oliver followed the tracks for some miles. 'They've got a decent-sized herd now, son,' Billy said.

They were now in the brush. It was easy following the tracks now. Maybe he had better wait for the police. There was only one direction the tracks could go now. They'd be there tomorrow. He'd go home and wait for the police to arrive.

It was mid-morning by the time the sergeant and his men arrived with Edward. They headed off after a quick drink.

Billy picked up the tracks again and led the way. They followed them to where on the Corker it had been considered impossible to penetrate further. The cattle tracks narrowed and still led on, disclosing a single file track through the precipices to the rocks above with sheer drops on either side. Here the land spread out into the flat plains and swamps of the Tops.

'We're getting close now, I think,' said the sergeant, riding close to Billy. 'Not too much noise now, boys. Keep your ears open. See if you can pick up anything.'

They rode silently. Only the sound of the horses' hooves on the soft earth could be heard.

Suddenly, the sound of a beast bellowing jerked them all alert. Then there were voices. They advanced quietly. Now they could see a mob of cattle in a good stockyard. Several men were busy branding cattle and drafting them off into different yards.

The sergeant and his men emerged from the trees. 'Hands up in the name of the law,' he shouted.

The rustlers were caught.

★　★　★

'But weren't you scared?' Etty asked her brothers. They had for the last hour regaled the household with their adventures.

'No. We had the police with us,' Oliver replied.

'But what about that part where there was just a narrow little track and you could fall down both sides?'

'You couldn't fall down both sides, silly,' Edward cut in. 'If you fell down one side you'd go right to the bottom! *Sploosh*!' he said dramatically, demonstrating with his hands.

Wilhelmina shuddered.

'Apart from catching the rustlers, it was a very worthwhile trip,' Billy said smugly.

'And why is that?' enquired Wilhelmina.

'Those cattle tracks showed us a way to the Tops,' he said triumphantly. 'We discovered a way onto the Barrington Tops. It's a rough trip up there, but once you get there, it's good grazing. It opens up a whole new area right across that plateau for grazing. There'll be a lot of people who will want to take advantage of that.'

The daily routine was tame in the extreme after the high adventure. Edward now considered his school days over. His dash to Maitland to bring the police back had put the seal on that. He was a man now.

Oliver reluctantly attended morning class, but it was hard to hold him after lunch.

35

Diversifying

Billy now added pigs to his farm. The house cows produced more milk than they needed, so he would put it to use. They were an interesting sideline. He had added to his grazing land, buying a property further up the valley. The pigs would help to pay it off.

Some of the men in the valley had gone into dairying. He considered this, but decided it was too risky. The milk had to be set in wide dishes for the cream to rise and set, then skimmed the next day. In hot, steamy weather, the milk could sour quickly before it got to the factory.

'You want to get one of these new milk separators,' Mr Fry told him when they chatted over a cup of tea after a delivery of cedar. Wilhelmina had gone on to do the shopping and was then going home.

'Separators? What are they?'

'A new machine invented. It's steam-driven. Copes with a lot of milk. You don't have to turn a handle. It separates the cream from the milk without having to set it overnight. You can separate it as soon as you milk, keep it in a cool place and take the cream to the factory two or three times a week, or however often you like. The cream keeps better because you can separate it more satisfactorily.'

'What next?' exclaimed Billy.

But already his mind was ticking over. All the farmers in the valley had the same problem: keeping the milk fresh and getting it to the factory in good condition. He'd look into it. It did not take long for him to decide.

When the time approached that he could be expected home after that trip, Wilhelmina listened as she darned socks by the oil lamp. Then she heard it, that full strong voice, singing at full blast. There he was . . . as usual.

She gathered up her darning and, sighing to herself, went to prepare for bed. He'd have to sleep it off — but not with her. She heard him unyoking the bullocks. The gate swung shut. 'Will, where are you?' She didn't answer. He mumbled something, then called again. 'Where are you, Will? Got something to tell you.'

She'd have to go and see what he wanted or he'd have all the children awake. She slipped quietly out to the kitchen. 'Hush. You'll wake everyone up,' she said softly.

'Got something to tell you,' he whispered thickly. 'Thought you'd want to know.' He looked at her, smiling foolishly, his eyes drooping.

Oh, how could he do this to himself? If only he could see himself. How ridiculous he was when he was like this.

'Be a good girl and I'll tell you,' he whispered.

She was busy making him a cup of coffee. She lifted the kettle and poured the water.

'I bought it,' he said again.

She turned from the stove to hand him the coffee, but he had slumped onto the table and was asleep. She stood staring at her husband. Then she went round the table and half pushed, half dragged him onto the sofa.

*   *   *

The news of Billy's separator spread rapidly up the valley. Men came to see what this latest thing was all about. Separator, eh? What was that? A large one operated by steam! They were using steam for all sorts of things now. Fancy! We'd had steam for so long and were only now finding its power to drive machinery.

Billy explained over and over about the separator. It would separate cream from the milk better than you could do it by hand. It could cope with large amounts — and you could get the cream to the factory in better condition than the hand-skimmed cream.

He had bought one and intended going further into dairying. But he was also offering to buy their milk, separate it and return their skimmed milk for pig-rearing. He would then transport the cream and sell it to the factory.

'The boys can take the dray and horses and deliver the cream three times a week,' he told Wilhelmina.

'If you think they can do it,' she responded.

'Of course they can do it. They can drive those horses as well as anyone.' It was quite a moment. 'You know, some of the fellows on those very small blocks have been having a pretty tough time. Their blocks are not big enough for anything but dairying. They have a bit of cultivation to feed their dairy cows, but they're not big enough for grazing. This will give them a chance to do a bit better, too.'

The idea caught on quickly and by the time the separator was installed, nearly all the farmers involved in dairying in the valley had arranged with Billy to sell their milk to him and, after separating, have the milk returned.

The machine was installed. Bert Goodwin was the first customer. He arrived straight after milking. Billy poured milk into the huge vat and started the engine.

Bert watched fascinated as the machine worked, the cream came out into the can and the separated milk flowed through the other spout into his empty can. 'Can't believe it, Billy!' he exclaimed. 'And you don't have to turn a handle or anything.' Billy smiled broadly.

'Suits me,' Bert said happily. 'We won't take long to finish here and I can take the milk straight home and feed my pigs!' He shook his head in wonder. The same sentiments were expressed by the other farmers as they followed.

The last one to arrive was a new settler from the very head of the valley. He arrived with a girl perched up on the front of the dray with him. He clattered the cans of milk down onto the floor and rolled them on their base rim into the dairy.

The girl jumped down and followed him in. 'Hullo, Billy,' the newcomer said. 'This is Rosy.' He indicated the girl.

She was a buxom lass. The first thing you noticed about her was her thick, curly, red hair. It was not auburn, not a deep beautiful copper, but a fiery beacon, shouting to be noticed. She lifted her eyes and looked at Billy, smiling.

They watched the separating and the creamless milk was returned.

She was a chatty little roly-poly thing, Billy thought — very friendly, with a sense of humour. You could have a joke with her. Jed hadn't said if she was his sister or cousin or what — just, 'this is Rosy'. Bit like a rose she was, too.

'Don't suppose you know of anybody wanting help in the house or work like that, do you?' Jed asked. 'Rosy wants a job.'

'A job, eh?' Billy considered. 'Go over and see my wife. She'll find a job for you. Tell her I sent you.'

36

Rosy

Wilhelmina heard the gate and looked out the window. Whoever was this coming? She was a stranger, not one of the valley people. She went through to the side door. 'You Mrs Foster?' the girl asked.

'Yes, I am Mrs Foster. What can I do for you?' What did this girl want? She lacked something of dignity. She was not dressed very neatly. But it wasn't just that. There was an air about her. She was too breezy in her manner. And her hair! Not only was it a flaming red (she couldn't help that), but it was full and loose, a mass of curls around her face.

'Billy said to ask you if you could give me a job. He said to tell you he sent me.'

'Billy? Do you mean Mr Foster?' Wilhelmina corrected her.

'Yes, I suppose so. They all just call him Billy. Nice, friendly man your husband, isn't he?' This was what came of Billy's lack of ceremony: this chit of a girl coming and talking with such familiarity of him.

'Mr Foster told you to ask me for work?'

The girl nodded, somewhat chastened.

'Come into the kitchen, then.' Wilhelmina turned and led the way to the kitchen. Why had Billy sent the girl to her for work? Did he know anything about her? 'What is your name?' she asked the girl as they sat down.

'Oh sorry,' she laughed. 'I forgot to tell you. My name is Rosy.'

'Rosy what?' Wilhelmina asked.

'Rosy Hale.'

'Where are you from, Rosy? Where is your home?'

'I come up from Morpeth with Jed. But I'm looking for work — live in.'

'Can you cook?'

The girl nodded.

I wonder how well, Wilhelmina thought. Perhaps her capabilities would exceed her appearance. 'Have you any references from former people you have worked for in a live-in position?'

The girl shook her head. 'Haven't had a live-in job before. Just came up with Jed and he says he can't keep me for long.' She looked around. 'I like it here. I'd like to stay.'

'Where are your parents, Rosy? Are they at Morpeth?'

'Got no parents,' she said breezily.

'Was your home at Morpeth?' persisted Wilhelmina.

'No. I was born in Sydney.'

'Is Jed a relative?'

'No. I said I just come up with him from Morpeth.'

She stood up and pushed her chair back. 'Can you give me a job or not?' Well! The cheek of her! Did Billy know any more about her? He must, or he wouldn't have sent her over, surely.

'I'll give you a trial, Rosy,' she said doubtfully. 'We'll try it for a month. Your work will be mostly in the kitchen — cooking and cleaning and generally helping. I usually do the cooking myself, but if you can take over part of that, it will be good.' She rose and walked to the door. 'I'll show you your room. Come along.'

Rosy had relaxed now. There was something she didn't want to tell. Oh well, if it didn't interfere with her work . . . and having no parents . . . she mightn't have had much training as she grew up if her parents had died when she was young.

'You'll need to get your things, so I'll expect you tomorrow morning,' Wilhelmina said.

'I can start now. Jed can bring my bag over when he brings the milk in the morning. Not much room in the bed over there — not very comfortable.'

Really! What did that mean? The girl was an enigma. What had Billy let her in for?

Rosy was duly installed in the kitchen. She was shown the bathroom and instructed to wash and tidy herself up. Wilhelmina gave her a clean white apron. 'Your hair now, Rosy. We must anchor it.'

'Oh, me hair!' Rosy exclaimed, running her fingers through her hair.

'Now that is something you must not do in the kitchen,' Wilhelmina exclaimed. 'It is not hygienic to be touching your hair or have your hair flying loose when there is food about.' She went to find combs and clips. She brought a piece of ribbon. Perhaps Rosy could plait her hair.

'I'm not a child!' she objected when this was suggested. Eventually, the fiery tresses were restrained to Wilhelmina's satisfaction.

To Wilhelmina's surprise, the new kitchen help proved to be quite a reasonable cook. She was keen and quickly picked up instructions she was given.

It was the girl herself that worried Wilhelmina. Her manner sometimes . . . she seemed to have a brazen quality about her. She was quite young. Was it wise to have her here in the house with boys growing up?

Perhaps she should give her a chance. She may not have had many in her life. Perhaps it was all ignorance. She'd try to instill in her a few of the graces of modesty expected of young ladies, even of servant girls.

★ ★ ★

The men of the local neighbourhood arranged a card game. They had talked about it for some time. Now it was arranged and was to be held in Billy's shed. There would be room there. And they would not be hampered by the confines of the house — and Wilhelmina's oversight, Billy thought.

Bert couldn't come. Beth was away at her sister's and Bert had to stay with the family. Sorry Bert can't come, Billy thought. Good mate, Bert — best of the lot, actually. The others arrived as darkness fell — Tom, Peter, Phillip, Jack. There were eight of them altogether.

The card game commenced after talk of the crops and stock — and rain! They all wanted rain. There was a good discussion on that.

Stakes for the game were limited. This was to be a friendly night of male mateship, not a game for high stakes. They could none of them afford to lose too much.

The game had been underway about an

hour. Billy's hand was promising. Jack had brought a bottle of rum. It had been passed freely to lubricate the working of the mind.

The door opened and Rosy entered, carrying a tray of steaming mugs. The whole shed seemed to light up with her entrance, the lantern light glinting on her hair. 'Thought you might be cold,' she said brightly. 'I brought you a toddy of rum each — warm you up.'

She swayed around the table, leaning over each man, placing a big mug in front of him. The aromatic steam and Rosy's perfume assailed their nostrils. She walked around the table, looking at their cards and watching the play. Billy was about to play a card. 'Uh! Uh!' she said, indicating a different card.

'Not fair. Not fair!' There was a general outcry of objection. 'No getting inside information.'

Rosy laughed and waved an airy farewell. 'Bring you another after a while,' she called, glancing over her shoulder.

'Where'd you get her?'

'She's the girl Jed brought back last trip south, isn't she?'

'Yes. What was that all about? Just picked her up, I hear.'

'She's a good enough cook anyway,' Billy said. 'Will's quite pleased with her cooking.'

'Might have more ways of pleasing a man

than cooking, I reckon,' contributed Jack. 'You know what you're doing having a girl like that under your roof.'

Billy played his card. 'That's mine, I think.' He raked the cards in. 'Have to keep your mind on the cards, Jack.'

It wasn't long before the door opened again and Rosy appeared with another round of hot toddies. 'That's the girl!'

Some of them had been imbibing freely from one or two more bottles that had been produced. Hands reached out to catch Rosy, but she swung away, laughing, and closed the door behind her.

'Fancy havin' that girl in yer house, right there in front of ya.'

Jack looked blearily at Billy. 'Bet ya take advantage of it.'

'I've got my own wife,' Billy replied, striving to see the marks on the cards. Was it a heart or a diamond? It was red anyway.

'Nothing like variety. Anyway, yer just scared o' yer wife. Scarey lady.' He pulled a face. 'Very ladylike.'

The others laughed, looking at Billy. 'Bet yer not game to put the hard word on her,' Jack challenged, indicating the direction Rosy had taken. 'Na. Too scared o' yer wife. Ole Wilhelmina. She wears the trousers, rules the roost.'

'Why would I want to do that?' Billy struggled. 'I tell you I've got my own wife.'

'Or she's got you. She plays the tune an' you dance to it. Ha ha. That's good. She plays the tune.' He looked stupidly at the others and played imaginary piano keys with his fingers. 'And you dance to it.' He laughed uproariously at his own joke.

Billy's male pride asserted itself. 'I don't dance to anybody's tune,' he stated thickly. 'I just don't choose to avail myself of all that may be offering.'

Jack threw back his head, laughing again. 'Doesn't choose to avail himself of all that is offering,' he mimicked. 'Won't be offering to you, anyway. Not a man. She'd only want a man. You're no man — scared of yer wife. Might throw you out.'

The others were leaning forward, mouths half open, eyelids held up with the difficulty of concentration. This was turning into a real show. The cards were forgotten.

Jack rose unsteadily to his feet. 'Not a man. Scared of ole Wilhelmina,' he jibed.

It was too much for Billy. He took another gulp of his toddy and rose with difficulty, leaning on the table. 'I'm not scared of any woman,' he declared.

'Well, prove it then. Prove yer a man. I saw Rosy.' His expression changed to a sickly smile. 'Sweet Rosy,' he breathed in deeply. 'Ah, sweet Rosy.' He came back to the matter in hand. 'I saw Rosy go into that room off the verandah, next to your kitchen. The light's gone out. Bet she's gone to bed.' He looked at Billy slyly. 'All nice an' soft an' warm.' He paused a moment. 'Bet you're not game to go in there and put the hard word on her.'

Billy's expression changed back again to one of contempt. 'Not scared of anyone. Any woman be glad to have me,' Billy boasted, stung.

The cards were now scattered over the floor. He trod a wavy path to the door and, after fiddling with the latch, pulled it open. ''Ere. Take the lantern so we can see ye — and see ye go in there,' Jack taunted.

Billy took the lantern. They watched, fascinated. Some of the others had sobered somewhat with the turn of events — hope old Billy knew what he was doing. The lantern danced slowly from side to side across the yard to the building. They saw it ascend the low steps and cross the verandah.

Then the door of the room opened and it went inside, the door closing behind it. It glowed softly through the window for a few minutes. Then the light went out. They watched in the pale light from the moon, but the door remained closed.

37

Caught in the act

Wilhelmina stirred. The moon was shining across the bed. Whatever time was it? Were those men still out in the shed? If they were, there would be more than cards afoot. There probably was, anyway. She reached for the little clock by her bed and turned it so the moonlight fell on the face. Three o'clock! Maybe they'd drunk themselves to sleep. She pulled on a wrap and slipped her feet into her slippers. She had better go and see if the lantern was still going. They could burn the place down if they were drunk and tried to light it again.

Her feet made no noise as she went quietly through the house. The kitchen was in darkness, but the moon fell on mugs on a tray on the table. No need to ask what was in them — you could smell it. Billy must have come and got drinks for everyone.

All was in darkness outside. There was no light showing anywhere when she looked out the window. Either they had drunk themselves to sleep or they had gone home. But where was Billy?

There was a sound outside. She moved quickly to the door and pulled it open. Billy was standing on the verandah with his hand on Rosy's door. The door was half open. Her mind reeled. What was Billy doing in Rosy's bedroom?

Then her shocked mind took in his appearance. His shirt was open and half out of his trousers. One bracer strap hung down over his elbow. He seemed to be having trouble getting it to stay up. His boots were in his hand. He looked up and saw her. She noted the shock on his face. 'Went into the wrong room, Will. Opened the wrong door.'

He was drunk. He reeked of rum. She backed away, a pain spreading through her chest, her throat clutched in a mighty grip.

He pulled the door shut with a bang. 'Oops! Sorry Rosy,' he said. Then, looking up, 'Sorry Will.' Sorry! He could say sorry!

She turned and ran back through the dark house, closed the door and turned the key. Then she threw herself on the bed and cried till there were no more tears. The ache was still in her chest. She felt as though her heart was being squeezed till every drop of blood had left it.

★ ★ ★

She saw the family about their business — the boys to the farm and the girls to the school room with Meg. Bridget and Sarah were washing in the washhouse. She could hear them talking and laughing down there.

She didn't think she would ever laugh again.

Billy, with all his lack of sophistication, with all his weakness when it came to drinking rum with his mates, had never for a minute given her cause to think he would ever be unfaithful to her.

Was this why he had sent the girl to her to ask for work? She had called him Billy so easily. Perhaps he had known her before she turned up with Jed. She had never discovered how the girl had come to be with Jed anyway. What was going on there?

But Billy? Hadn't she been a loving, responsive wife to him? He'd never complained. He seemed happy. They had a family.

The beds were made. The verandah swept.

Where was Rosy anyway? She hadn't done the washing up yet. A groan from the bathroom made her glance in. Billy was leaning against the washstand, clutching his head.

'You've got a headache?' she said flatly.

He looked up and groaned again.

Without answering, she turned and left

him. She went into the sitting room. Billy followed her. He stopped behind her where she was standing by the piano. 'I'm sorry, Will,' he said contritely.

'Sorry? For what?' she asked.

'For drinking rum — and getting drunk again.'

'Is that all?'

He looked up, frowning at her. 'What do you mean? I thought you'd be upset.'

'I *am* upset. I said is that all you're sorry for?'

He looked at her, not comprehending.

'What were you doing coming out of Rosy's room at three o'clock this morning?'

A wave of shock flitted across his face. 'What?'

'I said what were you doing coming out of Rosy's bedroom at three o'clock this morning with your boots in your hands and your shirt all undone and your braces falling down?'

'But I wasn't in Rosy's room,' he protested.

'Billy, I saw you with my own eyes. You had your hand on the doorknob and the door was open. If that doesn't mean you had been in there and were just coming out I don't know what it means.'

Billy slumped in a chair and put his head in his hands.

'It's no use feeling sorry for yourself, Billy.

I thought we had promised ourselves to each other for life, to no-one else; no affairs; just you and me.'

He lifted his head. 'But Will, that's the way it is. I love you. I don't want anyone else.' He was looking directly at her. Oh, those eyes, those blue, blue eyes she loved. That special expression was only for her. It had always been only for her.

'Then explain to me what you were doing,' she whispered.

He lowered his head again. 'I don't know, Will. Oh God! I don't know. I was drunk. Some of them brought bottles with them. Then Rosy came down with hot toddies, I don't know how many times. More than once. I thought you'd sent her. I thought that was funny.'

Was he telling the truth? Had he really blundered in and opened the wrong door just as she had come to the kitchen? But what about his clothes? Why so dishevelled?

Oh God, she loved him. In spite of it all, she loved him. But she wasn't going to share him with anyone. She had to know the truth. Oh God, help me find the truth, she thought. Please let it be as he said. He just stumbled into the wrong room.

'Rosy had no right to dispense rum without my knowledge. Where is she anyway?'

His look was unknowing.

'This is what happens when you get with other men and start drinking rum. You don't know what you are doing.' She walked over to the window. 'What time did the others go home?'

He shook his head. 'No idea, Will,' he mumbled.

She gave a disgusted grunt. The shed surrounds didn't look any the worse for wear. There were hoofprints around, that was all, and a saddle cloth on the fence. Someone was probably too drunk to notice he hadn't put it on.

But what about Billy's clothes? He looked as though he had just thrown some clothes on again when she opened the door and saw him. 'If you were just coming in from the shed, why was your shirt undone and your braces hanging down like that?'

He just shook his head sadly. 'I just don't know, Will. I can't remember a thing.'

★ ★ ★

The next few weeks were tense. Billy's recollection of the happenings of the night of the card game did not improve or change in any way — or so he said. What was the use to persist?

She found herself watching him. Are you becoming a jealous woman, imagining your husband has peccadilloes with every woman he meets? She chided herself. Trust — that's what marriage was built upon. That's what they had promised, 'forsaking all other, be faithful unto each other'.

Had Billy been unfaithful to her? Perhaps she would never know. Billy was as loving as he had always been to her. He tried to ignore the change in her. Gradually, the frozen thing inside her started to melt. Perhaps she had been wrong. Perhaps it was nothing more than a drunken mistake.

Rosy had continued after the month's trial. On principle, Wilhelmina would not sack her. If she was doing her work properly, she would stay. Her continual presence was an open sore, but if she sacked her, Billy would always think she didn't trust him and she would never come to terms with the question in her mind.

Rosy's excuse for her late appearance on the morning after the game was that she had stayed up late to take them a drink, thinking Wilhelmina would want her to look after them and knowing men like hot toddies when it is cold at night. Then she had simply overslept. She was sorry and it wouldn't happen again.

Something had changed in her. She was less flamboyant and seemed to be doing all she could to please. She was quieter somehow.

One morning, when Billy was busy with the separator, Wilhelmina had occasion to seek him in the dairy. Jed was just pouring the next can of milk into the vat. 'Morning, Mrs Foster,' he said in reply to her greeting. He waited till she had consulted Billy, then spoke again. 'How's Rosy? Fit in all right?'

She looked at him. She'd never taken much notice of him before. How blue his eyes were! Very like Billy's, really, but there was a harder expression in them. 'Yes. She seems to be doing all right,' she answered. 'Have you known her long, Jed? She's not a relative, I understand.'

'No. Not long. Just came back from Morpeth with me.'

So there, she told herself. You are no wiser. She went back to the house and walked through into the kitchen. Rosy was sitting on the chair near the window, her face ashen. 'Are you all right, Rosy?' Wilhelmina cried, hurrying to her side. 'What's wrong?'

'I don't know, Mrs Foster.'

'I just saw Jed over at the dairy and he asked me how you were. I told him you were all right and here you are like this. What happened?'

Rosy brushed her hair back. 'Oh sorry, Mrs Foster. I shouldn't do that. I know I shouldn't.' She burst into tears. 'You won't throw me out, will you, Mrs Foster?' she begged.

'Good heavens, girl, I won't throw you out for that. Why should I?'

Rosy lifted woebegone eyes to her. 'Oh, Mrs Foster. I think I'm going to have a baby!'

38

Facing up to things

The words swept over Wilhelmina like an icy blast of water. Going to have a baby, going to have a baby, going to have a baby. They bounded off every wall in her brain and echoed and ricocheted round. Her legs felt they were going to give way under her and she thought she was going to faint. She sat down heavily. 'What are you saying, Rosy?' she gasped.

Between sobs that wrenched her body, Rosy repeated, 'I'm going to have a baby.'

'Are you sure?' Wilhelmina appealed.

The girl nodded. Would she ask? Dare she ask? 'Rosy, who is the father?'

The girl's tears increased.

'Rosy, who is the father?' she repeated.

Rosy rocked back and forth. 'Don't throw me out. Please don't throw me out. You're the nearest to a mother I have ever had. No-one's ever taught me like you have. Say you won't throw me out, Mrs Foster. I can learn to be a real lady if you don't throw me out.'

Wilhelmina spoke firmly. She had to know.

'Rosy. Who is the father of this baby?'

The tears quietened.

'Well?'

'Billy,' she whispered.

'You mean Mr Foster?'

She nodded.

The cold frozen thing was back in her chest. What a fool she had been to believe him! How easily he could twist her round his finger. She loved him and wanted to believe he was innocent of any unfaithfulness. She was so gullible. 'Are you telling me the truth, Rosy? Because this is a very serious accusation to make. I shall certainly ask Mr Foster. I find it very hard to believe. My husband is not a man to take his responsibilities lightly. He is married and has a family. We have been happily married a long time.'

'He came to my room the night he had the men here for a card game. I took them hot toddies. I told you that. Then in the middle of the night he came to my room.'

'Are you asking me to believe he molested you?'

'No, Mrs Foster. He wouldn't do that. He's a nice man. He wouldn't molest anyone.'

'What are you saying then?'

'Just he came to me, to my room.' Then she added, 'There's something I haven't told you.'

Wilhelmina gazed at the girl in horrible wonder. What else?

'I had a hot toddy, too, when I came back and it made my head all wavy.'

'And?'

'I went to sleep. When I woke up he was there, asleep with me. The moon was still shining. But when I woke up in the morning he was gone. He'd picked up his boots, too. I'd told him to take them off because you wouldn't like dirt on the bed.' She started to cry again. 'You won't throw me out will you, Mrs Foster?'

Calmly, with the calmness of extremity, Wilhelmina stood up. 'Come along, Rosy. I think you should lie down a while. I don't care if no-one gets dinner today.'

She led the girl to her room, saw her lie down, then came out and closed the door. Quietly tying on her hat, she went along to the school room.

Mrs Richardson looked up to welcome her. 'Meg, I'm going out for a while. Would you please all get yourselves something for lunch? Rosy is lying down.'

Miss Richardson's eyes were wide. Something was wrong with Mrs Foster. 'Yes, of course,' she said quietly.

Wilhelmina found Billy down by the creek, mending a fence. He looked up as she approached. 'What are you doing here?' he said in greeting.

'Please leave what you are doing and come down here with me,' she said unsmiling.

Something was wrong. What was the matter with Will? He thought everything was all right again.

She went ahead down into the creek and sat on a log. He followed, ill at ease. He sat down beside her. 'Have you been talking to Rosy lately?' she asked quietly.

'No — not particularly — only at the table — or something like that. Why?'

She looked directly at him. 'She has just told me she is going to have a baby.' She watched his reaction. Shock; incredulity.

He looked away. 'Did you ask her who the father is?'

'Yes.'

'And?'

'She says you are.'

He put his hands over his face, shaking his head.

'She says you went to her in her room and that you went to sleep there with her on her bed.'

How could she be so calm? Why didn't she rant and rave at him? That's what he wanted to do to himself. What a fool he was to get drunk. Will was right. He'd have to stay off the stuff altogether.

'I don't know, Will. I just don't know.' He put his hand out to touch her. She flinched away. She wanted to scream at him not to touch her, never to touch her again.

His hand fell to his side. 'I'm sorry, Will. So sorry. I can't remember anything about that night after Rosy brought the drinks. Jack was saying something about her. I can't remember what. I just remember he made me mad.'

He waved his arms and let them drop helplessly. 'I wouldn't do that, Will. Surely I wouldn't do that. You know I only love you.'

She turned away. 'Tell Rosy that — and tell the baby when it comes.' She walked away, along the creek.

The water gurgled over the stones, making a gay little bubbling sound. How pure it was, crystal clear. She could see the grains of sand between the stones, the tiny forms of life moving under and around them. The dragonfly displayed the beauty of his colours and flight over the surface of the water. There were no murky secrets here, no hidden skeletons to trap you with their putrefying knowledge.

Was Billy the father of Rosy's child? Who could say? It was her word only. Billy was incapable of remembering. She had seen Billy herself coming from the room. He had been carrying his boots because Rosy had made him take them off so he didn't get dirt on the bed. The absurdity brought the tears. They simply flowed down her cheeks unchecked.

A koala climbed slowly down the tree across the creek from where she sat on a rock. She watched it. A baby was on its back, its little arms clasping the fur on the mother's neck — poor, little, defenceless thing.

What of Rosy's baby when it came? How defenceless it would be. What would Rosy do? She certainly couldn't stay here now. But she couldn't be turned out, especially now in this condition. Where would she go? Who would take her?

But the baby? If it was Billy's child, then he had a responsibility to it — and since she was his wife, she would have to make him see that. But how? How to fulfil that responsibility?

The tears flowed again. She thought of her own children, the four older ones and little Arthur. He wasn't so little now. He was a robust child. They all loved their father.

What of this one? If it was his child, wasn't it entitled to know and return the love of a father? She sat there, still. The turmoil within her was soothed by the creek and the creatures. The wind whispered comforting sighs in the leaves above her.

At last she stood up, capturing one last look at the bubbling, chattering water. A memory rose from somewhere in her mind, a memory of Allynbrook church and the voice of the minister: 'Have you ever done anything wrong?'

There had been convicts standing at the back of the church and she had thought, 'Silly man, of course they've done something wrong. Otherwise these people would not be standing there. They would be home in England.'

Then she had realised the question was for her, too. And they'd all prayed, 'Forgive us our trespasses as we forgive them that trespass against us.'

'Oh God,' she wept. 'I don't know if I can forgive Billy. I love him, but I feel so hurt, so besmirched by what he's done. I don't want him to touch me. Yet I long for him, for his arms around me, for the special look in his eyes, just for me.

'Help me to forgive him, Lord. As you forgave your murderers. I'll try, but I don't think I can do it just yet. And I don't think I can do it on my own.'

She stood a while longer. Then she made her way slowly home.

★   ★   ★

Rosy was in the kitchen cooking tea. Bridget and Sarah were setting the table. They looked up when Wilhelmina came in. 'Are you feeling better now, Rosy?' she asked quietly.

Rosy lowered her eyes. 'Yes, thankyou, Mrs Foster.' Then she lifted her eyes and looked at Wilhelmina. 'And Mrs Foster, thanks for not throwing me out.'

She found Billy with the children — Arthur climbing over him, playing with him and the girls pretending to curl his hair. She passed the room and hung up her hat and went to straighten her hair.

She spoke to the woman who looked at her from the mirror. 'You're a far cry from the concert pianist who would have no time for husband or family,' she told her, 'the great artist who would belong to her public, body and soul. As far as understanding life, you were just a babe in arms when the grand duchess told you those things.'

There was no chance for a private talk with Billy until it was bed time. The children were in bed and the house had quietened down. 'There are some things we must talk about,' she said quietly.

'I suppose so. But it's a bit late for talk,' he responded glumly.

'Perhaps in some respects. But in others it makes it essential.'

He looked up quickly. What was Will getting at now? 'If this baby is yours, you have a responsibility to it,' she said.

'What do you mean?' he asked quickly.

'I saw you and the children when I came in. They were playing with you, the boys talking to you. That's how a father should be with his children. If this baby is yours, then it has a right to that sort of thing, too.'

'For goodness sake, Will, how can that be?' he burst out. 'Don't be ridiculous.'

'I'm not being ridiculous. I'm facing up to things — and that's what you've got to do. That baby has as much right to you as a father as any of our children. It's not its fault that you couldn't control yourself. It will be your seed, the same as my children are. Since I am your wife, it is my responsibility, too. We are 'one flesh', remember?'

He winced.

'You must support me in the plan I propose to follow.'

'You have a plan? For what?' Billy jerked upright.

'For what we must do to fulfil our responsibility to your child. I want your wholehearted, undivided support and agreement.'

39

An extraordinary woman

They sat on in the half light of the verandah. Billy objected heatedly to Wilhelmina's plans. They were totally impractical and unthinkable.

Wilhelmina was adamant. The child was his. He must take responsibility for his actions. She would talk to Rosy in the morning and then, depending on whether or not her assessment was correct, she would go to visit her mother. Then, if all went according to plan, she would go to Etty in Sydney, taking Rosy with her.

'In the meantime,' she said, avoiding Billy's eyes, 'I would be obliged if you would sleep in the dressing room.' Billy put out his hand and started to speak, but she went past him and into the bedroom.

Rosy was very subdued when Wilhelmina came to her in the kitchen. Everyone else was busy in different parts of the house. 'Mrs Foster, can I talk to you?' she asked.

'What did you want to talk about, Rosy?'

'Mrs Foster, I don't want a baby!' She

burst into tears. 'I don't want a baby. I'm only young and I want to have some fun, travel around. I can't do that with a baby.'

'Don't you think you will love your baby?' Wilhelmina asked, remembering her own feelings for her babies.

'I just don't want it!' Rosy wailed.

So it was as she had thought. She was not in the least surprised. 'Are you quite sure about this, Rosy?'

'Yes, oh yes, Mrs Foster. I've been thinking awful thoughts, but I don't want to hurt the poor little thing.'

'I should hope not, Rosy.' She stood considering, trying to weigh up the girl, her emotions, her possible reactions. 'There is something I could arrange for you until the baby is born, I think — and then for the baby, so it will be cared for. But I have to speak to someone first. You are quite sure you do not want to keep the baby?'

'Yes. Yes. Really sure.'

★　★　★

Wilhelmina rode over the mountain to see her mother. It would not be the happy visit she would like, but she must have someone with whom to talk over the plan she had devised.

They sat long over a cup of tea. 'This is

Billy's child, Mama. I am his wife. I feel responsible for the welfare of that child.'

'I think you are being exceptionally brave, my darling. But if you think you can do it . . . then I support you wholeheartedly,' Sophia replied.

'Then I will write to Etty and see if she agrees. Do you think she will?'

'I feel sure she will. I think she will feel as I do that you are suggesting an extraordinary thing. But as I say, if you think you can do it, then go ahead. We will do our best to aid you in every way.' She kissed her daughter goodbye and put her hand on her knee as she sat on her horse preparatory to heading for home. 'You are an extraordinary woman, Wilhelmina. Papa would be proud of you.'

★ ★ ★

All was quiet when she reached home. Things had gone smoothly. With Miss Richardson, Molly and Sarah to look after things, they could do without her for a while. Drawing out paper and pen at her secretaire, she wrote the letter, signed it and sealed the envelope. Eddy could post it in the morning when he took the cream to the factory.

Now was the time of waiting. What would Etty think? Would she agree? The days went slowly. Life flowed on around her, almost as though nothing had happened. The children had their lessons. The boys did their chores, Eddy now working with his father all the time. Polly and Sarah laughed and talked or squabbled over their work as the mood took them.

Rosy was much more subdued than she was when she first entered the house.

At last, the looked-for letter arrived. She tore it open with trembling fingers:

My Dear Wilhelmina,
You are quite, quite wonderful, my little sister. Yes, most certainly I will aid you with all in my power in your plan. Just make quite sure in your heart, my dear, that you can do this thing you suggest, that the child will not suffer or be made to feel different in any way. If you can do this, if your plan is successful, then this will be a most fortunate child.

There was more in the same vein. She folded it and slipped it back in the envelope and put it in her pocket.

Now to find Rosy. The sound of chopping vegetables on the board guided her to Rosy's whereabouts. 'Rosy, sit down a minute. I want to speak to you.'

The girl looked around, apprehensive. She sat down, her attention riveted on Wilhelmina.

'Rosy, you are still sure you do not want to keep your baby?'

'Yes, oh yes, Mrs Foster.' The girl's eyes were pleading.

'Then I can make arrangements for you. Since you tell me this child is Mr Foster's child . . . ' She looked searchingly into Rosy's eyes. 'That is the truth?'

Rosy nodded. 'Then he has a responsibility to the child. I feel, as his wife, I too have a responsibility to the baby.' Her voice impressive, she continued. 'We will take the baby into our family and bring it up as our child, my child. I will be its mother.'

Rosy's eyes had opened wide, a look of astonishment on her face. 'Oh, Mrs Foster,' she breathed.

'There is one stipulation. I said I will be its mother and that is what I intend. The baby must never know, never guess anything different. I will be in every way, except the physical fact, its mother.' Her expression was commanding. 'The child must never know that I was not its physical mother. Do you understand?'

'Yes, Mrs Foster. But how can you do that? The children will know — the neighbours

— everybody will see me — and you — and know who had the baby.'

Wilhelmina shook her head. 'No, Rosy. The family can quite easily do without me for two or three months. I have written to my sister in Sydney. I have received a reply. Here is what we will do.

'I will take an extended holiday with my sister, ostensibly to seek medical attention. I am getting old for having babies. I shall take you with me. We will stay with my sister until the baby is born and you are on your feet. Then Etty will find work for you with one of her acquaintances in Sydney. That should get you under way to the life you say you want.

'I will bring the baby home — to its home. It will have to be bottle-fed, as I can't produce milk. But that will be part of my problem with this birth, as far as everyone else is concerned.'

Rosy had been listening with growing wonder. Now the tears trickled down her cheeks.

'Do you agree with all that, Rosy?' Wilhelmina asked.

'Yes. Oh yes, Mrs Foster. Thankyou. Thankyou.'

'I must impress on you, though, that you never tell anyone of this. The baby will be our child, my child. It must never know the facts

386

of its birth. Do you agree completely? No reservations?'

'Yes, Mrs Foster. Thankyou. I don't want a baby. Oh, how can I say thankyou enough?'

'Just keep our agreement, Rosy. That will be thanks enough as things stand.'

★   ★   ★

The baby was born, a beautiful little girl. 'Oh, look at her Wilhelmina,' Etty cried. 'Isn't she beautiful?'

Wilhelmina gazed at the tiny form. She was small, but quite rounded out, her little arms and legs curled. A soft fuzz of deep auburn hair covered her head, the little features clearly defined.

She was a beautiful baby. A great pang rent Wilhelmina's heart: Billy's child. 'Please God she will be my child, too. I shall love and care for her. I will make her my own. She will know love, the love of a family.'

'Is it all right, Mrs Foster?' Rosy lifted her head. 'You still want her?'

'Yes, Rosy, I still want her. She is a beautiful baby. Mrs Jones, Mr Foster, my mother and you and I will be the only people who will ever know she came to be my daughter in this way.'

Rosy closed her eyes.

The doctor had gone as soon as the birth was accomplished. He was busy, had many patients. The practice was growing daily.

Henrietta and Wilhelmina completed the cleaning up of Rosy and the baby. Henrietta sponged Rosy and sprinkled her own powder on the girl's skin. 'Oh, that's lovely,' Rosy sighed. 'You and Mrs Foster have been so good to me.' She was silent a minute. 'I don't deserve it an' all,' she added.

'My sister feels a responsibility for her husband's actions,' Henrietta said, continuing her sponging. 'He is the father, isn't he?'

Rosy was silent. Henrietta's hands stopped. She looked up. 'Yes, I think so,' Rosy said. Then, seeing Henrietta's expression said hurriedly, 'Yes. Yes, he is the father.'

'You are sure?' Henrietta's expression showed her consternation.

'Oh yes. I'm quite sure.' Then she added, 'It was the night of the card game it happened. That's when it was. I had a hot toddy, too. Otherwise it wouldn't have happened. I shouldn't have had it. But it did warm me up. Mr Foster is such a nice man. I liked him right from the start. He's so nice and friendly.'

'Yes, well never mind. You made me wonder for a minute whether you really are sure about this. Or whether there was someone else you had been involved with.'

Rosy was silent, enjoying the attention.

Wilhelmina bathed the baby, feeling the smooth, slippery little body under her hands. Was there ever anything like a new-born baby ... the wonder of it? So vulnerable, so helpless, it drew on your heart strings.

She dressed her and wrapped her firmly in a little rug. The fine hair covering her head now showed definite signs of being the same colour as her mother's in time. The little eyes opened. Oh Billy! They were still the slaty blue of the new-born, but there was a distinct impression of the blue of Billy's eyes. 'You will know your father, little one,' she whispered to the baby, cuddling her close. 'You will be loved.'

Rosy was soon on her feet and chafing to be off.

Henrietta had secured a position for her and, since she was so insistent, she was allowed to leave before Henrietta and Wilhelmina thought it wise. 'I'm all right. Now I just have me to look after I'll be all right,' she insisted.

She left them one bright morning and, after again thanking them profusely, she walked away, down the road, the sun glinting on her flaming hair.

Wilhelmina watched her go. 'I hope she

really can look after herself and doesn't let this sort of thing happen again,' she said to Etty standing beside her.

Etty turned away. 'Well, that is not your responsibility.' She looked back at her sister. 'You certainly have nothing to thank her for.'

Wilhelmina was silent. She looked at the baby in her cradle.

Who knows, she thought, who knows.

40

The little cuckoo

The baby was baptised Rebecca Sophia. 'After her grandmother,' Wilhelmina explained.

'But where does she get her hair from, Wilhelmina? Neither you nor Billy has red hair.'

'Oh, I dare say it is a throwback to some of our ancestors. I believe there were some on Billy's side who had red hair.'

Eliza and Etty played with her and fussed over her. The little, bright blue eyes soon sparkled and came to look for her brothers and sisters when she heard their voices.

'Fancy you not being able to feed this baby, Wilhelmina,' one of the up valley women said one day when they were all gathered round talking after church. 'You always had so much milk — and no problems before.'

'I must just be getting old for having babies,' she laughed. 'Arthur was quite a while after the others. Then this little one.'

Billy was very quiet, very reserved, but gradually, as he watched Wilhelmina, he relaxed and, before many months, he had succumbed to the baby's charms. He came in as Wilhelmina was bathing Rebecca in the nursery. 'This little darling of ours will soon be too big for this baby bath,' she said happily to him.

He looked at her quickly. 'Ours' she had said. She caught his expression and smiled. 'You know, for a moment I really forgot.' She wrapped the squirming baby in the towel and cuddled her close. 'She really is ours, anyway.'

Billy stood watching as she dried and dressed Rebecca. As he turned to leave the room she said softly, 'By the way, my bed is cold on my own. It would be nice if I had company to keep me warm.'

★   ★   ★

Rebecca, or Beccy as they called her, was the delight, the toy for the whole family. Each new achievement — when she could feed herself, her first words, first steps — was hailed as a wonder of wonders. It was soon obvious that, though she loved her father and sisters and brothers, she adored her mother.

Wilhelmina's praise filled her with glowing delight and her look of disapproval reduced her to tears. She followed her mother, trotting along at her heels, trying to do everything she was doing. 'Don't get under my feet, Beccy. I'll step on you,' Wilhelmina said frequently, whereupon little arms would be flung around her legs and the little face, looking up at her adoringly, would utter the words, 'Loves you.'

★　★　★

'You're very quiet,' Wilhelmina said as she and Billy lay in bed. 'A penny for your thoughts.'

He laughed. 'There's a place for sale over on the Allyn,' he said. 'Not far from 'Llanfylhn', actually. I was thinking about it.'

'Are you thinking of buying it?'

'Mmm. The boys are growing up, you know. Won't be long before they will be wanting to get out on their own, have a place of their own. Be good to give them a start. Then it would be up to them.'

'Yes, it would. But you got your own land. When we bought this place, you worked for it and did it yourself,' she reminded him.

'I know. But things here were just starting off then. There were opportunities. Land is so much dearer now and things are changing.'

She considered a moment. 'Do whatever you think,' she said. 'You've got judgment in these things. Why don't you go and have a look at it if you're interested? Then you'd know what you have to consider. Do you think we can do it if you think it's a good buy?'

'Get you to go over the bank statements with me tomorrow,' he said happily.

The moonlight filtered in through the lace curtains, the shadows dancing on the wall and the counterpane. Thank God she had done what she did. God's love, she mused — no-one was outside it. He had brought her to Billy. He had strengthened her in this turmoil in their lives. There was still a lingering ache at times, but she and Billy were back on their old footing — better, perhaps. It was a long while since the last bout with rum.

Her little girl, little Beccy, was a joy who had brought so much love with her. She had dropped into their lives. Rosy had been part of their lives for such a short time, really — and this little one had come into the family, like a cuckoo laying its egg in another bird's nest, she thought; just like a cuckoo.

She thought on the simile: her little cuckoo child. She smiled. That was it: her cuckoo child.

One day, Wilhelmina heard a soft thud as she entered the office. What was that? It seemed to come from the sitting room. She went to investigate. Rebecca was removing the red felt she kept over the ivory keys when the piano was not in use. She had laid it on the floor and was very carefully folding it.

'What are you doing, Beccy?' she asked.

The child looked up. 'Opened the piano,' she said proudly.

'Why did you open the piano?' Wilhelmina asked.

Rebecca looked at her in surprise. 'So I can play it,' she replied simply. How foolish you are, Mother. It is obvious that you have to open the piano if you want to play it.

'Do you want Mother to play?' she asked.

'No. Not now,' the child replied, striving to climb up onto the stool. 'I want to play.' She turned a smiling, confident face to her mother. Wilhelmina helped her seat herself. She looked at her feet hanging a foot above the pedals. 'Can't reach the pedals!' she cried in horror. 'Can't reach the pedals, Mother.' Her eyes filled with tears.

'Never mind. Your legs will grow,' Wilhelmina comforted. 'You can play without pedals till they are long enough.'

Reassured, the child turned her attention back to the keys. She pressed one carefully. Ping, went the note. She looked up in delight to her mother. She sounded another note, then note after note, black and white, but always listening after each one, sometimes playing one note several times.

A tentative surge of hope crept through Wilhelmina. This child, this cuckoo child of hers had an ear, an ear for music! It was there! Oh, she could see it in the expression on the little face.

This was not just a passing thing. You could see — the way she pressed a key and listened to the note and hit it a different way and listened again. Oh, if she savoured sound like this . . . If she really wanted to learn to make the most beautiful music the instrument was capable of . . .

'Would you like to sit there a little while and listen to the sounds you can make?' she asked.

The serious blue eyes looked up at her. She nodded.

'Call Mother when you want to get down so I can help you and you don't fall. Your legs aren't long enough to get down on your own, are they?'

★ ★ ★

Billy bought the property near 'Llanfylhn'. It was good, he said and, with hard work, could be better.

The boys were sent to repair the fences and other work needing to be done immediately. They camped there, working together and bringing things up to Billy's expected standards.

When autumn came, the corn was harvested and loaded on the dray and stored in one of the sheds. Now, in the evenings, the family gathered in the kitchen to help shell the corn needed for grinding and fowl feed.

Rebecca played around, going from one to another. 'Come on, Beccy,' Eddy said. 'Come and sit down beside me here and help me shell the corn.'

Beccy looked at the hard grains of corn as they fell from the cob he was shelling. Then she looked at her hands and put them behind her back. She shook her head.

'What's wrong?' he asked. 'Don't you want to help me?'

'No,' she replied. 'It would hurt my fingers. Then I wouldn't be able to play the piano like Mother.'

It was time for her to start learning, Wilhelmina decided. She was very young, but with such interest and enthusiasm! She wanted to encourage this to the greatest advantage. She waited till Beccy again opened the piano and climbed up on the stool. She had brought a footstool across and could now manage to get up herself.

Wilhelmina came in quietly and drew a chair up alongside the stool. 'Curl your fingers like this,' she said, demonstrating.

The little fingers curled and Beccy tried to

press the key. 'Can't do it like that, Mother,' she complained.

Wilhelmina persevered gently. 'Play on your tips like tip-toeing,' she'd say.

Soon, Wilhelmina found music for first melodies the other children had used. Beccy could read now. Miss Richardson, still part of their household, was delighted with her progress. 'This little one is like you, Wilhelmina. She has a real ability and interest in her school work. She's a teacher's delight. It is not work for her. She soaks it all up like a sponge!'

Wilhelmina smiled. Her little cuckoo child.

★ ★ ★

There was a fever of excitement throughout the house, throughout the valley. Wilhelmina had been baking all the day before. The girls had been ironing and putting the last touches to new dresses. Edward and Oliver had polished their saddles and bridles till they shone — it was a pity to use them to ride up the dusty roads. The phaeton had been cleaned inside and out.

It was the occasion of the valley sports.

People from all parts of the valley would be present. There would be foot races and horse races; novelty events galore; and broom-throwing for the ladies: a fun day for everyone. And not to miss an opportunity to raise funds and exchange the products of the valley kitchens to profitable ends, there would be a stall to raise funds for the church they were hoping to build before long.

The morning dawned bright and clear, with a slight breeze — a perfect day for the sports.

The big picnic hamper was packed with roast poultry, a large rooster from their own flock. There was homecured boiled bacon, cold salad, peach pies and apple pies and whipped cream, packed in glass and wrapped in wet paper to keep cool. There were cakes and home-made ginger beer.

'Now for the cakes for the stall, Lizzy,' Wilhelmina called. 'Bring me that big box from the pantry. Put a tablecloth in the bottom, then we'll wrap it right around and close the box so they don't dry out.'

There were sponges and chocolate cake, fruit cake and coffee cake and dainty little cream tarts and butterfly cakes.

'You've got enough for a stall of your own, Mother,' Etty declared.

'I was brought up in a German household renowned for its baking,' Wilhelmina declared. 'I can't let that reputation down.'

They set off, the boys riding and Billy and the female members of the household in the phaeton. The colourful parasols of the girls made a bright spectacle as they travelled along. Beccy also had her own parasol of which she was inordinately proud. There was great hubbub and excitement at the gate. People were congregating from everywhere. Vehicles were lined up and horses wheeling around, being exercised.

They made their way to the stall which had been set up in the shade of a large tree. The big box was handed down and Wilhelmina proceeded to unpack her offerings, while Billy took the phaeton to find a cool spot to leave it for lunch.

'Is that one of your sponges, Wilhelmina?' a woman asked, pointing.

'Yes, that is mine,' Wilhelmina replied.

'Well, I'll have that. I know your cooking.'

'Is Mrs Foster a good cook?' another newcomer to the valley asked.

'Just the best in the valley. No lady can come anywhere near her,' replied the first woman. 'You should just taste her blackforest cake.' She rolled her eyes and they all laughed.

The shouts and cries from the race track told them the races had started. Arthur came running to greet his mother as she made her way to the track. 'Look, Mother, I won my race!'

The egg and spoon race was followed by the apple and barrel race. It was great fun.

After lunch, the stock horses lined up for their race, their proud owners holding them back, the horses excitedly pulling at the bit. There was Eddy's horse and Oliver's horse, Tony Goodman's and Joseph Nolan's and a line-up of others waiting.

But the favourite for the big race was Prince Charming, a big, grey horse belonging to Jack Peterson. 'He's the only one in the race,' Jack boasted. 'Nothing here can come anywhere near him. He's a beauty. He's good around the stock, too. And knowing! All I have to do is call him and he comes. He always knows just what I want him to do.' He smiled, self-satisfied. 'Out on his own.'

Some of the listeners exchanged glances.

They were off! They thundered around the first lap. A big bay was out in front. He was pulling away. The field was pretty well bunched up. Around they came again. Edward was leaning far out over his horse's head, urging him along. Oliver's was tiring and dropping back. The crowd was wild with excitement, all on tip-toe. The third lap. Now they were coming up the straight. And here comes the big grey, his long legs striding out. He's passed most of the others. There were just Edward's piebald and Prince Charming in the race now. It's neck and neck. He's passed the piebald. He's over the line. Jack Petersen's Prince Charming wins the Valley Cup.

'Told you there was nothing could touch him,' Jack gloated. 'The best horse in the district.' He went to collect his winnings.

Rebecca waited at the stall, her money hot in her hand. 'A toffee apple, please,' she asked, passing over her money.

'That's the bastard child. That hair doesn't belong in that family, I tell you. It's just like the hair on that girl they had working there a while — just the same. Couldn't mistake it. She disappeared, you know. Nobody knows where she went. But the child's got her father's eyes.'

Rebecca took her toffee apple and turned to see the two women's eyes upon her. They turned away when they saw her looking at them. What were they talking about? They were looking at her. Were they talking about her hair? She went thoughtfully down to her mother.

Wilhelmina glanced to see she had her apple, then turned her attention back to the fun and laughter of the broom-throwing. Rebecca sucked her apple quietly for a while. Then she said in her piping little voice, patting Wilhelmina's arm for attention, 'Mama, what is a bastard child? Is it good or bad?'

41

Prince Charming

Wilhelmina almost dropped her parasol in shock. 'What did you say, Beccy?' Wherever had the child heard such a word?

'Mama, what is a bastard child? Is it good or bad?'

Wilhelmina pushed her way through the people gathered along the track. Taking Beccy's hand, she walked quickly to the phaeton. On the pretext of needing a drink, she pulled the hamper open to cover her confusion.

'Please Mama, what is it?' Beccy persisted.

'Wherever did you hear such a word?' Wilhelmina demanded.

'I was at the stall getting my apple and there were two ladies standing across under the tree. One of them said, 'That's the bastard child.' And when I turned around, they were looking at me. I think they were talking about me. I think they were talking about my hair. Is bastard good or bad? Am I that?'

What, oh what could she say? Who had said

this? Bright little Beccy with her active mind had sensed they were talking about her. But who? What did they know? Or guess? But what was she going to say to Beccy?

She took the child's hand in hers. 'I don't want you to use that word, my darling,' she said. 'It's not a very nice word. And ladies like you and I, and Lizzy and Etty and Grandma, none of us use that word,' she said seriously.

'Is it a swearword?' Beccy asked.

'In a way, yes.'

'But what does it mean? You know like you say not to say,' she bent forward and whispered 'bloody' in her mother's ear, her hand cupped around her mouth. Then stepping back continued normally, 'because it's a swearword and people don't mean there is blood everywhere, which is what it really means. Is it like that?'

'Something like that.'

'Yes, well what does it really mean?' She looked at Wilhelmina with questioning eyes.

'It means, my darling, someone who has a mother and father who aren't properly married. And that's not you, is it? Because you have Papa and me. So they couldn't have been talking about you, could they?'

Beccy smiled. 'Oh! I see. They must have just looked at me as I turned around.' She took a few licks at her apple. 'But I did think they were talking about my hair,' she said with a little frown.

★　★　★

There was consternation the length and breadth of the valley. Jack Petersen's horse Prince Charming was missing — disappeared. Jack had put him in the stable one night and next morning he was gone. But it was not only him. Jack's new saddle and bridle were gone, too. Jack had paid a lot of money for that saddle. He was a bit of a show-off; you know — real skite, too.

That horse of his! He was forever skiting about him. And, of course, him winning the Valley Cup at the race day hadn't made him any better. He'd make you sick the way he went on. In a way, it served him right. But then, a man didn't know whose horse might disappear next.

It had been reported to the police and they were coming. They'd be here next day to comb the district. 'It sounds like Thunderbolt to me,' Billy confided to Wilhelmina. 'The sort of thing he would do. Jack's always so loudmouthed about that horse. I don't know if it is really as good as he reckons. Don't know what it's like on the steep parts. If it doesn't come up to expectations, if Thunderbolt has taken it, it will be back in a week or so. Mark my words.'

He was thoughtful a few minutes. 'He may be a bushranger, but he's not a real criminal, you know. All circumstantial evidence against him. He does a lot of good to some of the real battlers. Money just appears — no name, no note — just a bag of money. No-one knows where it comes from. He never takes from people who can't afford it. And he never harms a woman.'

'In a way you admire him, don't you?' Wilhelmina asked.

He nodded. 'Wouldn't like to see the police catch up with him. Be some sad people if that happened.' He looked across the paddocks. 'Think I need to go round the stock in that lease paddock up on the Tops,' he said, standing up. 'Could you get a week's food packed up for me pretty quickly? I'll be heading off as soon as I've got a few things together.'

She put her sewing aside and went to pack the food. A week's supply, Billy had said. He must think he knew where Thunderbolt would be — or where his camp was. Looking over the stock would be an excuse if he happened to come across the police and the supply of food could be for an extended stay on the Tops.

She gathered the food and, tying it in a calico bag, carried it out to him. He had his roll ready, strapped behind the saddle. He kissed her goodbye and was gone.

The police were earlier than expected. Billy had not been gone more than two hours when they arrived. They came in and asked questions and looked all around. 'Sorry to bother you, Mrs Foster, but we have to search everywhere.' They were gone.

She had tried to delay them with a cup of tea, talking, but they hadn't stayed long. It was like a bloodhound on the trail, she thought.

The boys were surprised when they got home to find their father gone. 'That was a sudden decision,' Oliver said after they'd been told. 'Awfully sudden. He didn't say a word about it this morning. Did you hear about Jack Petersen's horse?'

'Bert Goodwin told us as we came past his place,' Edward added. 'Bert says, serves old Jack right. He's such a blather skite!' They laughed.

'Wonder who pinched it?' Oliver said.

'Horse, saddle and bridle.'

Wilhelmina looked at her boys. They were young men now. 'Your father thinks it was most likely Thunderbolt,' she said quietly.

They both looked at her surprised, then

dawning understanding moved across their faces. 'Y-e-s,' Edward muttered softly. He looked at his mother with a twinkle in his eye. 'And that may have influenced Father's decision to go up to the Tops and go around the stock up there. I hope he took enough food with him to see him for a few days. He might find he needs some food.'

'Oh yes. He took a good bag full. Have to look after the stock.' She smiled at them as she left the room.

Billy was back the next day. He met the police on the way back. They had lost the tracks, though. There were several tracks on the ground up the trail now. It almost looked as though the same horse had been up and down that narrow part several times. Anyway, it wasn't much use to go further. They'd been up and lost all the tracks where a mob of cattle had been driven.

Pity they couldn't get Jack's horse back for him, though. This lawlessness had to stop. There'd be heavier penalties introduced. People had to realise they couldn't do just as they liked.

Billy reported all the activity to Wilhelmina. 'And did you eat all the food I packed?' she asked.

'I left it for the wallabies,' he replied, grinning. 'Nice safe place where they'll know where to find it. They'd been around a little while before. There'd been a fire there. The ashes were still warm.'

Two weeks passed, then another breeze of excitement swept the valley, this time followed in most cases by laughter. Jack Petersen's horse had materialised back in his stable, none the worse for wear, with the saddle and bridle intact. A note was tied to the stirrup:

He's good, Jack.
But not as good as I thought.
Your estimation of him is a bit high.
He loses out once he gets into the mountains.
He's more use to you than me.
                    T.

P.S. Thanks for the loan of him.

'Jack will be livid!' Billy laughed when he heard it from the hired man. 'He'll be the laughing-stock of the valley.'

★   ★   ★

They were grown up now, Wilhelmina thought, all except Arthur and Rebecca. For that matter, Arthur was grown up, too.

Edward and Oliver had taken over the Allyn place and were working it on their own. Billy went over every so often, but they were capable young men.

Arthur was the only one now to help Billy here. He hired men when he needed extra help. And there is Rebecca, my little cuckoo child, she thought, who will soon be as old as I was when I played for Mr Chopin. She had taught Rebecca; trained her, coached her with untiring patience. And the girl had responded, eager to excel. She played for hours each day, the practice, like hers, no burden, no chore, but a means of achieving the excellence she craved. To listen to her was the delight of Wilhelmina's heart — to hear that crystal clear note through the house! She marvelled and thrilled at the persistence of the girl.

I'm too close to her, too involved emotionally. I have been away from the concert hall and its demands too long. She needs someone independent, someone who can judge her performance impartially. She needs the final polish that I cannot give her now.

Who was there she could consult? Who to judge the quality of Rebecca's performance? Who to put the final touches so that the jewel could shine in brilliance? She opened her secretaire and took out paper and pen.

'My dear Etty,' she began.

42

Etty's letter

Three weeks passed before the reply came from Etty. Wilhelmina took it to her room and sat down in the chair by the window. Several newspaper clippings fell from the envelope as she took out the folded sheet.

Etty's neat hand began:

My Dear Wilhelmina,
I am sorry to have been so long in answering your letter. I have been combing Sydney and I have been attending performances. I talked to musicians far and wide. It seems to be the general consensus that the most appropriate teacher to give the finish to Rebecca's music is Mr Heinrich Grosinover. He is, I understand, a great teacher and is also an eminent performer. He has groomed many of the principal pianists in Australia today.

I suggest you bring Beccy down here to me. I shall look after her. She can then not only receive the finishing you say is necessary, but also gain experience in performing. I am told this is a very important part of a concert musician's development, not only in technique and presentation, but in personal confidence and stage presence.

After a year or two, she should be ready for her full debut into a concert hall career. This is, of course, if your estimate is endorsed by Mr Grosinover.

She went on to write of Alister and the social life of Sydney.

Wilhelmina scanned through the clippings. They were mostly reviews by the critics of various performances of Mr Grosinover: 'a masterly musician', 'he goes to the soul of the music' and so on.

Wilhelmina folded them and replaced them in the envelope. Beccy to go to Sydney for two years' training and preliminary experience! She would be leaving home when she went to Sydney. It was most unlikely she would ever return to live here. It would really be saying 'goodbye' to her, her little cuckoo baby.

This would have been how Mama and Papa had felt when she told them of the grand duchess' offer of patronage. But then, there were the other factors. I wonder what would have happened had there not been the problems, the dangers that Papa anticipated, she thought.

But back to the present and to Beccy. There was no such reason to restrict her. Etty would look after her. She would have her opportunity. If Mr Grosinover did not think she had the potential, there was no harm done. But he would not so think, she was sure of that. She must tell Beccy and decide when they could go.

As she went in search of Rebecca, footsteps sounded on the verandah. 'Anyone home?' a man's voice called. She hurried to the door. Jed Raby stood there with his hat in his hand. 'Billy home, Mrs Foster?' he asked.

'He will be shortly,' she replied.

'I'd like to have a word with him,' Jed said.

'Certainly. He won't be long. We are just going to have a cup of tea. Will you join us?'

He followed her to the kitchen, where Beccy was making the tea.

Whatever did Jed want to see Billy about? She hadn't seen him for years. Billy had long gone out of the separating business with the milk. Most of the valley folk still in dairying had bought their own hand separators and there was a factory quite close now. What could he want?

He sat down at the table and Wilhelmina passed the cake. He took a piece and bit into it. Beccy put down a cup of tea beside him and passed the sugar.

He watched her as she moved around the table, an odd expression on his face. 'Pretty hair, hasn't she?' he said. 'Really catches your eye.' He paused as though considering something. 'Know who her hair reminds me of? That girl I brought up from Morpeth years ago, Rosy. Remember? Hair just like hers — just like it.' He sipped his tea.

Wilhelmina held her breath. She couldn't think of a word to say.

Beccy sat down beside him. 'Fancy anyone having hair like mine,' she said. 'I hate it. I get called 'Carrots'. I wish my hair was dark like Mother's.'

Wilhelmina let her breath out slowly. 'Beccy, I think I can hear Father coming. Get another cup, please.'

As she spoke, Beccy and Jed both looked at her directly.

Again she caught her breath. Side by side like that, the colour of their eyes was identical. The similarity of the eyes was uncanny — the same colour, the same shape, with the little tilt at the corners.

Beccy jumped up and poured her father a cup of tea.

'Billy, Jed has come to have a word with you. Have a cup of tea, then you can get on with your business. Beccy and I have things to do, too.'

Billy sat down. Wilhelmina felt quite shaken. What did it all matter now? Rebecca was hers, her dear daughter.

Billy looked across the table at her. 'You got your letter, I believe. I met the mailman and he said he'd left one for you from Sydney.'

She glanced up and met Billy's gaze. What was wrong with her this morning?

Billy's eyes and Jed's were so alike — but Billy's had a gentler expression. His whole face was different. Jed had a closed look. He lived on his own and was not used to smiling. She sighed. She and Becky left the men to their discussion.

With the news, Beccy was beside herself with excitement: dear Aunt Etty to say she could stay with her — and for doing all this arranging!

It was decided they should travel to Morpeth and catch the steamer to Sydney the next week. It would not leave much time for preparation, but they had prepared clothes in anticipation, believing Etty would be able to arrange things satisfactorily.

★ ★ ★

415

The journey was accomplished with a modicum of discomfort. Etty's welcome was profuse. It would be such a thrill for her to help set Rebecca on her career. Now for the audition with Mr Grosinover.

Wilhelmina's mind was filled with the memory of the day she had seen Mr Chopin alight from his carriage and enter the palace at Heidelberg, his slight figure wrapped in a greatcoat. She fancied she could feel the cold of the Baden winter — the snowflakes falling against the window and settling on his hat and greatcoat, the moment when the grand duchess had sent for her, of Mama's concern, of her secret exhilaration.

★　★　★

Rebecca buttoned her coat. She would go alone, she said. She was so excited that she needed a short while alone. The journey in Aunt Etty's coach would give her that. Brampton the driver knew the address and would wait for her to bring her home again.

'Just remember all you have been taught, my darling,' Wilhelmina said. 'Mr Grosinover is looking for your potential. He does not expect the performance of a concert pianist yet. He is assessing your ability, your potential, in order to decide if he is willing to accept you as a pupil.' She kissed Rebecca. 'I have no doubt he will be pleased with you.'

Rebecca ran down the steps and entered the coach. Brampton flipped the reins and she was on her way. They listened to the clip-clop of the horse's hooves as she was borne away.

43

Preparation

The time of waiting was unbearable. Time and time again, she went to the window, but no coach appeared. What would be happening now? What would Mr Grosinover ask Rebecca to play? What was he like? Would he set her at ease?

But why was she worrying like this? Surely she was more nervous for Rebecca than she herself had been all those years ago. Rebecca was just as confident as she had been. She also lost awareness of anything else when her fingers touched the keys.

How could it be that this great affinity existed between them, this affinity of soul, of perception, of love of the excellence in performance? None of her blood flowed in Rebecca's veins, yet she was closer to this child than to any of the other children. They were not children now, she thought. I am getting old.

But Beccy, her dear cuckoo baby — even yet, through this dear child, she may realise some of her dream. It would not all be lost. All that talent, gift, perseverance — not all for nothing, not wasted, if Beccy succeeded through her.

At last, they heard the carriage approaching. She flung the front door open as Beccy ran up the steps and threw her arms around her. 'Oh Mama, he liked my playing! He liked it!' She was crying and laughing at the same time, hugging her mother and Aunty Etty. 'He said he would be delighted to take me as a student,' Beccy told them. 'He believes I have great potential.'

Wilhelmina wept. She could see Mr Chopin walking slowly across the room, standing by the piano and saying, 'That was a truly remarkable performance for one so young, Miss Wilhelmina.' She could see the grand duchess and her pleasure and satisfaction. Then he had said, 'I shall look forward with delight to working with you.' It all sounded so familiar — and it was as though it had all been yesterday.

Now would begin the hours of intense practice and the polish that Mr Grosinover could give, to make the difference between good and great.

⋆ ⋆ ⋆

Wilhelmina returned home. Rebecca was safely set on her final stage of development. It would take time, time for the polish and time for experience, experience in the art of performance. 'Keep the letters and all your news coming to me,' she called as they waved her goodbye.

Etty put her arm around Beccy. 'We will,' she called. 'And I'll take great care of her.'

The weeks passed, each one bringing news of Beccy's progress and of the theatres and concerts they had attended. Beccy's knowledge and critical appraisal of other performers was also growing. Her whole outlook was being rounded out.

Then began her own performances — her appearance as an unknown pianist at concerts in obscure theatres, then at large private residences and then the great excitement of an invitation to perform at Government House. His Excellency had stood and applauded her and congratulated her personally. 'I shall remember the name,' he said. 'I shall look for it in lights at the Theatre Royal.'

Her experience was growing. Now came the press reviews, the praise. Where had this gifted and accomplished young performer been hiding? The excellence of her performance was quite extraordinary for one so young!

Etty sent all the press reviews and Wilhelmina went over and over them. She pasted them all in a folder and left it in pride of place in the sitting room. Rebecca was gaining confidence, developing a stage personality to complement her musical performance — and she was becoming known.

★　★　★

Then finally came the news of an invitation to perform as the 'Principal Musician' at a 'Gala Performance' at the great Theatre Royal.

'It is just like you have described theatres in Europe, Mama,' Beccy wrote. 'There are rows and rows of seats and the galleries and dress boxes on each side on every level. Oh, it is grand! And I shall be playing there.'

Rebecca must have a new dress to suit the occasion. Etty would have to be entrusted to help her in her choice. They must go! Oh, there was no doubt. They must be there for this great occasion. Billy agreed. Of course they must go. They would travel down and arrive in Sydney town a few days before the performance.

★　★　★

To go to the theatre! How long was it since she had been there? This new Royal that Beccy spoke of may be grand to her eyes, but it may not equal the grand theatres of Europe. But oh, it would be wonderful! And her own Rebecca was playing — the chief musician; billed on the program as the principal artist!

They sent paper clippings of the advertisements and advance notices of the gala performance. The Sydney orchestra would be in attendance with the reigning conductor at the rostrum.

She must find something to wear, too. She must do Rebecca credit. She may meet some of the dignitaries and she must be dressed suitably, so Rebecca was not embarrassed. There would hardly be time to find something when she got to Sydney. She must make something and take it with her.

She smiled to herself. Would it be possible that there was still something she could use in the old trunks, the old court clothes from so long ago? There may be something she could alter or combine. She went to look out the old trunks.

Henrietta and Rebecca had been to many shops and dressmakers. At last they found something they both thought was the answer, something just right. It was a taffeta dress — blue, the colour of her eyes, the wide neckline displaying the milky white of her neck and shoulders. It allowed freedom of movement for her arms and altogether seemed ideal. They paid for the dress and came out onto the pavement in front of the shop.

A woman was just alighting from a carriage. She glanced at them, then turned back to look again. Then she continued on her way down the street. Rebecca grabbed Etty's arm. 'Aunt Etty. That woman. Did you see her?'

'Yes, Why? Do you know her?'

Rebecca nodded. 'A long time ago, when I was a little girl. She was talking to another lady. She was looking at me and she said, 'That's the bastard child.' I asked Mother about it. I didn't know what it meant then, of course, but she said they couldn't have been talking about me. I never forgot it, and I never forgot her face. That was her. I know. I've always wondered why she called me that.'

Etty moved her parcels. 'I shouldn't worry about it, dear. People say strange things sometimes.'

★ ★ ★

Henrietta met Billy and Wilhelmina when they arrived in Sydney. The wharf was crowded with people. The throng quite dazzled Wilhelmina. It had been a good journey, but now the real excitement was about to begin. Alister was due home the morning of the concert and would be able to attend, too.

The morning of the big day dawned cool and cloudy.

'So much better if it is not too hot in the theatre — and for Beccy, with her performance. It is more comfortable if it is a little cool,' Alister said when he arrived.

They were to have a light evening meal and arrive at the theatre in good time to settle themselves in the dress box Alister had reserved for them. Beccy, of course, would be at the theatre for rehearsal and would remain there in her dressing room, refreshments being sent in to her.

At last all was ready. The carriage was brought to the front door. They climbed in and the carriage door was closed. They were off to the grandest occasion: the gala performance, where Miss Rebecca Foster was billed as the principal artist.

44

The dream of a lifetime

The excited buzz of the theatre rose to them as they entered the box. The theatre was filling quickly, the attendants busy guiding patrons to their seats.

The light glistened on the satins and silks of the dresses and the jewels of the ladies in the dress circle, men in their dark evening suits, starched shirts and high collars escorting them. Oh, it was a grand occasion! Not since they had left Europe had she been to such a dazzling gathering.

The orchestra was tuning up, the various players finding their seats and adjusting their music. The lights dimmed. Now the conductor mounted the rostrum to a great applause of welcome. He bowed. Then, ensuring the attention of all the orchestra, he lifted his baton. It was wonderful — the music, the response. But it was all just a preliminary, Wilhelmina thought. The principal artist will be last on the program, the second half.

At intermission, refreshments were brought to the box. Alister had thought of everything.

He was looking most elegant in his evening suit and the latest most fashionable touches on his shirt.

She glanced at Billy. He looked most unfamiliar in his evening clothes. He caught her eye and smiled. There was a twinkle in his eye. He really did look the Norse god in all this elegance. He really was handsome. 'A bit different from a big do in the valley, isn't it?' he said softly. Then, his eyes roving over her, he added, 'You really look very beautiful, Will — and much too young to be the mother of the principal artist.'

The lights dimmed again. The orchestra was in place. A slim figure, a vision in sky blue, topped with a glorious titian head, made her way to the piano to a tumultuous welcome. The sound died away and a hush fell over the theatre as she lifted her hands.

Then it began.

They were lifted into another world — theatre, performance critics were forgotten. The notes commanded or enticed, wooed or beseeched, or took them tripping along in a dance, or stirred emotions of deep longing, yearning.

Composition after composition followed, weaving from one to the next. At last, the final one on the program was finished. The last notes died away. There was silence. No-one moved.

Then Rebecca lifted her hands from the keys and, as one waking from a trance, looked around.

Then it came: the thunderous applause, the acclamation that went on and on. The audience was on its feet, cheering, the restraints of polite English theatre audience swept away. Rebecca, flushed and glowing, bowed and bowed, kissed her hands and threw to them. Bouquets were piling up as they were handed to her and placed along the front of the stage. Still the acclamation continued. She had them in the palms of her hands.

Tears poured down Wilhelmina's face. The great well of thankfulness, of joy, of achievement threatened to engulf her. She had been right. She had succeeded.

At last, Rebecca held up her hands for silence. Gradually, the noise subsided and the audience reseated. 'My dear, dear friends,' Rebecca began, 'thankyou. Thankyou for your reception of my music.' A light burst of clapping again started up.

Rebecca held up her hand again. 'This is a wonderful occasion for me,' she continued. 'There is one in the audience tonight to whom is due the greatest part of my success.

This is my dear mother, who played in the palace of the grand duchess of Baden, before the master Francois-Frederick Chopin himself. As my tutor, dear Mr Grosinover, accepted me as a student, so Francois-Frederick Chopin accepted my mother, to train her for a career as a concert pianist, under the patronage of the grand duchess. Due to political upheaval, that was not to be. I dedicate this night to Wilhelmina Foster, my mother.'

Again the hush was broken by a smattering of applause and again Rebecca held up her hand for silence. 'I would now like to play for you something that is not on your program.' She held up a manuscript. 'This is a composition by my mother, written when she was fifteen years old.'

She moved back to the piano. The hush fell again and the magic began anew.

As she finished, she stood and, smiling, threw kisses towards their box. The audience was on its feet again. There were cheers and calls for the composer. It was too much! Too much! The tears flowed.

'Go on, stand up!' Billy cried, urging Wilhelmina forward. 'They want to acknowledge you. Stand up.' She stood, moving forward to the edge of the little balcony.

The applause washed over her, the lights

shone, the faces uplifted to her. She bowed, again and again. Still it went on. She lifted her arms in acknowledgement. Then, turning to the stage, she held out her arms and, kissing the fingers on both hands, threw them to Rebecca.

The orchestra struck up the notes of 'God Save the Queen'. They stood and sang lustily. Voices rose, the hubbub of sound washing over them.

As they gathered their cloaks, an attendant entered the box. 'A bouquet for Mrs Wilhelmina Foster,' he said.

Wilhelmina put out her hands to receive them. A bouquet for her? She picked up the card:

To my dear Mama, to whom I owe all the wonderful things of my life.
With all my love,
Beccy.

She read it again. Then her eye fell on the embellishment of the card. It was leaves. And a nest. And a bird.

The bird she realised, in a fresh wave of shock, was a cuckoo.

We do hope that you have enjoyed reading this large print book.

Did you know that all of our titles are available for purchase?

We publish a wide range of high quality large print books including:
Romances, Mysteries, Classics
General Fiction
Non Fiction and Westerns

Special interest titles available in large print are:
The Little Oxford Dictionary
Music Book
Song Book
Hymn Book
Service Book

Also available from us courtesy of Oxford University Press:
Young Readers' Dictionary
(large print edition)
Young Readers' Thesaurus
(large print edition)

For further information or a free brochure, please contact us at:
Ulverscroft Large Print Books Ltd.,
The Green, Bradgate Road, Anstey,
Leicester, LE7 7FU, England.
Tel: (00 44) **0116 236 4325**
Fax: (00 44) **0116 234 0205**

Other titles published by
The House of Ulverscroft:

CAROLINE

Daphne Saxby Taylor

'The deed is done, Caro. The land is mine. We haven't got anything on it yet — but the land is mine.' William couldn't hide the pride in his voice from his fiancée. The trek to remote north-east South Australia was soon to begin for this pioneering couple. But disaster was to strike Caroline, leaving in its wake a haunting legacy of pain and guilt. A present-day researcher, looking into these past events, has the task of getting to the bottom of it all. To her surprise, she finds herself bringing release and peace 'across time'.

THE COUNTESS AND THE MINER

Olga Sinclair

Countess Anastasia and Irena, a peasant girl, were worlds apart, but when Duncan MacRaith learned that Lord Eveson had raped Irena, he rushed to the big house intent on revenge. Now, with Eveson's departure, the Countess finds him a welcome diversion in her unhappy marriage, and the pair talk, drink vodka and lose all inhibitions. The Countess and Irena both become pregnant, but Irena fears that Eveson had fathered her baby. And then war breaks out in Russia and Duncan disappears whilst serving on the front lines. Irena must battle to find him and a future for herself.

RETURN TO ROSEMOUNT

Patricia Fawcett

Together, Clementine and Anthony Scarr had co-founded the school known as Florey Park on the headland. Then, after Anthony's tragic death in a car accident, Clemmie's priorities changed to making sure his memory remained untarnished for their two daughters, Nina and Julia . . . Clemmie is delighted when her grown children return home — Nina due to a doomed love affair, whilst Julia's reason remains a secret — along with Julia's feisty daughter, Francesca. And then Nina meets Alex and the promise of a new relationship blossoms . . . But, outside the beautiful gardens of Rosemount, forces are shifting that will threaten their happiness.

THE UNCONVENTIONAL MISS WALTERS

Fenella-Jane Miller

Eleanor Walters is obliged, by the terms of her aunt's will, to marry a man she dislikes: the irascible, but attractive, Lord Leo Upminster . . . Leo finds Eleanor's unconventional behaviour infuriating, her beauty irresistible and their agreement not to consummate the union increasingly impossible. It is only when he allows his frustration and jealousy to drive her away that he realizes what he has lost . . . Meanwhile, in her self-imposed exile on a neglected country estate, Eleanor becomes embroiled in riots and treachery. In a desperate race, can Leo save both her life and their marriage?

WINDS OF HONOUR

Ashleigh Bingham

The Honourable Phoebe Pemberton is beautiful and wealthy, but is the daughter of the late, disgraceful Lord Pemberton and Harriet Buckley . . . Phoebe escapes her mother's plans to teach her the family business of wringing profits from the mills. She dreams of running away, and, when she learns of her mother's schemes for Phoebe's marriage as part of a business transaction, she calls on her friend Toby Grantham for help . . . But Harriet's vengeful fury is aroused, leaving Phoebe tangled in a dark and desperate venture.

A LADY AT MIDNIGHT

Melinda Hammond

When Amelia Langridge accepts an invitation to stay in London as companion to Camilla Strickland, it is to enjoy herself before settling down as the wife of dependable Edmund Crannock. Camilla's intention is to capture a rich husband, and her mother is happy to allow Amelia to remain in the background. Camilla attracts the attention of Earl Rossleigh, but the earl is intent on a much more dangerous quarry, and it is Amelia who finds herself caught up in his tangled affairs . . . A merry dance through the Georgian world of duels, sparkling romance and adventure.